George P. Emswiler

Poems and Sketches

Consisting of Poems and Local History; Biography; Notes of Travel....

George P. Emswiler

Poems and Sketches
Consisting of Poems and Local History; Biography; Notes of Travel....

ISBN/EAN: 9783337228354

Printed in Europe, USA, Canada, Australia, Japan

Cover: Foto ©Andreas Hilbeck / pixelio.de

More available books at **www.hansebooks.com**

POEMS AND SKETCHES:

CONSISTING OF

POEMS AND LOCAL HISTORY; BIOGRAPHY; NOTES OF TRAVEL; A LONG LIST OF WAYNE COUNTY'S PIONEER DEAD, ALSO MANY NAMES OF THOSE WHO LOST THEIR LIVES IN DEFENSE OF THEIR COUNTRY, DURING THE LATE REBELLION, AND WHOSE HONORED REMAINS ARE INTERRED IN THIS VICINITY; WITH MUCH INTERESTING AND INSTRUCTIVE MISCELLANEOUS MATTER;

BY

GEORGE P. EMSWILER.

CAREFULLY COLLATED AND ARRANGED BY THE AUTHOR.

RICHMOND, INDIANA:
NICHOLSON PRINTING & MFG. CO.,
1897.

Dedication.

———

This little volume is lovingly and reverently dedicated to the memory
of three noble souls,

Martha Agnes Finley,   Attilia R. Goodrich,

and my dear, devoted mother,

Elizabeth Mitchell,

all long since departed from the confines of this sad world,
into the abodes of peace and rest eternal.

PREFACE.

THE contents of this volume consist of an hundred and fifty, or more, poems, on a multitude of subjects; also, several interesting papers on local history; sundry biographical sketches of former citizens of note; several old and interesting letters written in days of "auld lang-syne;" some miscellaneous matter, pertinent and impertinent; some brief sketches of travel; and a long list of pioneer names, with age, and date of death, directly from the records, whose bearers have passed, in the fullness of time, to the ever-silent shores beyond; also, a partial list of Wayne county's soldier dead: forming, in the aggregate, an exceedingly interesting collection, rare and valuable, to be found nowhere else in print. The material has been collected and wrought out, at various times and intervals, to beguile the tedium of an idle hour, and was begun in the author's boyhood days and continued on down to the present time, with *no* thought, whatever, until recently, of putting the matter into its present form. None of the contents have, therefore, been worked up, mechanically, with the purpose of making a book. He has no apology to offer for any defects of composition or arrangement, as we are all human and liable to err, and, besides, in his case, circumstances compelled him to be his own tutor and the architect of his own fortune. He does sincerely wish the offering were more worthy, but, such as it is, he has determined to submit it to an ever-tolerant public, hoping it may at least amuse, should it fail to edify or instruct, the reader.

THE AUTHOR.

CONTENTS.

———

MISCELLANEOUS POEMS.

The World's Columbian Fair   1
The Great Pullman Strike   4
The Stars   8
Musings   9
Garfield School House 11
Life 12
Time 13
His Loving Spirit Fills All Space 15
"If a Man Die, Shall He Live Again?" 17
Contemplation 19
"Be Not Like Dumb-Driven Cattle" 20
The Bell at Saint Paul's 22
Niagara 24
Lines to a Late November Butterfly 26
Thoughts Suggested by the Closing Year 29
Robert Burns 31
The Lunatic, the Lover, and the Poet 33
To a Departed Sister 34
Abandon 35
Indolence 36
Departing Summer 38
The Snow, Dec. 2d, 1893 39
Some Cool Reflections on a Gas Fire 40
Thoughts Suggested at "Fountain Square," Cincinnati, O. 41
Thanksgiving of the Poor 43
Aimless Thoughts 44
Scenes and Reflections at "Yearly Meeting" 45
Musings (written while the snow was falling) 49
Pictures of Winter 51

Some Characteristics of Our City's Servants 53
Lines Suggested by the Recent Death of a Friend . . . 55
The Toiler's Lament 57
March 13th and 14th, 1893 58
Master Willie May 59
Early Spring 60
Creation's Heirs 61
A Public Wedding at Old Pearl Street Church 62
When Life is Young 63
A Wail at the Weather 64
Enigma 65
To One Departed 67
Random Thoughts 68
Lines to a Belated Grasshopper 69
The World a Theatre 70
To Evan Wright 71
Lines Suggested by a Visit to Benj. and Emily Strattan . 72
Toil On 73
A Doggerel on a Departed Canine 74
Impromptu Lines Suggested by an Old Bonnet 75
To an Absent Brother 76
The Chase 77
A Sabbath Afternoon in Summer 78
A Fragment 78
Musings 79
Impromptu Lines to March 80
To One at Rest 81
Early Autumn 82
Could Prayers Avail 83
The Day We Celebrate 84
March 11th, 1896 85
Passing Away 86
I Know No Misanthropic Hours 87
Old Letters 89
Early Spring 91
My Love and I 92
Lines to a Butterfly 94
When First We Met 96
Retrospection 97

Just as Thy Nature Urges 99
Crinoline 100
Memento Mori 101
Autumnal Musings 102
The Robin 103
Two Translations 104
In the Days When I Went Tipsying 105
Some Reflections in a Country Churchyard 107
The Rose 108
Artlessness in Art 109
Lines to a Late Rosebud 110
Sleeves, and Hoops, and Bustles 111
Passing Away 112
Mary Had a Little Dog 113
Lines Suggested by the Tolling of Pearl Street M. E.
    Church Bell 115
The Rain — A Protest 116
A Boyish Dream 118
May 19th, 1894 119
To E. J. S. 121
To Miss Sarah F——y 122
An Humble Tribute to Nelson Stanley 123
To Rachel M. Atherton 124
To Miss Mary Rambo 125
Impromptu Lines to Nellie Smurr 126
To One Who Loved, Not Wisely, but Too Well 127
Lines on the Death of a Favorite Cat 128
Apostrophe 128
Seeking Gold 129
Stanzas on the Early "Gold Fever" 131
To Christian Rathfon 132
To Isaac Kline 133
Impromptu Nonsense 133
A New Year's Greeting to William L. John 134
Avoid Extremes 134
To William L. John, on His Eighty-eighth Birthday . . 135
These Are Weary Days of Waiting 137
To William Parry 138
To William L. John, Aged Ninety-one Years 140

To Dr. T. H. Davis 141
Thoughts of Autumn. 142
December 8th, 1894 143
The Curfew Bell Will Ring To-Night 144
I Hate That Drum's Discordant Sound 146
Charles H. Burchenal 147
Henry R. Downing 148
Never Do Thou Stoop to Conquer 149

POETICAL LETTERS.

To Claudius Byles 152
To S. F. Smurr 153
To My Sister 156

THE SEASONS.

New Year's Morning, 1893 158
A Day of Gloom — February, 1894 159
Winds of March 161
An April Morn 162
A Morning in May 163
Reflections on a Morning in May 164
In the Sunny Days of June 165
July 167
In August — The Harvest is Over 169
August 170
September — Summer Wanes 172
Autumn — October 174
November 175
Farewell to December 176
Let Every Tongue Rejoice 178
Summer Salad 180
A Summer's Day 182
Autumnal Leaves 184
To Winter 185

RELIGIOUS POEMS AND SENTIMENTS.

O, Why Should We Mourn? 186
In Lent 187
At the Last 188

Christmas 190
Thanksgiving Day 191
Random Thoughts 193
And This Is True 194
"Be Just, and Fear Not" 195
Some Reflections 195
As I See It 196
Jewels Are Jehovah's Trust 197
Jesus — A Triple Acrostic 198
"Just as I Am, Without One Plea" 199

ALBUM PIECES.

To Beauty, for Miss Biles 202
To Miss Mary Mason 203
To Gabriella Newton 204
To Miss Mary Finley 205
To Mary E. H—t 206
To Mary Ellen Ward 207
To Elmira Basset 208
To Rebecca D. Strattan 209
To Sarah F. 210
To Miss Rebecca Meek 211
To Julia A. Brady 211

VALENTINES.

To Miss Margaret McCoy 213
To Miss Phœbe C—f—d 214
To Miss Rebecca D. Strattan 215
To Miss Rebecca Meek 216
To Miss Mary Rambo 216

LOCAL HISTORICAL SKETCHES.

My Recollections of Richmond — Paper No. 1 221
My Recollections of Richmond — Paper No. 2 234
My Recollections of Richmond — Paper No. 3 250

xii CONTENTS.

BIOGRAPHICAL.

General Sol Meredith 258
Alfred Kayne 259
Judge James Perry 263
Irvin Reed 267
Senator John Yaryan 270
William Parry 274
William L. John 276

OLD LETTERS OF PIONEER TIMES.

Andrew Finley, Jr. (No. 1) 282
Andrew Finley, Jr. (No. 2) 285
Rebecca Bradbury 287
Susan Finley 288

MISCELLANEOUS SKETCHES.

Court House Removal 290
How Richmond Met a Crisis 291
Richmond's Postmasters 292
David Hoover's Memoir 295
A Relic of War Times 311
Some County History 321

HISTORICAL.

Recollections, Etc. 325
A Trip to California 328

WESTERN SKETCHES.

An Old Time Elopement 333
Early Railroad History at Richmond, Ind. 337
Early Railroading Between Richmond and Anderson . . 344

MISCELLANEOUS SELECTIONS.

Canal-Boat Trains 351
Our Navy During the War 353
War Prices in the North 355
War Prices in the South 359
Cotton Mather and the Friends 361

The Optimist 363
The Children of the Desert 365
Chronology of Plants 369
Shells, Fossils and Flowers 372
Travel — Notes by the Way 373

PIONEER DEAD.

First Settlers — Place of interment unknown 400
Earlham Cemetery 401
Maple Grove Cemetery 412
Friends' Old North Side Cemetery 412
German Lutheran Cemetery 413
German Catholic Cemetery 414
Irish Catholic Cemetery 416
Hoover Burying Grounds 417
McClure Family Cemetery 418
Friends' Ridge Cemetery 419
King's Cemetery 420
Goshen Cemetery 421
Elkhorn Cemetery 423
Chester Cemetery 424
Centerville Cemetery 426
Boston Cemetery 427
Recent Deaths 429

THE SOLDIER DEAD.

Maple Grove Cemetery 431
Earlham Cemetery 432
Elkhorn Cemetery 432
Boston Cemetery 432
Lutheran Cemetery 432
German Catholic Cemetery 433
Irish Catholic Cemetery 433
Public Cemetery 433
Old Catholic Cemetery 433
Kennedy's Chapel 433

God Bless Abraham Lincoln 434
Farewell Poem 435

MISCELLANEOUS POEMS.

THE WORLD'S COLUMBIAN FAIR.

Thou great White City by the lake,
    Thou rare conception of the mind ;
A dreamy fancy crystallized,
    The proudest work of humankind.

The world thy equal ne'er has seen,
    Nor will it soon compete with thee ;
In grandeur thou wilt stand alone
    For ages that are yet to be.

Here all the universal world
    Has stored the choicest things it holds
Of skill, or wealth, or pomp, or power,
    That we may see what life unfolds.

Here mines reveal their richest ores,
    And forestry displays its woods,
The watery world its wondrous stores,
    And cultured fields their fruits and foods.

Here we behold rich gems of art,
  And treasures fair as ever sought,
To please the mind, or touch the heart —
  From earth's remotest regions brought.

From Europe and from Afric's soil,
  From Asia and its vast domain,
From East and West, come works of toil,
  And lessons for the busy brain.

Here science and mechanic art
  Declare the progress of the world,
And merchandise from every mart
  Where'er a flag has been unfurled.

Swart natives from the torrid zone,
  With such as dwell in regions drear,
And ocean's distant islands lone,
  And every continent, are here.

Behold what energy has wrought !
  What grand results of brain and skill !
The climax of creative thought,
  A wonder to amaze and thrill.

In gratitude for priceless dower,
  We celebrate a country's birth —
The grandest, freest, best : the flower
  And fruitage of the smiling earth.

All Hail, Columbia ! May thy years
　　Exceed the years of Greece and Rome,
And may a happy people's cheers
　　Forever greet thee: ''Home, sweet home.''

And thou, Chicago — Freedom's pride,
　　A very queen by Nature blest,
Whose feet are laved by wind and tide :
　　The crown and glory of the West —

To thee belongs a meed of praise
　　For what thou hast conceived and wrought :
The grandest work of latter days
　　By which the nations have been taught.

Here thronging millions come to see,
　　From every foreign clime and zone,
Admire and praise thy works and thee –
　　Supremest effort man has known.

OCTOBER 12, 1893.

THE GREAT PULLMAN STRIKE.

[Engineered by Eugene V. Debs, President of the American Railway
Union, culminating in riot and bloodshed, on Saturday and Sunday, July
7th and 8th, '94, at Chicago, Illinois, when Federal and State troops were
called out to quell the disturbance, after hundreds of cars had been
burned, with much other railroad property, amounting, it is claimed, to
over two million dollars.]

The times are all in a turmoil ;
　　There is striking on all the roads —
Determined to boycott Pullman,
　　Regardless of means or modes.

A spirit of evil possesses
　　These toilers, against the rich,
Who vent their spleen with torch and force
　　And the aid of the railroad switch.

They complain of a serious grievance,
　　Which, granting it may be just,
Can never excuse their dreadful work,
　　Which tramples all rights in the dust.

Destruction of cars by hundreds,
　　With marvelous wealth of freight :
Live cattle and hogs and horses,
　　And products from far-off States.

Switches and towers and tracks
    Are broken and burned and wrecked :
In their devilish round of destruction
    They never a moment reflect.

They side-track Pullman sleepers,
    And hinder the Government trains,
And tie up travel and traffic,
    Both eastward and over the plains.

All properties owned by the roads,
    Wherever they chance to be found,
Are wrecked by these anarchist hordes,
    Or burned, in their hate, to the ground.

And still these elements flourish ;
    The unions of all the trades
Are being called off from labor,
    In sympathy's various shades.

They are bound upon conquest, they say,
    Determined to rule or to ruin ;
And, worse than the beasts of the forests,
    They haven't the sense of a " Bruin."

The spirit of evil is rampant ;
    The country is wild with commotion ;
And, like a contagion, is spreading,
    And widens from ocean to ocean.

Having quitted their places of labor,
    To join with the vagabond host,
They are out on a raid of destruction ;
    And to ruin the rich, is their boast :

Forgetting that money is needful
    To furnish employments for all,
And that bread, and a home, and apparel,
    Are wants of the great and the small ;

That idleness ends in distress,
    Demoralization and crime ;
That labor alone tends to bless,
    Ennoble, and make us sublime.

Then why should such envy exist
    As capital seems to create ?
Without it no labor could live,
    Nor happiness come to the State.

Then cease all this turbulent fury ;
    Go, each to his engine or brake ;
You cannot afford to be idle :
    Your course is an awful mistake.

Be just to the laws of the land,
    By being good citizens, all ;
Avoid being tools of a leader,
    To serve his behests or his call.

Be honest, and faithful, and prudent ;
  Provide for the comforts of age ;
And should disaffection surround you,
  Keep aloof from its frenzy and rage :

For those who command you seek glory,
  And are drunk with the power they hold,
And simply repeat the old story
  A thousand times acted and told.

Their reign will be brief, we may trust,
  For the State and the Nation, at hand
With their forces and loyalty, must
  Compel the vile mob to disband ;

And as the promoters of crime
  May speedily hang for their sport,
Or serve a life sentence of time
  From whence they may never report.

July 9, 1894.

THE STARS.

From childhood's earliest hours till now,
  My thoughts have vainly striven
To comprehend those orbs of light,
  Those star-lit lamps of heaven.

And, oftentimes, my soul hath dwelt
  In rapture, wild and free,
As contemplating them I knelt
  To ask from whence they be —

To know that high Almighty hand,
  Whose boundless power and love
Created, and sustained, and planned,
  Such countless worlds above ;

Whose sweet, mild radiance comes to earth
  Like gem-drops, through the air,
And shining on, through endless years,
  God's providence declare.

May my freed spirit take its flight
  Some calm, bright, holy even',
Drink in one draught of their pure light,
  And sweetly pass to heaven.

December 17, 1850.

MUSINGS.

———

"The remembrance of youth is a sigh."

Once fondest illusions of promise and hope
 Shed a halo of gladness around,
And the sigh, and the tear, and the cares of to-day,
 Could not in my presence be found.

But change is inherent in all that has life,
 And constancy never was known ;
The castles we builded, in battle and strife,
 Like leaves have been scattered and strown.

For a shadow like that of the passage of clouds
 O'er the glow of the Mid-Summer sun,
Will shade, in its turn, ev'ry brow with a care
 Ere the goal of ambition is won ;

And the maid on whose cheek blend the lily and rose,
 And the youth who, so happy and fair,
In his ardor aspires to be wealthy or great,
 Will each be the victims of care.

I, too, had bright hopes of the future in view,
 And an aim that was noble and high,
But, alas ! for my dreams, for they vanished in air,
 Like the vapory mists of the sky.

I feel no such buoyancy boyhood displayed,
  Which, in fullness of soul, effervesced ;
But instead, with a soberness suited to age,
  For many a long year have been blessed.

Thus many a fond hope has been blighted in blooming,
  And many a fond heart has been crushed ;
Its sorrows within its own bosom concealing ;
  Its mirth and its gleefulness hushed.

Still, I love to go back to the shadowy past,
  And muse o'er the pleasures it brought us ;
The many fair visions, too fleeting to last,
  And the frostwork of bliss that was wrought us.

For the Spring-time of life, tho' a glorious cheat, .
  Has food for reflection and ruth,
And its joys — evanescent, entrancingly sweet —
  Seemed real and lasting as truth.

Note.—Written in 1854 ; revised in May, 1891.

GARFIELD SCHOOL HOUSE.

[Erected by Dr. Joel Vaile, in 1854; removed by Ebon Louck, in June, 1894, to whom has been given the contract for a new building.]

I saw thee builded, and have seen thee fall,
Dismantled and demolished, to thy basement's wall ;
A once proud structure of a former day,
Like all things earthly, thou hast passed away.

A temple, truly, where the youthful mind
Was fed and fostered and to good inclined.
For two-score years thy purpose served us well,
But in mem'ry only wilt thou henceforth dwell.

Some statelier structure will supply thy place,
Combining elegance, as well as grace ;
For pride and riches, with their siren song,
Have won the worship of the thoughtless throng.

Uncultured minds no higher joys can know
Than vain display, or garish, tawdry show ;
While modest worth has vanished far away,
Or sought the precincts of some by-gone day.

The old simplicity, that once prevailed,
Is jeered and hooted, and by gibes assailed ;
Our robes are scarlet : that they catch the eye,
And flash and flourish, common sense defy.

The world at large is out on dress parade,
For even learning apes the showy maid ;
With surface gilding, on a mental ground,
It seeks to dazzle and appear profound.

Delusive shams, instead of wholesome truths,
Are doled, "ad libitum," to ardent youths ;
While things essential to our weal or woe,
Must find solution as through life we go.

Let common sense be your unfailing guide ;
Be self-reliant, shunning shams and pride ;
Take naught for granted — follow wisdom's plan :
Think for yourself, and prove yourself a man.

JUNE 18, 1894.

LIFE.

Life is a mysterious mystery,
Which none may solve, of all humanity ;
Supreme reflection of a Great First Cause,
Controlling being, under Nature's laws.

Akin to light, which doth illume the day,
It shines, in splendor, but to pass away ;
No seeking will the story ever tell —
It may be soul or spirit, energy or spell.

It seemeth like a breath, a shadow fleeting,
Which stirs the vital currents, and the pulses beating,
And may evanish, like the misty air,
Or linger strangely, after we despair.

A real something, yet we see it not ;
An unseen force — alas ! we know not what ;
We call it life, but can explain no more,
Though we all learning and all thought explore.

To that High Power which no eye beholds,
We leave the problem, till His will unfolds :
We only know vitality and being
Bring power of action, loving, hating, seeing.

JUNE, 1893.

TIME.

Time is the measure of the ages past ;
  A miracle of power, invincible, sublime ;
An ever-active force, an ocean vast ;
  The grand inheritance of every clime.

The instrument and glory of the Great I Am ;
  The day of Deity, which doth not pause,
But worketh and evolveth, in a peaceful psalm,
  Eternal duty, through eternal laws.

At His behest, unnumbered distant spheres,
  Through time and space, revolve their devious
    rounds,
And so continue, in the countless years,
  Through regions knowing neither metes nor
    bounds.

A vasty deep, an endless, measureless degree,
  Is Time — the mighty arbiter of all ;
Nations and empires yield themselves to thee :
  They rise, in splendor, and in time they fall.

Thou art a conqueror without a peer ;
  Thou comest and thou goest like the viewless
    wind ;
Thou fleest swiftly as the charioteer,
  And dire destruction in thy path we find.

JUNE 28, 1893.

HIS LOVING SPIRIT FILLS ALL SPACE.

In temples of the glorious woods,
  Where God's first altars rose sublime,
There men, of various climes and moods,
  Erst knelt to Him, in ancient time.

The mighty oak, the towering pine,
  Which sheltered, and ascended high,
Were fane and spire, the most divine
  That ever pointed to the sky.

Man here communed with Nature's God,
  In silence and in solitude,
And saw, without the chastening rod,
  That all His ways and works were good.

No glittering show, no vain display,
  Which man alone regards as great,
Distracted thought from Heaven away
  To empty forms and pomp of state.

The sun by day, the moon by night,
  And all the countless orbs that shine,
Were proof to them of power and might,
  Forever loving and divine.

Go forth, my brother ; seek the hills,
  The sparkling streams, the vales of green,
The boundless plains, whose grandeur fills
  The soul with awe : there God hath been.

Behold the glorious earth and sky ;
  Breathe in the ambient air of heaven ;
Expand thy soul ; prepare to fly
  From narrow creeds that men have given.

His loving spirit fills all space :
  Not only temples built by hands,
But everywhere He sheds His grace —
  From mountain peaks to ocean strands.

Sunday, August 2, 1891.

"IF A MAN DIE, SHALL HE LIVE AGAIN?"

———

" Ah, whither strays the immortal mind
    When coldness wraps this suffering clay?"
When this fair world we leave behind,
    And death and darkness veil the day?

Will it go hence to distant worlds,
    Beyond the ken of mortals given,
To live again, where life unfurls
    Existence in a joyous Heaven?

Elysian fields where happy souls,
    Beloved and loving, ever dwell?
Where bliss eternally unrolls
    Some new delight no tongue can tell?

Shall we rejoin our loved ones there,
    And know them as we knew them here,
Exempt from toil, and pain, and care —
    Inflictions of this mundane sphere?

Will naught but happiness and bliss
    Fill up the hours of endless years,
And everlasting praise dismiss
    The fleeting ages, free from tears?

Or shall we be condemned and doomed
   To endless years of woe, instead,
Or in forgetfulness, entombed,
   Remain till age on age is sped?

Alas! for us — we do not know
   What is our destined end or aim;
Why we have lived, nor where we go,
   Nor e'en from whence, at first, we came.

O! Thou Supreme, Almighty Power,
   Reveal to us these hidden things,
That we may know Thy will, each hour,
   Freed from the doubt and fear it brings.

These secrets, Lord, on us bestow,
   Who see Thy works and still are blind;
Whose eyes behold, where'er we go,
   Some unsolved myst'ry of the mind.

September 30, 1892.

CONTEMPLATION.

We dwell amidst unnumbered worlds,
    In unexplored and boundless space,
Wherein supreme creative power
    And high intelligence, we trace.

We view, with an admiring awe,
    Great suns and systems as they roll —
Obedient to a common law,
    Fixed, from the first, for their control.

Beneath the all-resplendent stars —
    A panorama, vast and grand —
A streaming light of shining bars
    Illumines air, and sea, and land :
    Amid all these we nightly stand

Upon the crest of this great ball —
    Yclept the globe, or Mother Earth —
Revolving — with its kindred, all
    In mighty orbit — since its birth.

Hereon, for countless ages past,
    Millions of millions lived and died ;
For a brief space they dwelt, and passed,
    And others, still, their place supplied.

So it has been, and so will be
  Till Time itself shall be no more,
And all mankind are called to see
  That Being whom we all adore ;

That Great First Cause — our fathers' God —
  Through whom we live and have been blest,
Who chastens us, with mercy's rod,
  And giveth His beloved rest.

How wonderful are all His works !
  How fraught with wisdom all His ways !
What mystery abounds and lurks
  In all His countless years and days !

MARCH 20, 1893.

"BE NOT LIKE DUMB-DRIVEN CATTLE."

" Be not like dumb-driven cattle :
  Be a hero in the strife ; "
Be not led by others' teachings,
  But evolve thy own true life.

Hail mankind as loving brothers,
  Have a lofty aim in view ;
Do the right to self and others,
  Only goodly paths pursue.

Honor those whose worth and wisdom
   Count for more than gems or gold,
But forbear to fawn or truckle,
   And be neither bought nor sold.

Ne'er forget thou art a freeman,
   In a land of liberty ;
Where the plowman or the seaman
   Dares a Senator to be.

Let thy daily life proclaim thee
   Moral, merciful and just ;
Doing for thy friends and neighbors
   Works of love, and not of lust.

Think for thyself ; let manhood shine
   Resplendent over all thou dost ;
To wisdom let thine ear incline,
   And virtue be thy guest and host.

So wilt thou be complete in all
   That the Supreme decreed for thee ;
Let superstition's shackles fall,
   For truth alone can make thee free.

By energy and faith, I trow,
   And self-reliance, most divine,
Thou canst compel the world to bow
   And worship at thy chosen shrine.

Then " be not like dumb-driven cattle :
    Be a hero in the strife ; ''
Press onward in the din of battle,
    And evolve a nobler life.

God has meant that every being
    Should grow stronger in the right,
And at last attain perfection,
    For acceptance in His sight.

NOVEMBER 15, 1893.   .

THE BELL AT ST. PAUL'S.

Full many a time thy tones I've heard
    Ring out, in years gone by,
And listened till my heart was stirred,
    And echo made reply.

Thy sad, sweet notes have wondrous charms,
    In every peal and swell,
And fill my soul with joy so full
    That language fails to tell.

I've loved thee well, and loved thee long —
    In truth, I love thee still,
As thou dost call the careless throng
    To worship, if they will.

Thou art to me a cherished friend,
  Cemented by long years,
And mayest sometime mark my end,
  In sadness, if not tears ;

For often dost thou sadly toll
  For some dear friend or brother ;
Some cherished sister, passed away,
  Or dear, devoted mother.

Oft have I heard from stately towers,
  In regions far away,
Sweet bells ring out, in morning hours,
  In joyous clang and play ;

But nowhere else on earth, to me,
  Have such sweet notes been rung
As flood the vibrant air from thee,
  And issue from thy tongue.

Still ring the call to praise and prayer,
  As oft in days of yore,
Till hope invites to climes more fair,
  Beyond this mundane shore.

Aye, ring in tones distinct and clear,
  Melodious, sweet, and long,
Till every sin-sick soul has cheer,
  And faith in God is strong.

And when thy mission is fulfilled —
　　Should that good time e'er come —
And truth from error is distilled,
　　Then, only, be thou dumb.

And now, farewell, thou dear old bell ;
　　Ring for the thoughtless world ;
Ring loud and long, His mercies tell ;
　　Love's banner floats unfurled.

SUNDAY, JANUARY 7, 1894.

NIAGARA.

Thou wondrous marvel of the world !
Whose floods for ages have been hurled
Into far depths, unseen, below,
From whence thy surging waters go !

Thou art sublime in might and power,
And, flowing on through time's long hour,
Hast rolled impetuous o'er these rocks,
And dashed to foam, in deafening shocks.

Thy roar — a never-ceasing sound —
Ascends from hidden caves, profound,
Where boiling waters seethe and foam,
And mist and fury find a home.

Amazed at sight of thee, we feel
An awe that words cannot reveal ;
A shrinking fear, wrought by thy frown,
As mighty torrents pour them down.

Full many a luckless wight, long dead,
Since fleeting eons hence have sped,
Has drifted down, in dire dismay,
To thy deep, yawning gulfs, away.

The Indian, in his frail canoe —
To all his native instincts true —
Pursuing hind, or fallow deer,
Across thy bosom, year by year,
Or vengeful foe, in horrid hate,
Has met, upon thy brink, his fate.

So his white brother, far less rude,
Has ventured forth, in thoughtless mood,
To where thy restless waters flow,
And, leaping, thunder down below.

Nor these alone, but Nature's throng,
Whom instinct blindly leads along
And lures to death, upon thy wave,
Beyond the power of help to save.

Pour down thy floods while time shall last,.
Tremendous torrent, swift and vast,
Far into mystic depths below,
And rear aloft thy radiant bow.

Triumphant work of Nature's God,
Evolved ere man the earth had trod !
Emblem of power and might, for aye,
Sublimely grand, Niagara !

MAY 10, 1894.

LINES TO A LATE NOVEMBER BUTTERFLY.

[On Thursday. November 13th, while out driving, the day being warm and pleasant, I saw. at a short distance in advance of me, a very beautiful butterfly, sporting in the sun as in the early days of Summer.]

'Twas the thirteenth of November,
And a day to long remember,
For the sun was shining brightly,
And my team was tripping lightly,
   As we traveled down the road.

I was musing o'er the past,
And the shadows it had cast,
When I lifted up my eyes,
And I saw, with glad surprise,
   What the circumstance bestowed.

'Twas a miracle, indeed,
That the season seemed to breed,
In its solar warmth and light,
And, with marvelous delight,
  I beheld a butterfly !

Happy spirit of the air,
Flitting lightly, here and there,
Like a harbinger of bliss,
Come to beckon us from this
  · To some fairer world on high —

Cheer us ever, beauteous thing ;
Hover round, on sportive wing ;
Pleasant thoughts forever bring :
Youthful fancies, boyish dreams,
Flowering meads and babbling streams,
  Of the golden days now flown.

When a romping, gleeful child,
Many an hour have I beguiled
In pursuit of such as thou,
Whose fair presence charms me now,
  Though to manhood I have grown.

Ignis fatuus fancies flit,
Still, across my brain, and sit,
Just as thou art wont to do,
On some object strange and new ;
  And as quickly come and go.

Given still a score of years
In this vale of joys and tears,
We may never chance to see
Other winged sprite like thee
  Linger till the cold winds blow.

Such a charm, in chill November,
We shall cherish and remember,
For like seasons come not often,
Its asperities to soften,
  That we dare forget them soon.

And the soul that is not better,
When to Nature it is debtor
For its charms, to mind or eye,
E'en of bird or butterfly,
  Must be sadly out of tune.

NOVEMBER 13, 1890.

THOUGHTS SUGGESTED BY THE CLOSING YEAR.

And now another year is past,
  A twelvemonth more of life is sped,
Borne onward to that ocean vast
  Where all preceding time has fled.

Like atoms on a flowing river,
  Humanity is drifting on
To find its goal — returning never —
  Till all now living shall be gone.

The thought is sad, yet Nature's laws
  Are absolute, as were the Medes',
And if the contemplation awes,
  'Tis the most kindly of His deeds.

In youth a buoyant spirit reigns,
  And we are confident and strong ;
At middle age strength still sustains,
  And promises a voyage long.

Old age appears to us at last,
  With sunken cheeks and grizzled hair,
And tells us that our prime is past —
  A truth our feelings all declare.

With steps uncertain now, and slow,
    A staff required for our support,
We totter on, as down we go —
    Of circumstance and time, the sport.

Worn out, at last, we sink to rest,
    From life's concerns and troubles, free ;
At peace with all the world, and blest
    Throughout a vast eternity.

As forest trees grow old, and die,
    And younger forms arise instead,
So, reader, will both you and I
    Go hence, ere many moons are sped.

Deplore it not, for Nature's ways,
    Like justice, are the ways of God ;
Probationary years and days
    Lead homeward, and by all are trod.

Life here prepares us for the skies —
    If, happily, such heavenly spheres
Await — to which we may arise,
    Triumphant, through our toils and tears.

Rest, surely — if naught else — is ours,
    In dreamless and unending sleep :
Blest gift of the supernal powers,
    For souls quiescent cannot weep.

December 20, 1893.

ROBERT BURNS.

Truly, the youthful Burns was gay ;
A happy reveler in his day ;
His years were ever June or May,
          And bloomed with love.

He knew not care, but everywhere
Had amours with Eve's daughters, fair,
Who seemed inclined his flame to share,
          In cot or grove.

A rustic, all unschooled, and free,
With native wit, in full degree,
Endowed with wondrous sense to see,
          As well as know.

A peasant born, he wrote with skill,
He plowed and planted at his will,
And on himself the most of ill
          He did bestow.

But, after all, his soul was great,
And far beyond his low estate,
Which was too humble to elate
          So clear a mind.

He stood alone and had few peers,
And none, for opportunity and years ;
And later times will greet with cheers
    Aught he designed.

He was dear Scotia's noble son ;
Lowly and lofty, all in one ;
The friend of all, the foe of none
    Except the proud.

He loved the right, despised the wrong,
And hurled his pointed shafts of song,
In language keen, as well as strong,
    At the vile crowd.

He was the child of Nature, too ;
To all its loving instincts true,
And celebrated all he knew
    Of its fair charms.

Long may his nobler thoughts endure —
The tender, sympathetic, pure,
The heritage of rich and poor —
    Through time's alarms.

JANUARY 30, 1894.

THE LUNATIC, THE LOVER, AND THE POET.

———

"The lunatic, the lover, and the poet
  Are of imagination all compact;"
We write it that you read it and may know it,
  For the saying is not questioned as a fact.

The vagaries and visions of the lover
  Tell of heaven upon earth unto him,
For the joys of his heart we discover
  Welling up, through the soul, to the brim.

So the lunatic, in mental aberrations,
  Hath visions of magnificence and glory,
Though descended through the lowliest of stations,
  Or the scion of a king famed in story.

While the poet, no less ardent, taketh flight
  To the starry and the distant fields of air,
For the lofty and the beautiful delight,
  And his spirit ever seeketh what is fair.

So he pictureth a world aglow with bloom,
  And his sky becomes as radiant as heaven;
While a ceaseless longing doth his soul consume
  As he pleadeth that his weakness be forgiven.

" The lunatic, the lover, and the poet
Are of imagination all compact ; "
We write it that you read it and may know it,
For the saying is unquestioned as a fact.

July 24, 1893.

TO A DEPARTED SISTER, AGED SIXTEEN YEARS.

God, in his goodness, placed thee here,
With sisters dear and brothers,
To glad the heart of thy fond sire,
And cheer a doting mother's.

But short, alas ! thy earthly stay
With those thou lov'dst so dearly,
For Heaven's decree ne'er brooks delay,
And thou hast passed thus early.

'Twas hard, indeed, to give thee up,
E'en for that brighter shore,
Whose holier joys, shall fill thy cup,
Than earth e'er held in store.

Farewell ! my sister ; life has cares
  Too rude for human flowers ;
Transferred to fairer climes, thy soul
  May bloom in happier bowers.

A sweet remembrance thou shalt yield
  While life to us is given,
And at its close we trust to meet
  With thee, dear one, in Heaven.

TUESDAY, JANUARY 16, 1855.

ABANDON.

Give to me the hawthorn's shade
  On a hot and sultry day,
A novel of some interest
  To read, when down I lay ;
A brown " Havana roll " to puff,
  A " lucifer " ignited,
And after all, a good, sound sleep,
  And I shall then be righted.

A. D., 1850.

INDOLENCE.

I was languid and aweary,
    For the day was long and hot,
And though I sought amusement,
    Its resources I had not.

I had read and read, and pondered,
    Till a stupor filled my brain,
And I sat and read, and wondered
    If I had not best refrain.

So I yielded to the promptings,
    And sought a shady nook,
With the air and sun about me,
    A pencil and a book.

And to beguile the moments,
    As in silence they went by,
At some poetic stanzas
    I thought my hand to try.

So while the breeze was wafting
    Its coolness o'er my brow,
And song-birds trilled their laughter,
    I undertook my vow.

I framed these simple verses
　　As you behold them here,
Without a special object —
　　That seemeth very clear ;

And if they lack perfection,
　　Or energy or wit,
Or seem to want direction,
　　It comes from lack of grit.

For Summer's heat and indolence
　　Deprive us of our powers,
And this must be my sole defense
　　In these oppressive hours.

Perhaps when Autumn days return,
　　Fresh vigor they may bring,
With inspiration that shall burn
　　Till loftier strains we sing.

So, fare you well, for we must go,
　　A duty to perform :
The clouds are rising in the west,
　　With promise of a storm ;

And should a cyclone sweep our path,
　　It would be "versus" then ;
So I had better cease, or wrath
　　May wrest this scribbling pen.

TUESDAY, JUNE 20, 1893.

NOTE.—A storm was actually arising at the time this was being written.

DEPARTING SUMMER.

———

"The harvest is over, the Summer is ended."

Now forests wave a long and sad adieu,
 And trembling leaves, in sorrow, seem to sigh,
Because of thy departure, and alas ! to view,
 Not distant in thy train, chill Autumn nigh.

Thou comest and thou goest like a dream,
 And earth bewails her Summer beauties, flown ;
While Time moves onward, like a passing stream,
 And seasons vanish, but go not hence alone :

For man and matter, all that Nature knows,
 Tends to the final goal — Eternity ;
Each living thing a debt to Nature owes,
 Both great and small of earth's fraternity.

Then, wherefore should we sadden at thy leaving ?
 For thou again mayst cheer us with thy rays ;
But when poor mortals are called hence, no grieving
 Will ever render back departed days.

Note.—Written August 31. 1848; re-written and amended July 23, 1891.

THE SNOW.

———

" Here we come, and there we go,"
Say the little flakes of snow ;
" Down we fall, at Nature's call,
Silently or in a squall.

" Children greet us, glad to meet us ;
To their merry cries they treat us ;
Happy days and gleeful plays,
Romping in their childish ways."

They enjoy the snow, at least,
Coming from the north or east ;
Coasting here, and gliding there —
Splendid sport, I do declare.

See them rolling up a ball —
Now so large, at first so small ;
Then, again, they pile it high,
And to form a man, they try.

And anon they build, in sport,
What they term a snowy fort ;
Then they rear a monument,
Till their slender strength is spent.

And, at last, too cold for play,
Cease to revel for the day,
And, with hasty steps, retire
Homeward, to the cheerful fire.

E'en the cold, ungenial snow
Makes the childish heart to glow ;
While to those mature in years
Its enchantment disappears.

DECEMBER 2, 1893.

SOME COOL REFLECTIONS ON A GAS FIRE.

I sit and freeze, I sit and freeze ;
I shake and shiver, yawn and sneeze ;
I pray for heat — instead, I freeze ;
I almost swear — and yet I freeze.

I long for warmth of sun or breeze,
And yet I freeze, and yet I freeze ;
Confound the gas ! I wish I could
Convert its vapors into wood.

That genial warmth might cheer my soul,
And give my chattering teeth control ;
Revivify my powers of life,
And end this frightful frigid strife.

But, lo ! a chill pervades my frame,
With dire forebodings, ill of name,
Because I'm cold, so very cold —
The fire burns low — so cold, so cold.

We pray the powers that be for aid,
And trust that help be not delayed ;
We pray for honest, righteous pressure,
And less of daily scanty measure :

That we through future times remaining
Shall have less cause for just complaining.

DECEMBER 31, 1892.

THOUGHTS,

Suggested by the Ever-Thronging Multitude About Fountain Square.
Cincinnati, Ohio, September 5. 1894.

Come, thou, with me, and see the world go by,
And mark its phases, while the moments fly ;
Its ceaseless turmoil and its endless strife,
To seek a fortune, or sustain a life.

Like ocean's tides, in constant ebb and flow,
It surgeth hither, and doth yonder go ;
Some aim or purpose every act declares,
And in pursuit, nor toil nor labor spares.

While hope of gain is urging some along,
The love of pleasure seemeth full as strong ;
So all go headlong, as their wills incline,
To Mammon's altar, or to Folly's shrine.

Some speed on foot, and some on flying cars
Propelled by cables or electric bars ;
While here and there, and back and forth they rush,
In one mad conflict and unheeding crush.

Each rising morn beholds the fray begun,
At dewy eve it is not wholly done ;
So we, poor humans, in this restless world,
Are ever onward and still onward hurled,

Till our sad lives are weary, worn and wan,
And gladly yielded, that we may be gone :
For pleasure-seeking and pursuit of gain
Are disappointing and invite to pain.

MONDAY, SEPTEMBER 10, 1894.

THANKSGIVING OF THE POOR.

Give thanks — and for what? For a year of
    hard times?
For numberless strikes and for countless crimes?
For murder and robbery, arson and theft,
By graceless scoundrels, whose hands were deft?

For squalor and poverty, pinching the poor,
Who cannot keep want away from the door ;
Whose labor has lessened and wages reduced,
Good morals degraded, and virtue seduced?

For law-makers pandering unto the rich,
And aiding in schemes the gist of which
Meant millions of money to combine and trust,
Thus filling their coffers, and pampering lust?

For evils like these, and multitudes more,
We are asked to give thanks and forget to deplore
The wrongs that we suffer, and crush out the life
Of the poor and the lowly, in unequal strife.

Nay, never, we cannot give thanks for our lot,
So long as the comforts of life we have not ;
It is all very well for the rich man to tell
Of his gold and his gains, in a way that is ''swell:''
But, alas ! we have sorrows, and cause to complain
Of the tyrannous rich and monopolists' reign.

Sunday, November 25, 1894.

AIMLESS THOUGHTS.

This is an hour of idleness,
   With scarcely any aim in view ;
Alone with self can I express
   My aimless thoughts to even you.

I write that time may swiftly fly —
   However fruitless what I write —
And therefore will not seek to try
   To make of worth what I indite.

My thoughts are circumscribed and pent,
   And neither range aloft nor far,
And if on some high mission sent,
   Would fail to greet the nearest star.

They could not mingle with the spheres,
   Nor compass all of Nature's laws ;
Nor gain the triumphs due to years,
   Explain results, or state the cause.

" Will not some power the ' giftie gie ' us "
   To soar aloft from earthly clods,
And from our mental shackles free us,
   To think and act the part of gods?

SUNDAY, JANUARY 14, 1894.

SCENES AND REFLECTIONS AT " YEARLY MEETING."

[This Sketch is almost literally true, and is preserved not for any literary merit (for it possesses none), but simply as a memento of the times. This scene occurred at the old brick meeting-house north of the railroad, on Sunday, October 1, 1854.]

Behold that moving image there —
That rosy, buxom, country fair ;
She struts with honest pride of face,
But sadly lacks the art of grace.

She proves, at least, her limbs are strong,
As she divides the yielding throng ;
And if her mind is not well stored,
Her head has freight enough aboard.

Its gear is venerably old —
A sight well worthy to behold ;
Its plumes and ornaments, once gay,
Have sadly paled and drooped away.

Her dress is of a gaudy hue,
For nothing else, of course, would do ;
While from her waist a ribbon, fair,
Floats out upon the breezy air.

About her neck a strand or two
Of showy beads attract the view,
While sundry rings, of shining brass,
Bedeck the fingers of this lass.

She deems herself the favored belle
Of home, and neighborhood as well,
And therefore, as she little cares,
Assumes some unbecoming airs.

She talks and laughs, both long and loud,
Regardless of the gazing crowd,
And seeks to find her simple beau
And plighted flame of long ago.

They meet, at length ; each fond desire
Has set their willing hearts afire,
As flushing cheeks and radiant eyes
The truth most fully testifies.

He bows, and takes the proffered hand
And clasps it, while they chat and stand,
Remarking of the num'rous fair,
Each other's health, and how they were.

Of standing, weary, they retreat
To an obscure and vacant seat,
And hold a conversation there
Quite worthy of the rustic pair.

Says he to her, '' Be seated, Sue,
And post me up on all that's new ;
And tell me, is it true that Harry
And Belle Grimes intend to marry?

And if it would not be as well
(But then, you know, we mustn't tell)
To have our own dear wedding day
To come about the first of May?''

They spoke of this and then of that,
And held a long and social chat,
Unconscious of the busy throng
That passed them heedlessly along.

With fondest love and seeming haste,
He twined his arm about her waist,
And softly whispered in her ear
Words that only she might hear.

At this juncture I retreated.
Causing me to be defeated
As a witness of their ways
And such languishing displays.

Then, seating me without the throng,
I pondered, silently and long,
Bethinking me of changeful life :
Its varied scenes of love and strife ;

And how these twain were all untaught
In all its ways, in act or thought.
I felt a deep emotion thrill,
As every heart, responsive, will,

Whene'er it sees a verdant pair
So free, and so devoid of care,
Confiding in each other's love,
Not doubting each will faithful prove.

O ! unsophisticated pair,
All ignorant of Fashion's rules,
You have never known the care
Taught us in its tyrant schools !

May you live and love together,
Happily, for many a year,
Stemming life's tempestuous weather,
Smiling, spite of toil and tear.

Sunday, October 1, 1854.

MUSINGS,

Written while the snow was falling, Sunday, January 18, 1852.

See how gently falls the snow,
  Wheeling from its airy height,
Decking earth and forest-bough
  With its flakes of virgin white.

Not a scene on earth so cheery
  Ever greets my longing sight —
Though it be to some so dreary —
  As the snow-flake in its flight.

Boyish visions float around me,
  As I wander back through time,
Calling up the sports of childhood —
  Sports of merry winter-time.

Sleds and skates, and hill-sides sloping,
  Chase of rabbit round the hill :
Treed and captured — caught at last,
  Yonder by the distant mill.

Weary many a time, and oft
  Almost frozen, with the sport,
As we rolled us huge round snow-balls,
  Fashioned men, or snowy fort ;

Or with skates, upon the surface
  Of some pond or glassy lake,
Long excursions o'er its bosom —
  Oft returning — we would take ;

Or, when home-returned, would gather
  Round the hearth at even-tide,
And with song or tale enraptured,
  Cause the hours to swiftly glide.

Mirth and glee and gladness, all,
  Filled our cups with joy so high
That when now I think of them,
  They are thought of with a sigh.

But our boyish days soon leave us,
  And a few years, how they tell :
We have quit our skates and sledges —
  Bade to childish sports, farewell ;

And instead of hill-sides, sloping,
  Or the icy surface wide,
We prefer the stately highway
  And a coach, wherein to ride.

Thus it is : when youth departs us,
  And the boy becomes a man,
He discards the sports of childhood,
  In accord with Nature's plan.

PICTURES OF WINTER.

———

Mark ye, how the fleecy snow
Circles to the world below,
Mantling hill and plain and glen,
Hut, or castled haunt, of men.

See how varied every form,
As the flakes, 'mid driving storm,
Heap their added treasures higher
Over ground and tree and spire.

Bounding children hie to school,
Cheeks aglow, in air so cool,
Happy in the drifting snow,
Pealing laughter as they go.

Hark ! the merry call of bells !
How their melody up-wells !
Cheer-instilling every feeling,
And such happiness revealing.

Joyous youth and maiden fair —
Neither conscious of a care —
Glide like spirits o'er the snow,
Whispering something soft and low.

Seated round the glowing fire,
Mother dear and child and sire,
Happy, cheerful, loved, and warm,
Housed securely from the storm. .

Now, behold the lot of those —
Poor, and shelterless from snows,
Biting frosts and driving rain —
Doomed to poverty and pain.

Shun them not — the vagrant poor —
Open wide the heart and door ;
Lend them aid, relieve distress :
'Twill promote your happiness.

Nor forget that all mankind,
Whether simple, poor, or blind,
Are our brothers, sisters, dear,
Whom we should protect and cheer.

Kindly acts and worthy deeds
Are the sowing goodly seeds,
That may germinate in mold,
To return a thousand-fold.

NOTE.—Written first March 22, 1869, and amended and extended
January 26, 1893. .

SOME CHARACTERISTICS OF OUR CITY'S SERVANTS.

———

" A little learning is a dangerous thing,"
And small experience doth its miseries bring ;
So, little minds who wield official power
Are petty tyrants — lordlings of an hour.

A pompous manner and an owlish air
Declare the wisdom that they have to spare ;
They never reason, for they know not how —
And he that cannot is a fool, I trow.

Some wield the hammer, and some work in wood ;
Some deal in spirits, it is understood ;
And one, at least — the wiliest member, far —
Doth often "smile" to dedicate the bar.

A very Nestor, of peculiar kind,
With wit and cunning to divert the blind,
He poses leader of this weakling host,
Whose combined wisdom is a ghastly ghost.

Yet such as these, whose lack of wisdom's ways
Will scarcely serve them thro' the Summer days,
Assume to rule us, with an iron rod,
And ask obeisance to their beck and nod.

Such creatures squander what our labor hoards,
In fruitless journeys and at festal-boards ;
In new creations of some park or street :
In ways and manners ever indiscreet.

The people's rights are treated with disdain,
For haughty servants, now, the power maintain ;
Whose countless blunders stamp them heedless
     fools,
For lack of knowledge taught in common schools.

One son of Vulcan, with a noisy jaw,
Assumes importance, to inspire with awe ;
While Master Turner, with his swollen head,
Is so inflated that his wits have fled.

And e'en '' His Honor,'' like a chronic curse,
Is ever scheming to do something worse ;
A little conscience is a dangerous thing,
And untaught minds a constant misery bring.

May fortune grant that when this rule shall end,
Some wiser council may our needs attend —
Men who have brains, ability and worth,
And not abortions of ignoble birth.

Monday, July 10, 1893.

LINES,

———

Suggested by the death of an esteemed friend, in a neighboring city.

Once more we mourn the "loved and lost,"
   The friend of earlier days,
Whose winsome ways and loving heart
   Were themes of constant praise.

Hers was a soul sincere and true,
   Artless and free from guile,
Making more happy all she knew,
   With charmed speech and smile.

No group of friends was e'er complete
   Without her presence there,
To lend its hallowed influence — sweet
   As incense to the air.

In later years, when duty's cares
   Came, as our cares will come,
She was as sunlight to the home,
   And to complaint was dumb.

A helping hand was ever hers
   To lend, in times of need —
No thought of toil such souls deters —
   She was a friend, indeed.

And when affliction sore befell,
  And weary days of woe —
With suffering, only she could tell
  And only she could know —

It was her last sad trial here,
  Ere rest, eternal, came :
She bore it with a martyr's cheer,
  She bore it in His name.

In peace and rest her weary breath,
  Like sighing zephyrs, fled ;
She hailed the change — which we call death —
  They tell us.   She is dead.

OCTOBER 29, 1894.

Mrs. Lida Johnson died at Indianapolis yesterday, after a prolonged illness. She was a sister-in-law of Calvin R. Johnson, and a daughter of the late Benjamin W. Davis. Mrs. Johnson's early home was in Richmond, and her acquaintances are many.—October 25, 1894.

THE TOILER'S LAMENT.

Have I been born a life-long slave,
  To labor in the sun —
To work from morn till dewy eve,
  And still be never done?

Can I ne'er have release from toil,
  Or get a rest from care?
Must I keep on this tread-mill round,
  And have no time to spare?

I have no leisure of my own
  To think or even pray —
I simply am a slave for bread,
  And have been, day by day.

I am a thing for others' use,
  To bow at their behest —
The servant of some lordling's power,
  Without release or rest.

Will not the fates increase my store,
  To free me from this yoke —
If not on this, some kindlier shore,
  My lot, at last, revoke?

Or am I doomed to live a slave,
  To work through storm and sun,
And toil from morn till dewy eve,
  And still be never done?

SATURDAY, FEBRUARY 3, 1894.

MARCH.

"Its fickle fancy ranges,
And knows of naught but changes."

To-day it snows, a chill wind blows —
  'Tis Winter in the Spring;
The day before we did adore
  The sun's warm shimmering —

At sixty-five (as I'm alive)
  The mercury stood, serene;
At twenty-eight to-day, we state,
  The temperature is seen.

With changeful strife the times are rife,
  And prone to wayward ways;
We love them not, for hard the lot
  Of humans in these days.

MARCH 15, 1893.

MASTER WILLIE MAY.

Suggested by his photo.

Ho ! bright little elf, in a duplicate self,
  Thou miniature image of man ;
Thou copy in photo, thou shadow in toto,
  Thou hindrance to peace and to plan.

We love thee most dearly, we love thee sincerely,
  Thou restless young creeper and crawler ;
But when thou wouldst master, we look for disaster,
  For mighty art thou as a squaller.

A conqueror, truly, and often unruly,
  We sometimes are wholly confounded ;
Anon thou art playful and civil and, truly,
  Thy goodness of heart is unbounded.

Thou joy of the household, thou symbol of love,
  And a master of mischief, forsooth,
We pet thee and spank thee, by turns, little dove,
  For fretfully cutting a tooth.

February 26, 1894.

EARLY SPRING.

How delightful in Spring,
 When the sun's cheerful rays
Invite us to wander
 O'er meadows and '' braes.''

How elated the soul,
 As we gaze on the scene :
The earth newly robed
 In a vestment of green ;

Loudly thrilling their notes
 To the Being of Love,
Happy warblers unite
 With the plaint of the dove ;

Little rills, as in gladness,
 Go bounding along,
Gayly threading the vale
 With a murmuring song ;

While tiny flowers peep
 From the earth, broken up,
Exhaling perfume
 From each fairy-like cup.

Oh !   Who can behold
   Such an Eden as this,
And feel that the world
   Was not formed for his bliss?

A dreamy delight —
   Far beyond my control,
As I look upon Nature —
   Steals over my soul !

February, 1852.

CREATION'S HEIRS.

There is not anything that God has made
That should be hidden or should make afraid,
Of all the mysteries of all the years,
In this, our world, or e'en the distant spheres :
For we are His, and His creation ours,
And all co-workers, whom his bounty dowers.

We are His children, and our Father He —
From Him we came and unto Him we flee ;
Formed in His image, as Himself declares,
We are His only and Creation's heirs.

September 24, 1895.

A PUBLIC WEDDING AT OLD PEARL STREET M. E. CHURCH.

[The building was an old, one-story frame structure, with two front doors—and for many years has been doing duty as a third class dwelling, on the west side of South Tenth Street, near Main. The contracting parties were highly respectable citizens, but for prudential reasons the names are not given. He is, however, a wealthy manufacturer, and the "best man" a flourishing banker, of Knightstown, in this State. No tickets of admission were required in those days, and the performance was open to all. The description following is literally true.]

I sat amid a waiting throng ;
Silence reigned profound and long ;
Every optic nerve was strung,
And auditory fibres rung ;

While, ever and anon, the shout :
"They come ! They come !" was heard
    without.
In gay and glee, a happy pair—
The bride, the fairest of the fair—

Were seen to cross the threshold o'er,
Succeeded by some couples more.
They passed adown the spacious aisle
To meet the parson, who, the while,

Arose, in sanctimonious mood,
To meet the groom and "ladie goode."
Attendants stood on either side,
To see the "nuptial knot" was tied.

When all was o'er, and " Hymen's bands "
Were linked about their gentle hands,
They bowed in silence, and withdrew,
To where no vulgar eyes could view,

Nor meddling spirits interpose
Annoyance to the heart's repose.

Angelic love — most heavenly flame,
Whose mission is to soothe and tame
The wildest passions of the breast,
And calm them into perfect rest —

Mayst thou forever hold thy sway,
And never pass from earth away.

MARCH 3, 1850.

WHEN LIFE IS YOUNG.

When life is young, and joys forever new
Succeed each other in the distant view,
The fancy pictures images ideal,
Stamps them perfection and proclaims them real.

But as we wander on, through weary years,
Scathed and neglected, and bedewed with tears,
We, all too soon, shall comprehend the truth
That fiction mingles in the dreams of youth.

NOVEMBER 10, 1861.

POEMS AND SKETCHES.

A WAIL AT THE WEATHER.

[Suggested by the remarkable gloom of March, which was supplemented by severe cold and snow, lasting to the 7th of April, 1891.]

Sol's genial ray doth oft display
    Its fervor in the Spring,
But in this year hath lent no cheer,
    Nor kindly offering.

But clouds, instead, in gloom, have shed
    Their tears, in rainy sadness,
Till man, distressed, hath been depressed,
    Impatient, unto madness;

While Phœbus' car still rides afar,
    And frost and snow prevail,
And song of bird is rarely heard,
    But chilling winds assail.

No floral forms yet dare the storms
    That bluster round the world,
But seek repose beneath the snows,
    With scarce a leaf unfurled;

Nor bud of tree, as yet, we see
    Expanded into bloom,
But seem as dead as life were fled,
    Imprisoned in a tomb.

We prithee, sun, thy course to run,
 And shed thy genial rays,
So we may feel not woe, but weal,
 As in the former days ;

For thou art life, and life were strife
 Without thy influence shed,
And this fair world, from sunlight hurled,
 Must soon be dark and dead.

April 10, 1891.

ENIGMA.

I am seen in the air,
 Though in earth I am not,
Save "beautiful Erin,"
 That "bonnie, bright" spot.

The Indian's fair bride,
 In her merriest glee,
Proudly calls me her own
 As I be ! As I be !

I have ne'er been in love,
  Though its victim I am,
Contending for beauty,
  Or bearing the palm.

But, with the glad victor,
  And in his bright shield,
I am seen to stand forth
  In the midst of the field.

I know not the foe,
  But in strife I advance,
With an arm that is strong,
  And an uplifted lance.

I am found, it is said,
  With the patriarchs old,
Inmingled with virtues
  That never were told.

While mistress and maiden
  Each give me a part
In all their affections,
  And choice of a heart.

Now, reader, be kindly,
  And tell me my name,
And thou shalt be sharer
  In all of my fame.

JANUARY 9, 1849.

TO ONE DEPARTED.

The storm of life is o'er, and death has closed the scene ;
Remorseless time has rent the viewless chain
Which coupled earth and old eternity and main,
And thou art launched upon the dark unseen.

No mortal eye hath e'er beheld the future,
And yet, alone, thou goest forth to seek its shores.
Beware ! Or thy frail bark may founder, and no more
Return to harbor.   Have thou all secure ;

For we have never kenned what lies beyond the vale,
Nor will we ever, till the spirit's boundless flight,
Unloosed from thraldom, doubt and brooding night,
Hath seen afar some fleet of heavenly sail.

O ! May'st thou safely reach the shores of that fair
    stream,
Where joys eternal ever shine and loom
Like noon-day suns, to dissipate the gloom,
Or stars of promise, 'mid the soul's effulgent gleam.

May heaven's high King receive thee to His fold,
And grant thee all the pleasures of the hosts above ;
Where thou canst praise Him for His boundless love
And mercies infinite, by mortal tongues untold.

SUNDAY, OCTOBER 22, 1854.

RANDOM THOUGHTS,

Suggested by a thunder-storm, attended with hail and rain, during the
night of January 28th, 1893.

'Mid lightning's flash and thunder's crash,
  The hail and rain descended,
And spread its stormy deluge far,
  As light and darkness blended.

The snow, which lay for many a day,
  Heaped on the frozen ground,
In haste departed on its way
  To river and sea and sound.

Farewell ! and may it not return,
  To chill us with its greeting,
For its cold presence we shall spurn,
  And shrink from such a meeting.

We long for Summer's sun again,
  With genial airs of heaven,
To woo, with zephyr's soft refrain,
  The birds and flowers, at even'.

Happy, indeed, our lives should be
  Were sunshine never-ending —
A paradise for thee and me,
  Around the world extending :

Where birds are always on the wing,
   And flowers are ever blooming ;
Where tuneful souls delight to sing,
   And know no cares, consuming.

Pray Heaven to grant a realm like this —
   Where peace and love are dwelling —
That we may revel in endless bliss,
   Beyond the power of telling.

JANUARY 28, 1893.

LINES TO A BELATED GRASSHOPPER,

Found stranded on the chilly confines of Autumn, Wednesday, November 26, 1890. Mercury 34°, and a very miserable day.

Pray, Mister Grasshopper, why tarry here?
The summer is gone, and the winter is near.
You'd better seek shelter away from the cold,
Or hie to the South, would you live to be old.

The winds from the north will soon silence your
     song,
And you cannot expect to live here very long ;
For the frost is a mighty destroyer of hosts,
And you insects will all be converted to ghosts.

So get you away, and go hence, where you came,
If you wish to preserve your existence and name.
We cannot encourage the presence or stay
Of wand'ring intruders, who seek only prey ;
So take to your wings, and away and away !
And return not again for a year and a day !

THE WORLD A THEATRE.

Night's radiant lamps illume
   The firmament on high,
And earth, the mighty theatre,
   Has for its dome the sky.

Upon its monster stages .
   All mankind, arrayed
For ages upon ages,
   Have each their parts displayed.

Some acts are worthy of their authors,
   Some are not ;
The better will survive all time,
   The worse be soon forgot.

A. D. 1850.

TO EVAN WRIGHT,

———

Who was a fellow-clerk of the writer's boyhood days, with the dry
goods firm of Strattan & Wright, of this city. Mr. Wright was a
very estimable young man, and died of consumption — the result of
too close application to business.

Fare thee well ! departed spirit,
   God to thee has given
More than all the joys of earth —
   Eternal life in Heaven.

Troubles more shall ne'er assail,
   Nor pains of sickness ever,
For thou hast made thy home the sky,
   And earth shall know thee never.

The angel hosts shall welcome thee,
   High in that holy place,
Where naught but mercy, truth and love
   And happiness we trace.

Sin is unknown in that bright sphere,
   And sorrow cometh not ;
Nor passions, to distract the soul,
   Which are a mortal's lot.

Then fare thee well ! departed one,
 For God to thee has given
Far more than all the wealth of earth —
 A home with him in Heaven.

APRIL 22, 1849.

LINES

Suggested by a visit to "Forest Home," the country seat of Benjamin and
Emily Strattan, whose many kindnesses to the writer can
never be forgotten.

Old Time's resistless car may speed,
And crown the world with many a deed,
Ere we shall all have left this sphere,
And all the heart holds sacred here.

Our days may reach the utmost span
Appointed to the years of man,
And compass many a round of joy,
Unmixed with aught of care's alloy.

But few shall be more bright than this,
More fraught with hallowed dreams of bliss ;
Long may our recollections glow
With memories of this long ago.

JANUARY 1, 1855.

TOIL ON.

Toil on, toil on, for thy life and mine
Were but idle gifts, were they left supine.
Then work, and of wealth, to a bounteous store,
Shall fortune on thee, from her treasury pour.

And the idle may gaze, in their wonder, at will,
And envy thy riches, in idleness still ;
Whilst thou hast laid up, like the provident bee,
Good store for the winter of life — as we see.

They, thoughtless and negligent, shrouded in rags,
Whose tatters shall flaunt in the breeze — filthy flags,
Fit emblems of beggarly wretches — whose hours
Were wasted in idleness, earning no dowers.

Then mock not my efforts at striving to win
A name and life's comforts — it is not a sin.
I'd scorn to be idle —'tis a shame of such dye,
'Tis alone fitly kin to deceit and a lie.

Let me labor, while life and my health me are given,
That when I have passed this sad vale into heaven,
I may do so all conscious of duty fulfilled,
As the Maker designed and the Master has willed.

JANUARY 27, 1856.

A DOGGEREL ON A DEPARTED CANINE.

[This poem refers to a favorite terrier, the property of a neighbor, who prized him very highly for his many good qualities. The dog became demoralized and vicious through the acts of mischievous urchins, who would torment him in passing, and who afterward poisoned him.]

Alas ! and alack ! for the manes of poor Jack ;
   He has gone to his dreamless repose ;
He peacefully yeilded his breath, at his death,
   And surrendered his checks at the close.

He faithfully served his kind keepers in life,
   Though some of his traits were displeasing ;
His barking propensities led into strife
   With impish young urchins, for teasing.

But even poor humans may err, and a cur
   Is surely not better than they ;
Then why should we stress his few faults, which
       were less
   Than some we commit ev'ry day.

So, a truce to his weakness — at times he had
       meekness
   Quite up to the mark of his betters :
He was playful and civil, a good-natured
       " divil,"
   Sans tricks, or a knowledge of letters.

Farewell, to his dogship ! His voice never more
Shall awaken our slumbers at even ;
But instead, may be heard on Plutonian shores,
Dog Island, or Mount of Ben Nevin.

OCTOBER 21, 1875.

IMPROMPTU LINES,

Suggested by an old bonnet. once the property of Mrs. Grace Vausant,
made in 1838. and exhibited by the writer at a meeting of the
Historical Society, held in the new court house,
Saturday, May 20, 1893.

Full fifty years ago in style ;
Pray do not curl the lip or smile ;
For she who wore me then, like you,
Was happy, for my form was new.

But time, resistlessly as fate,
Puts all we cherish out of date ;
And that fair hat you wear to-day,
Will scarcely see its fiftieth May.

MAY 20, 1893.

TO AN ABSENT BROTHER,

For some years resident at New Orleans, Louisiana.

Dear brother, shouldst thou chance to see
  These lines — from one you love —
I ask that thou remember me,
  In palace, hall, or grove.

Though time and distance sever us,
  The joy may yet be ours
To meet on life's broad stage once more,
  'Mid childhood's vernal bowers.

Should stern misfortune be thy lot,
  Or sickness, cold, attend,
Be humble, for Jehovah will,
  In love, the meek befriend.

Then fare thee well! my brother dear,
  Till we shall meet again ;
That health, prosperity, be yours,
  My prayer is — Amen !

October, 1847.

THE CHASE.

"A little nonsense, now and then,
Is relished by the best of men."

Albicore, in wondrous haste,
Sped away, across the waste ;
In pursuit went horse and hounds,
With accelerating bounds ;
Allectation being great,
Each has sought to know his fate.
Herpetologists are they,
Yet they scarcely dare to stay,
But pursue their chase so far
That fatigue and many a scar
Has unfitted them to go
Otherwise than sure and slow.
Pabulum is what they need,
Both the rider and the steed ;
Peonity, to drive ahead,
Left them less alive than dead.

[See Webster for definitions.]

February 20, 1895.

A SABBATH AFTERNOON IN SUMMER.

What stillness broods on all around !
How dead the silence seems !
Its depth is fathomless ! no sound
Is heard, though Nature teems

With life : the Sabbath reigns supreme,
And sheds its holy influence far
As Andes' peaks — 'neath sunlight's gleam —
Or distant Alps, or twinkling star.

Sunday, July 20, 1856.

A FRAGMENT.

Dear brother, how often I think of the past,
And muse o'er the pleasures it brought us ;
The many fair dreams that we fancied in youth,
And the frost-work of bliss that was wrought us.

I sigh, when the images dearly beloved,
That in childhood so fondly we cherished,
Arise in my mind, and present to my view
But a wreck of the hopes that are perished.

A. D. 1851.

MUSINGS.

———

I sigh to see the changing leaf,
　For Autumn days are here ;
I sigh to know that life is brief,
　And age is drawing near.

'Tis sad to know that wintry winds
　Will come at Nature's call ;
'Tis e'en more sad to know that Death
　O'er Nature spreads its pall.

Our lives are all a fleeting show ;
　No lasting joys are given ;
We dwell amid fair scenes below,
　But soon fond ties are riven.

The leaf that now is sere, was green,
　In Summer's early time ;
The aged man we just have seen,
　Was youthful in his prime.

But soon, alas ! the years go by,
　And soon the young grow old :
For ev'ry living form must die,
　And mingle with the mold.

Let us so live that when our years
  Have reached life's utmost span,
We may triumphantly go hence,
  Obedient to His plan.

SUNDAY, SEPTEMBER 25, 1892.

IMPROMPTU LINES TO MARCH.

Thou art a most unlovely month,
  Whose elemental strife
Afflicts us, through the day or night,
  With dire experience rife.

Sunshine to-day, to-morrow rain,
  With wind and storm the next,
Alternate, with their sad refrain,
  Till all mankind are vexed.

Thank heaven ! Thy race will soon be run,
  Thy iron rule be o'er ;
And sleet and snow and gloom be done,
  And nature smile once more.

THURSDAY, MARCH 26, 1891.

TO ONE AT REST.

M. A. E.

Thou dear departed, fondly loved —
  For many a year at rest —
Thy soul long sought its last repose,
  Forever to be blest;

Yet, countless times since thou hast gone
  Have I remembered thee :
By night and day, in crowds and lone,
  Thy form has haunted me.

Thy absence here has left a void
  Which none can ever fill
As thy deft hand and brain were wont
  When thou wert with us still.

Thou wert so good and true and kind —
  Thy worth no words can tell :
Thy even-tempered, noble mind
  None living could excel.

Thou didst a hallowed influence shed,
  As roses shed perfumes,
And though thy spirit long has fled,
  Its incense ne'er consumes.

We ofttimes pray to be with thee —
    Lone, wandering here below —
And when, at last, from life set free,
    May we each other know :

Such is my earnest, fond desire —
    Naught else could lend such bliss —
And to that end my hopes aspire,
    In climes more fair than this.

MARCH 10, 1894.

EARLY AUTUMN.

How sadly and mournfully sighs the soft breeze,
    As it lightly disports with the leaves,
Like one who in sorrow bewaileth a friend —
    The Autumn wind seemingly grieves.

Alas ! It may well, for the Summer is gone,
    With its bright sunny face, and its flowers ;
The garden is changed to a desolate spot,
    Where so often I lingered for hours.

E'en while I discourse, I can feel the rude blast —
    Which so lately was balmy and bland —
At first like the delicate touch of a friend,
    Anon like some rude, clutching hand.

The breeze, which so late seemed a whispering sigh,
    Has passed over valley and hill,
To return, with the boreal blasts of the North,
    With a breath that is icy and chill.

SUNDAY, SEPTEMBER 10, 1854.

COULD PRAYERS AVAIL.

Could prayers avail to hasten Spring,
And usher in its sunny days —
Methinks it very long delays —
I'd leap for joy, and shout and sing.

It seems so chill to see the snow —
A cold, white mantle on the ground —
The landscape looks so dreary round ;
The spirits feel no genial glow.

Thank Heaven, delay cannot be long —
The sun seems warmer even now ;
And folks will soon begin to plow ;
And birds, in glee, renew their song ;

The grass grow green, the flowers bloom,
The trees put forth the budding leaf —
And may the time be very brief
When all the air will be perfume.

Sunday, February 18, 1894.

THE DAY WE CELEBRATE.

The glorious Fourth was ushered in
    With rush of rocket, skyward sent,
And cannons' roar, and crackers' din,
    While Babel sounds with those were blent :
Huzzas and shoutings, born of glee —
The soulful language of the free.

The people, in their might, appeared,
    To manifest their joy, once more,
For Liberty — whose tree was reared
    By patriots on these happy shores ;
With joyful hearts, they thus expressed
How we, through freedom, have been blessed.

Long may we keep the sacred trust
  To us confided by our sires —
Whose forms have crumbled into dust,
  But whose brave deeds still prompt these fires !
Let each returning natal day
Find no less fervor and display !

And long was kept the revel going.
  Blue lights, and red, that flash and flare,
Lit all the heavens aflame and glowing,
  While smoke, like incense, filled the air.
Away ! away ! dull care, away !
Glad millions celebrate to-day.

July 6, 1895.

MARCH 11TH, 1896,

Brought the heaviest and most persistent snow of the season.

And still and still and still it snows,
And still and still and still it blows,
And thus and thus and thus it goes
  In Winter's cheerless time.

Alas ! alas ! alas ! how cold,
And bleak and bleak and bleak the wold,
As I, as I, as I am told,
    In all this North-land clime.

O, haste ! O, haste ! O, haste ! dear Spring ;
Come birds, come birds, come birds, and sing ;
And Flora, Flora, Flora, bring
    Thy glorious train, to charm the year.

Shine out, shine out, shine out, O ! sun,
Till frost, till frost, till frost be done,
And light and heat are well begun,
    And longed-for Summer here.

MARCH 11, 1896.

PASSING AWAY.

Lo ! the days pass away, and the seasons decay,
    While the years bear us speedily on,
Like the tireless waves when the mad ocean raves,
    Which arise and subside, and are gone.

Our youth, like a dream or a phantom, doth seem
    So brief in its glory and bliss,
For 'tis scarcely attained until bound and enchained
    To some duty it cannot dismiss.

We plod day by day our life's rugged way,
  With the hope of reward and return,
Till the joys of desire, with our forces, expire,
  And leave but the ash and the urn.

All weary and worn, with a spirit forlorn,
  We welcome the earth as a mother :
Our form 'neath the sod, and our soul with its God,
  We rest from life's turmoil and pother.

July 26, 1895.

I KNOW NO MISANTHROPIC HOURS.

I know no misanthropic hours—
  I have no hatred for my kind :
God's love is everywhere, and ours
  Should not be to ourselves confined.

All men are brothers in this world ;
  All women should be sisters, dear ;
And over all should be unfurled
  Love's sacred banner, with its cheer.

Why should we envy those in power?
  Why should we hate the man of wealth?
To him who strives, some honest dower
  May come, by labor, void of stealth.

The world is wide enough for all —
  No conflict need arise to me ;
We should not soar that others fall,
  Nor hamper others' liberty.

His blessings every soul enjoys,
  Without a stint, or limit given,
Yet man his fellow-man annoys,
  By evil schemes not born of Heaven.

Good will, at least, if not great love,
  Is due to every mortal man :
It is not much, but Heaven above
  Includes it in her mystic plan.

Then let not misanthropic hours,
  Nor even moments, thus controlled,
Subject thee to its evil powers,
  But let love rule — that is pure gold.

OCTOBER 14, 1895.

OLD LETTERS.

A True Story.

" Old letters, old letters ; lo ! what have we here ?
A name for each friend and a date for each year ;
Old time-eaten records — lo ! how they recall
The memory of kindred, friend, lover, and all."

Here is one that was written in " thirty-three " —
It is yellow with age, as yellow can be ;
The paper is rough, without sign of a rule,
And is folded and sealed in the primitive school.

The modern envelope and stamp were unknown,
So it had to go forth on its journey alone ;
The missive was written ten miles away,*
And posted at Richmond, with little delay.

The charges were high in the early time,
For postage upon it is marked a dime ;
Its destiny hence was Yellow Springs,†
And three days' travel a message brings.

The times were slow, and the roads were bad,
And the gift of a letter was rare and glad ;
The sender thereof, long absent from home,
Now writes to a sister for news, to come.

He says he is lonely, unhappy and "blue,"
Yet his prospects are good, with plenty to do ;
But somehow a restless condition of mind
Will afflict him at times, however inclined.

He declares his intentions, if all goes well,
To make the acquaintance of some Hoosier belle ;
With more of the sort, in a gossiping way,
But little to interest us of to-day.

A letter that follows — of "thirty-six" —
Shows that he yielded to Cupid's tricks ;
And one, that was dated in "thirty-eight,"
Tells how the *baby* had walked of late.

Long since, all the parties hereto concerned
Unto God and His keeping their souls returned ;
And the baby above, in her after life,
Became to the writer a loving wife.

Thus Time, on his tireless pinions, doth fly —
To-day we are here, and to-morrow we die ;
We act our brief parts as they fall to our lot,
Depart and go hence, to be gone and forgot.

*Near Abington, Wayne county.
+Yellow Springs, near Springfield, Ohio.

MARCH 14, 1894.

EARLY SPRING.

Farewell ! Clouds and storms of Winter,
  Spring returning breaks thy chains ;
Smiling sunbeams loose thy fetters,
  And in air dissolves thy reign.

Sweet and dewy exhalations
  Greet us from the fields around,
While the distant forest echoes
  And re-echoes joyous sounds.

Music made by feathered minstrels - -
  Songsters of the upper air —
Happy in their vocal praises,
  Free, alike, from toil and care.

Shrub and floweret rise in gladness ·
  From the teeming mother earth ;
Cheered by ray divine, of Phœbus,
  Nourished by her into birth.

Praise we then the Gracious Giver
  For his bounties, manifold ;
Resurrected life rejoiceth,
  That it never groweth old.

MARCH, 1850.

MY LOVE AND I.

Just two score years ago to-day —
　It seems not half so long —
Since we assumed life's wedded ways,
　Happy as birds of song.

Our lives were fair, and not a cloud
　Obscured the love that shone ;
A buoyant hope our souls endowed,
　For cares were all unknown.

Thus we set forth on times broad sea,
　Our faith in each was strong ;
We prayed for health — our only plea —
　And that our lives be long.

Ours was a charming cot and grounds,
　With fruits of various kinds,
Embowered with vines within its bounds,
　And flowers by heaven designed.

Our home a joyous Eden seemed,
　Contentment made us blest ;
Our lives were all we e'er had dreamed,
　Each evening gave us rest.

Success attended all we did,
　No effort proved in vain ;
The road to fortune ne'er was hid,
　The way seemed broad and plain.

Thus year on year went swiftly by,
　In labor, love and joy,
With not a tear, nor e'en a sigh,
　To add to life's alloy.

At length a direful day arose,
　When all our hopes were high ;
Ill-health disturbed our fond repose —
　A fiend of evil eye.

It came as with a stealthy tread,
　Scarcely observed or seen —
A thief, ill-omened, all may dread —
　My love and self between.

She was the shining mark it sought,
　And claimed her for its own —
Such priceless jewel gold ne'er bought
　Such blight we ne'er had known.

She sickened, and for many a day,
　Un-murmuring, bore her woes
With more than human fortitude,
　Till came at length the close.

That was a sad and hapless day,
  When she passed hence from life,
Compelled to tread death's cheerless way —
  My own dear, cherished wife.

Since then we oft remember her
  As one long laid to rest :
A soul too pure for this cold world —
  Loved, sanctified and blest.

FEBRUARY 14, 1895.

LINES TO A BUTTERFLY.

Poor little butterfly !
  So weary and cold !
Brief was thy summer's day,
  And soon it was told !

The cheer of the sunshine,
  The bloom of the flowers,
Delight thee no longer,
  In Autumn's chill hours.

And alas ! Nevermore
  Wilt thou flit o'er the fields,
Or seek in the rosebud
  The nectar it yields.

The clover is blighted,
  The wild-flower is dead ;
The forest is leafless,
  Its beauties are fled.

But the sheen of thy wings,
  And thy glorious flight,
Were the regalest things
  That e'er gave me delight.

And thy memory ever
  We fondly shall cherish —
A vision of beauty
  That never can perish.

A spirit of gladness,
  A joy to the heart —
We quit thee with sadness,
  Forever to part.

Thy journey is ended,
  Thy day-dreams are o'er ;
Thy flight is suspended —
  Farewell, evermore !

'Tis the story, in brief,
  Of the great and the small :
We all have our day,
  And the end comes to all.

NOTE.—The aforesaid butterfly had fallen to the walk, beside the house, benumbed by the cold.

NOVEMBER 1, 1890.

WHEN FIRST WE MET.

—

Impromptu Lines to Mattie.

'Tis true I loved thee dearly then,
But, O ! I love thee better now,
And trust, supported by His will,
To keep through life the sacred vow.

I feel thou art too good for me —
Deserving more than I can give —
But if thou wilt but trust in me,
I'll love and serve thee while we live.

I know no happier hours than those
Which swiftly sped when at thy side :
Each moment seemed so fraught with joy,
For thou hast been my only pride.

O ! may we long enjoy that bliss —
The brightest boon to mortals given ;
That love which springs from kindred hearts —
The utmost wealth this side of Heaven !

FEBRUARY 19, 1855.

RETROSPECTION.

—

When we remember all —
  The past of by-gone years —
Fond memory doth recall,
  Our eyes are filled with tears.

How thoughtless childhood fled,
  With all its cares and joys ;
The hopes and fears now dead,
  Since we were careless boys.

How youth advanced apace,
  And aspirations wild
Took boyish fancies' place,
  And we ignored the child.

At length, to manhood brought-
  At least so told the years —
A goal we long had sought,
  Upon life's way appears.

New duties now devolved
  Upon our manhood's powers ;
Nor could we be absolved
  Through all its weary hours.

Life's conflict now was on,
  Its labors had begun ;
And ere the day was gone,
  A victory must be won.

We strove with faith and prayer,
  We labored long and true,
The world's success to share,
  And crown our hopes anew.

The end was blest, in part,
  With worldly wealth and store ;
But oh ! alas ! fond heart,
  What disappointments sore !

The friends we loved have passed,
  Beyond our mortal ken,
To peace, at least, at last,
  Out from the homes of men.

Fond hopes we once enjoyed,
  Of long continued bliss,
Were blasted or alloyed —
  So we the dream dismiss.

Thus have we wrought and sought ;
  Thus have we lived life's day ;
Much of our gain was naught,
  Nor do we long to stay.

A few brief years of care,
    Spiced with a joy or pain,
And we shall sojourn where
    None will return again.

The morn of life is hope,
    The noon is care and toil ;
Its eve hath little scope,
    But endeth all turmoil.

JUNE 13, 1893.

JUST AS THY NATURE URGES.

Just as thy nature urges, weep or smile,
Yet let not faults nor follies thy true heart beguile ;
If sunshine enter, let thy soul bestow
Some marks of favor, lest it quickly go.

If shadows wing their way across thy path,
Let sadness hold its sway, instead of wrath ;
But through all seasons and all coming times,
May joy-bells cheer thee with their happy chimes.

FEBRUARY 21, 1893.

CRINOLINE.

We are coming, Flora Flimsey,
    We are coming right along ;
We are coming, Flora Flimsey,
    Full an hundred thousand strong.

We are coming with a hustle,
    We are coming in great troops ;
We are coming in a bustle,
    We are coming with our hoops.

We are coming, dearest Flora,
    We are coming like a storm ;
We are coming, very mighty,
    We are coming to reform.

And you'll be glad to see us —
    With an awful swell and dash —
For ev'ry sister's soul of us
    Is bound to make a mash.

The men will all go crazy
    When they see us in our skirts ;
It will make them feel so mazy —
    We're a jolly set of flirts.

We will capture all the women,
   And we'll captivate the men ;
And when we've captured everything
   We'll change the fashion, then.

But we'll never cease our striving
   After novelties and men,
Till we convert the masculines
   To Crinolines again.

MARCH 2, 1893.

MEMENTO MORI.

A Double Acrostic.

Mysterious, unknown realM —
Endless and eternal — wE
Meekly bide our time, till death shall whelM
Earthly ambition in that world, sublimE,
No eye of mortal e'er hath seeN.
The future surely dawns when life is spenT.
O! teach us, then, Thy will to dO;
Make all our strivings end and aiM
On Heaven and Thee, to center; O!
Reward our faith, our spirits cheeR,
In thee to die — so Lord, may I.

WRITTEN IN 1876.

AUTUMNAL MUSINGS.

When the leaves begin to fall,
  And the chilling winds are wailing,
Sadness shrouds us like a pall,
  For the Summer's glow is failing.

Winter's most unwelcome presence
  Follows Autumn's footsteps, fast,
With a snowy, cheerless mantle,
  Over dying Nature cast.

Songs of birds and bloom of flowers
  Cease to cheer or charm the world;
Silence reigns, and beauty slumbers—
  Happy, gleeful wings are furled.

Come, O! come, thou joyous season
  When the earth renews her prime:
Herald of re-animation—
  Summer's prelude, most sublime!

Earth and air with life now teeming,
  Floral forms, in splendor, glow;
Nature now—a Heaven, in seeming—
  Makes a Paradise below.

OCTOBER 21, 1890.

THE ROBIN.

All hail ! fair bird, in russet dressed !
Thrice welcome, as our Summer's guest !
Build in thy Northern home a nest,
    And rear thy callow young.

Thy advent heralds coming Spring ;
Make glad expectant hearts, and sing,
Till all the welkin round thee ring,
    And thy glad notes are sung !

Thou knowest well the time of flowers —
When sunshine gladdens all the hours,
And Nature sheds her gentle showers,
    To vivify the world.

When forests don their vernal dress,
The earth sends forth her fruits to bless,
'Mid sights and sounds of happiness —
    A glorious dream unfurled.

Who would not be a joyous bird,
Whose notes of rapture all have heard ?
A gift on thee alone conferred,
    And Heaven-designed.

Could I but fly, I'd fly with thee —
Thou pure, blithe spirit, wild and free —
O'er all the world, its charms to see,
Of Nature, art, or mind.

FEBRUARY 3, 1893.

TWO TRANSLATIONS

Of the Following German Stanza.

"Das meer ist tief, das meer ist weit,
Doch gehet Gottes Herlichkeit
Noch tiefer als das meeres grund,
Noch weiter als das erdenrund."

The sea is deep, the sea is wide,
Yet God's great glory doth abide
Still deeper than the ocean's ground,
Still farther than earth's utmost bound.

The sea is deep, the sea is wide,
Yet God's great glory doth abide
In regions deeper than the sea,
And farther than earth's boundary.

JULY 30, 1889.

IN THE DAYS WHEN I WENT TIPSYING.

In the days when I went tipsying —
　A long time ago —
The bars and taverns were so thick,
　I had n't far to go.

And thus I wasted precious time,
　Nor knew how came it so —
In days when I went tipsying,
　A long time ago.

I traveled down the paths of sin
　As fast as I could go,
And soon became a wreckless man —
　As surely you must know.

I shuffled cards, and played at dice,
　And wandered to and fro ;
I lost my health, I lost my wealth,
　And gained, instead, but woe.

My wife, at length, deserted me
　For drinking rum and wine ;
For she, the jewel, never could
　Companion with the swine.

I revelled still, in sottish ways,
  With boon companions old,
Till rags and misery were my lot —
  The gutters and the cold.

Despised and hated of my kind,
  I had nowhere to go ;
And often prayed that I might die
  Amid the drifting snow.

But I reformed — became a man —
  And ceased to drink and revel ;
And now, that I am sane once more,
  I loathe that liquid devil.

NOTE.—The first verse of this song is very old; the remainder was built up from it.

FEBRUARY 25, 1889.

SOME REFLECTIONS,

Suggested by the presence of a rose-bush, in full bloom, at the head of
a grave in Elkhorn cemetery.

A rose-tree, in its glorious bloom,
Stood guard above a silent tomb ;
Its flowers were gay, its leaves were green,
Its perfume filled the air, serene ;

And though the year was waning fast,
And wintry storms must come, at last,
Its ruby petals, bright and fair,
Still sought new life from sun and air.

It was a token love had given —
A hint of holier joys in Heaven ;
Its buds were blessings, unawares ;
Its exhalations, silent prayers ;
Its thorns were human ills and cares.

Its brief existence told that we
Should likewise shortly cease to be ;
That as we lived, so should we die :
Then let our aims be pure and high.

WEDNESDAY, NOVEMBER 19, 1890.

THE ROSE.

The Rose, the Rose, the beautiful Rose !
The queenliest flower of all that grows !
A gift of the gods to May and June,
When Nature's charms are all in tune !

When Phœbus shines with a ray subdued,
And birds are busy with nest and brood ;
When the sky is bright and our hearts are light,
And the world partakes of Elysian delight ;

When woods are green and fields are fair,
And sounds of joy fill all the air,
And laughing brooks, meandering by,
Reflect and mirror a cloudless sky.

Then hail to the Rose, the glorious Rose !
The queenliest flower of all that grows !
A gift of the gods to May and June,
When Nature's charms are all in tune !

MAY 24, 1894.

ARTLESSNESS IN ART.

There is an artlessness in art,
   All women know,
Which they employ to wound the heart,
   With Cupid's bow.

To-day she wreathes herself in smiles,
   To-morrow, frowns ;
The next, it may be, she beguiles
   With newest gowns ;

A ringlet or a ribbon, fair,
   From waist or neck ;
A pin, or charm, a "bang" of hair,
   A "beauty" speck.

Whatever be the means employed,
   She bears the palm ;
She rules all nations, and the "tribes"
   Of "Uncle Sam."

September 1, 1895.

LINES

———

Suggested by some late rose-buds, on a bush in our front yard.

A rose-bud strove in vain to bloom,
　The season strove to kill it ;
And thus it failed to shed perfume,
　For Nature failed to will it.

November's chilling winds were keen,
　Too keen, its soul to cherish ;
So, humbly, it was shortly seen
　To bow its head and perish.

Thus many a human soul has bowed
　Before life's chilling storms,
And died — from out the thoughtless crowd
　Of striving human forms.

This world holds dearth of sympathy
　Too charily bestowed ;
And while some loving hearts there be,
　It has not freely flowed.

To Him who lets no sparrow fall
　Without His loving care,
Let all His needy children call —
　To Him direct your prayer.

NOVEMBER 18, 1892.

SLEEVES, AND HOOPS, AND BUSTLES.

———

Thou latest of wonders, O ! feminine sleeve —
    Which fashion prescribes for the fair —
When will the dear creatures of thee take their leave,
    Some other new folly to dare ?

Thou clearly deformest and makest a fright
    Of those who are patrons of thee :
However they may in thy fullness delight,
    We nothing of beauty can see.

Some decades ago it was hoops, in extreme,
    With a form so distended, alas !
The climax of folly was reached, it would seem,
    For scarcely two persons could pass.

Next followed the bustle — a rearward display —
    Most vulgar contrivance, indeed :
Which flourished a season, and then passed away,
    As fashion some new fad decreed.

Thus, weakness and wickedness constantly tend
    To display and extravagance, ever :
The " hoop " and the " bustle," the old " Grecian
        bend,"
    With the " sleeve " as the latest endeavor.

Why not, for a change, sew wings to the back,
    And make the fair creature a bird —
To seek, in new regions, an untrodden track,
    Far away from all styles so absurd?

September 14, 1895.

PASSING AWAY.

The days, the weeks, the months, the years,
Fly swiftly, as revolving spheres —
Or some vast river's restless flow,
Upon whose bosom hence we go.

The child to youth, the youth to age,
Till we attain life's latest stage,
When mercy, with her mystic wand,
Conducts us to that unknown land.

Where all, at last, in death shall sleep,
Profound and silent, long and deep,
No sound of trump shall break the spell —
Farewell ! ye worldly cares, farewell !

Released at last, at rest for aye,
We yield this tenement of clay,
And seek a home with Nature's God,
Where none but spirit forms have trod.

December 15, 1892.

MARY HAD A LITTLE DOG.

———

A True Story.

Mary had a little dog ;
  His fleece was black and tan ;
And ev'rywhere that Mary went,
  He just as surely ran.

He went with her up town, sometimes ;
  And when she went a-shopping,
His antics made the people laugh,
  Wherever she was stopping.

He wore a tiny little bell,
  That made a dainty clatter ;
And came with such a nervous rush
  That ev'rything would scatter.

He loved to put the cats to flight,
  And sought them, here and there ;
But when they scampered out of sight,
  His " bark " was on the air.

His mistress taught him many tricks,
  To please herself and friends,
And had him double up like sticks,
  Uniting both his ends.

He'd stand upon his hinder legs,
  And thus would strut around,
And, leaping over Mary's " pegs,"
  Would sit upon the ground.

This little imp would leap, or lie,
  Or run, or roll, or stand ;
And grin and whine, or feign to die,
  Or bark, at her command.

He was a cunning little brute
  As ever you did see —
He'd nestle down in Mary's lap,
  Or climb upon her knee.

She prized him for his many pranks —
  So unlike any other ;
He had no little sisters, dear,
  Nor had he any brother ;

But Mary, in the fullness of
  Her sympathetic heart,
Would say she was his dear mamma,
  Because he was so smart.

And now I've told you all I know
  About this little creature,
Except — his master was a man,
  His mistress was his teacher.

Märch 20, 1891.

LINES

Suggested by the tolling of the Pearl Street M. E. Church bell, for
divine service.

How sadly sweet its echoes float,
　How many a tale 't could tell,
If 't had the power events to note,
　And tongue could speak as well.

A daily record of our sins,
　And those which are forgiven,
Might be tolled out upon the air,
　Or wafted up to Heaven.

Although its tones breathe not in chimes
　A language, realistic,
They hint to us of fairer climes —
　Supremely grand and mystic.

We pray Thee, Lord, that we may be
　More worshipful and lowly ;
That we, at last, Thy Face may see —
　Renewed, redeemed and holy.

Then ring out cheerily again —
　Thou dear old Sabbath bell ;
Far over hill and vale and glen,
　Let thy sweet echoes swell.

Recall the erring wanderer home,
  To seek the house of prayer —
Though far in distant lands he roam —
  That he may worship there.

For He who grants His blessings here,
  Will, in his boundless love,
Prepare for all his children, dear,
  A home with Him above.

Then ring out cheerily again —
  Thou dear old Sabbath bell ;
Far over hill and vale and glen,
  The joyful tidings tell.

SUNDAY, OCTOBER 15, 1854.

THE RAIN.

A Protest.

It is all very plain
That the rain rains rain,
In a dull, monotonous,
And sad refrain.

The grass may grow,
And the flowers may blow,
But I like not rain,
With its sad refrain.

For the sunshine, fair,
And the balmy air,
Have a charm for me
That I feel and see.

So, away with the rain
And its sad refrain,
For it makes me " blue,"
Which is all too true.

And the world were brighter,
And our hearts were lighter,
If the sun shone more
On this mundane shore.

So we pray Thee, then —
Again and again —
That the sun may shine
With a light divine.

For we love not rain,
With its dull refrain —
Which makes us sad,
When we should be glad —
Because of its doleful,
Dull refrain.

MARCH 22, 1893.

A BOYISH DREAM.

In youth the world's a circus-show,
And women angels, here below.

Maiden of majestic mien —
Robed in modesty, serene —
Thou art my ideal queen :
Gentle, and divinely fair ;
Pure of speech, and culture rare ;
Goodness beaming from thy face,
Lends each charm a living grace.
Artlessness, in every art,
Of thy nature is a part ;
With a heart to love inclined —
Tender, lofty, and refined ;
Dreamy orbs, of limpid blue,
Mirror Heaven's cerulean hue ;
Cheeks, with rosy health aglow,
Show the spirit's happy flow ;
Ebon locks, and teeth of pearl,
Make of thee a peerless girl :
Dignified, and calm as even' —
Fit for Paradise, or Heaven !

May I, then, on bended knee,
Ask that thou wilt hear my plea?
I would be a slave to thee;

I would worship at thy shrine —
Consecrate my life to thine —
If thou wilt be only mine.

Only promise this to me,
And I swear that I will be
All that thou couldst ask of me.

Time shall ever prove me true —
Distant though I be from you —
Death, alone, the tie shall sever :
While we live, I 'll love thee ever —
Aye, forever and forever.

MONDAY, JULY 20, 1891.

MAY 19, 1894.

With bluster, rain and snow, combined,
And cold, at thirty-six, to find
We are to cheerless thoughts inclined ;
So, prithee, pass without delay,
Thou dreary, nineteenth day of May.

But yesterday men died of heat,
While passengers upon the street ;
The air was wrought to high degrees,
Which soon became a boreal breeze —
And now, alas ! we almost freeze !

The rose-tree, with its radiant bloom,
Is cold and chill, amid the gloom ;
For its dank leaves and shrunken form
Are martyrs to an Arctic storm ;

While bird and beast and lordly man
Suffer alike — as best they can —
From Nature's all-perverted laws,
For which we can assign no cause.

More fickle than the ways of men,
Climatic changes seem ; and then
If Nature's charms our hearts beguile,
With balmy breeze, or sunny smile,
Some disappointment lurks the while.

Stability has no place here ;
Each day and week and month and year
Doth still its various changes bring'—
To man, and every living thing
Upon the earth, to which we cling.

SATURDAY, MAY 19, 1894.

NOTE.—On the 17th inst. deaths from sunstroke were reported in various parts of the country, since which we have had snow, frost, and cold weather, to date.—May 31, 1894.

TO E. J. S.

———

Think not that I forget, Lizzie,
  Think not that I forget ;
Though time and distance sever us —
  Think not that I forget.

I love thee far too well, Lizzie,
  To cease to love thee yet ;
And while the rose and lily bloom,
  I never shall forget.

I often muse o'er happy hours
  We spent when e'er we met —
The happiest of our lives, Lizzie —
  I never shall forget.

Then think not I forget, Lizzie,
  O ! think not I forget ;
Though time and distance sever us,
  I never can forget.

January 20, 1848.

TO MISS SARAH F——,

On Receiving a Basket of Flowers.

Dear lady, may the joys of life
  Be thine, through many a year,
With countless friends, to cheer thee on
  Thy pilgrimage, while here.

May all thy deeds with love be fraught,
  Life's destiny to fill ;
Fresh hopes renew thee every morn,
  To bear each rising ill.

May mem'ry's choicest roses bloom,
  Thy pathway to adorn —
Still fragrant with life's early dews ;
  Of beauty, all unshorn.

May flowers, such as thou didst send,
  Receive thy tender care :
Fit emblems of thyself, fair one —
  Bright, beautiful, and rare ;

And lastly, though not least, dear girl,
  Accept my kind regards ;
And, though they seem but trifling gifts,
  They are my best rewards.

JULY 15, 1854.

AN HUMBLE TRIBUTE

TO A DEAR, DEPARTED FRIEND, NELSON STALEY.

Thy gentle spirit winged its flight
    To regions in the sky ;
And dwells with its Creator, there,
    To never, never die.

Though friends and kindred mourn thy loss,
    They vainly shall deplore ;
For thou hast bid adieu to earth,
    And will return no more.

On California's distant plains —
    Washed by Pacific's wave —
A gentle mound marks the sad spot
    Where thou hast found a grave.

Alas ! dear Nelson — many a sigh
    Is heaved for thee, I ween ;
And many a tear, in silence, steals
    Down beauty's cheeks unseen.

Full many a heart that beat for thee,
    Still notes its happier hours
As those which passed when thou wert near,
    And counts them memory's flowers.

E'en now, methinks I hear thy voice —
  Its tones distinct and clear —
Now rich and deep, in song outpoured ;
  Now sprightly, yet sincere.

Alas ! that thou didst die so soon —
  So soon from us depart ;
For all who knew thee loved thee well —
  Thee and thy noble heart.

But thou hadst numbered all thy years,
  And couldst no longer stay ;
For He who rules in wisdom, sent
  And beckoned thee away.

MARCH 13, 1853.

TO RACHEL M. A————.

[This is the writer's earliest poetical venture extant.]

I 've loved thee, dearest, to distraction :
Loved thy every word and action ;
Loved thy form and features, fair,
And loved thy very auburn hair.

I 've often fancied thee divine ;
As often fancied thou wert mine,
And fancied — as I truly might —
A life with thee were pure delight.

Then, dearest, may I hope return
Of love, that constantly doth burn
Within a heart that cannot rest
Until, by thee, 'tis truly blest?

TO MISS MARY R——,

On Receiving a Bouquet of Flowers.

Thank thee, kindly lady, fair,
For thy gift, so choice and rare ;
And believe it gave me pleasure
To receive so fair a treasure.

Roses bright, of various hue,
Clasping sparkling drops of dew ;
Fresh, and blushing, from the stem,
Vieing with the fairest gem —
Fit for regal diadem.

June, 1851.

IMPROMPTU LINES

Sent, with a Gift Book, to a Little Nine-Year-Old Miss.

This book, my dear, has ''natural gas''
  Pervading all its pages —
Designed to cheer the heart of youth,
  Whate'er, by chance, the age is.

So read it o'er, and ponder well
  Its fancies, facts and follies,
And you, perhaps, may wiser grow,
  While playing with your '' dollies.''

A happy New Year ! little *Nell ;
  May love and cheer surround you,
And nothing worse than joyous mirth
  E'er trouble or confound you !

*Nellie Smurr, Brook Haven, Mississippi.

TUESDAY, DECEMBER 25, 1888.

TO ONE WHO LOVED NOT WISELY, BUT TOO WELL.

Sad news, dear friend, of thee I hear,
While I had fondly hoped that cheer,
Such as once dawned and promised fair,
Would reign, instead those clouds of care.

For once thy joyous hopes were young,
And none but happy songs were sung ;
And naught was seen of thee, or heard,
But some familiar note was stirred :

The soul could lend a willing ear,
The heart bestow a happy tear,
And all was joy, delight and pleasure,
Far beyond belief or measure.

But, O ! how darkling comes the night,
When disappointment dooms to blight
The hopes and loves of other years —
Resolved, at last, to sighs and tears.

Alas ! alas ! may Heaven protect thee,
Guide and guard thee, and direct thee,
And, like an absentee from home,
Return thee — ne'er again to roam.

MARCH 23, 1852.

LINES ON THE DEATH OF A FAVORITE CAT.

Alas ! for poor puss — how I grieve at her death !
She departed this life 'cause she got out o' breath ;
I 'm so sorry, yet cannot help thinking that she
Is far happier now than when staying with me ;

For the joys that surround her in that feline sphere
Surpass all her happiest moments while here ;
And such a rare sport she 'll have — think of it, cats !
What a blissful emotion that — chasing such rats !

For there, it is said, they are monsters in size,
And the taking 's considered a capital prize ;
May she revel in bliss, 'mid her fond occupation,
And receive all the credit due, filling her station.

MARCH 25, 1852.

APOSTROPHE.

Eternal powers ! but grant this element of bliss :
   My soul be filled with love for all mankind ;
That none may know to hate, nor see to fear,
   Thy humble instrument, who, seeing, yet is blind.

SUNDAY, SEPTEMBER 24, 1854.

SEEKING GOLD.

———

[Suggested by the discovery of gold in California. One of the writer's
earliest efforts.]

El Dorado sands that shine,
Sparkling in the secret mine,
Cheering heart of him who delves
'Neath the rocks' projecting shelves ;

Where no day-star, gleaming bright,
Sheds on him its ample light,
Giving forth refulgent rays,
Adding to the golden blaze —

Say ! hast thou the power to will
Wealth to him who labors still,
Toiling in the cheerless earth,
Where vain treasures take their birth,

And the nights of ages roll
Fancied visions o'er his soul,
Starting dreamy phantoms forth,
Seemingly of wondrous worth ;

Rearing airy castles high,
Pendant 'twixt the earth and sky ;
Richly decked with treasure o'er,
Brightly sparkling, evermore?

Such are dreams of him who delves
'Neath the rocks' projecting shelves.
Hast thou, then, the power to will
Wealth to him, or to fulfill

All the dreamy visions he
Fancies are reality?
Or to give that soul content —
On the search of treasure bent —

Who, expectant, hopes the '' powers ''
Will strew o'er him golden showers?
Foolish man, to question thus.
If thou wouldst be of the just,

Seek for wealth in God, alone —
At the altar and the throne —
Not in metals, nor in stone.

Vain delusions !   Vile desires !
Cease existence !   Quench your fires !
Man, too oft, the dupe of dreams,
Seeks the substance in its gleams.

STANZAS

———

Written during the early "gold fever" in California.

Adieu ! to the scenes of my childhood ;
　Adieu ! to my kindred and all ;
I haste to the land of the stranger,
　To rise amid fortune, or fall.

Hope, kindly beaming, shall guide me,
　On land or on turbulent main ;
And, as a bright spirit, shall point me
　To fair California's plain.

When there, amid wealth, I will revel,
　As did Montezumas of old —
In halls richly furnished with silver,
　And sparkling with gems and with gold.

Yes, such were my visions at parting,
　But, alas ! disappointment was mine !
Then stay, honored stranger — believe me ;
　The same cruel fate may be thine.

December 24, 1848.

TO CHRISTIAN RATHFON,

Who died upon the plains, in an overland journey to California, in
1849; having started from East Germantown,
Wayne county, Indiana.

Christian, thou no more art with us ;
  God receive thy spirit ;
Mayest thou in Heaven rest thee —
  All its joys inherit.

Now thy toilsome journey 's ended,
  Thou wilt meet no more
Friends or kindred, who once loved thee,
  On this mundane shore.

Far amid the desert fastness,
  In a stranger's land,
Death o'ertook thee and detained thee,
  At his fell command.

Golden dreams are vanished now,
  Earthly cares are ended,
And thy spirit — we may trust —
  To its home ascended.

August, 1849.

TO ISAAC KLINE,

On the Return of His Poem Entitled "Johnson's Vanity of Human
Wishes."

Friend Isaac Kline, this book of thine
　Gave me profoundest pleasure ;
I conned it o'er, admired its lore,
　And found a very treasure.

Accept my thanks : a kind act ranks
　Far higher than good wishes ;
The mind needs mental pabulum,
　And this a first-class dish is.

SEPTEMBER 24, 1892.

IMPROMPTU NONSENSE,

On Seeing a Cat Upon the Floor.

The cat can lie upon the floor —
　And thus can lie at will —
But I can lie upon my feet,
　Walking, or standing still.

FEBRUARY 28, 1890.

A NEW YEAR'S GREETING

To my esteemed friend, William L. John, Esq., in his seventy-ninth year.

Good native sense, keen wit
And genial ways
Have won you friends, and doubtless
Length of days.

May added years, with peace
And plenty, crowned,
Attend you still, through all
Life's devious round.

And should ill-fortune or
A foe assail,
Retrieve the first, and o'er
The last prevail.

Sunday, January 7, 1883.

AVOID EXTREMES.

Be neither very grave nor gay,
But uniformly kind and cheerful;
And happiness will ever stay
To dissipate the sad and tearful.

Sunday, January 25, 1891.

TO WILLIAM L. JOHN, ESQ.,

—

On His Eighty-eighth Birthday.

A helpless, puling infant,
  In a mother's careful arms,
Nursed to sturdy boyhood,
  By her love and winning charms ;

Then a self-reliant youth,
  Soon developed to the man —
As the tree that was a sapling
  Hath fulfilled its Maker's plan —

A wealth of brawn and muscle, .
  A brain of power and will,
To conquer native forces,
  Or to wield a trenchant quill.

Of such endowments Nature,
  Unsparingly, bestowed,
And well hast thou maintained them,
  Along life's weary road ;

For thou hast been the victor
  When other men have failed,
And, like the Roman Lictor,
  Hast often been assailed ;

But now art past the zenith
   Of manhood in its prime,
And leavest shining records
   Upon the sands of time.

Thy sun is now declining,
   And evening shades appear,
Yet may'st thou still be strengthened
   Through many a month of cheer ;

May vigor that has lengthened
   Thy years to eighty-eight,
Accord thee full an hundred,
   And not a jot abate.

So prays a friend that loves thee,
   And long has known thee well,
And wishes health and happiness,
   But would not say farewell !

SEPTEMBER 6, 1893.

THESE ARE WEARY DAYS OF WAITING.

These are weary days of waiting,
  For the coming of the Spring,
When the chill shall be abating,
  And the happy birds shall sing ;

When the sunlight shall be stronger,
  And the grass begin to grow ;
When the days at last are longer,
  And evanished all the snow ;

When the forest trees are decked
  In their robes of leafy green,
And the ground beneath is flecked
  With the shadows and the sheen ;

When the flowers begin to rise
  And expand each tiny cup,
And, ablushing, ope their eyes
  To the sun that wakes them up ;

When the butterfly and bee,
  Like gay spirits, haunt the air,
And the sunshine, like the sea,
  Shall be present everywhere —

O, then we shall be happy,
    And rejoice in life renewed ;
For the earth will seem an Eden,
    And its Giver very good.

So, farewell to the Winter,
    With its chilling winds and snow ;
For its frigid seasons freeze us,
    And we gladly see it go.

FEBRUARY 21, 1894.

WILLIAM PARRY.

[A man of most extraordinary will, energy and ability. He was mainly instrumental in the construction of the Fort Wayne railroad, and was its President for a number of years. None of his friends will ever forget his hearty greetings, nor the friendly grasp of his powerful right hand.]

Gone hence from the world and its devious ways —
Alike unconcerned for its censure or praise ;
Thy weary mortality under the sod,
And thy spirit at rest in the mansions of God.

Thou wast manly and upright, a leader of men,
And hast aided thy fellows, again and again ;
Thy kindly demeanor, thy cheerful address,
Will long be remembered, to praise and to bless.

The clasp of thy hand was the key to thy heart —
The index of feeling, and absence of art ;
Neither guile nor deception e'er entered thy soul,
And were foreign to thee as the sun to the Pole.

Direct in thy speech, unassuming and true,
Fidelity marked what thy hands had to do ;
No man was more truthful, no friend more sincere —
Thy presence was sunshine to all who were near.

A halo of goodness encircled thy brow,
And thy hearty salute I can hear even now —
A welcome not doubtful to all thou didst know —
In return we can tender but tears, as they flow.

Farewell !   Nevermore shall we see thee again —
Thy counterpart cannot be found among men :
Thou wast simply thyself, to the utmost degree —
God's symbol of manhood, pure, noble and free.

April 14, 1894.

TO WILLIAM L. JOHN.

————

Died October 17, 1896.   Aged ninety-one years. one month and eleven days.

As fruit, at maturity, falls from the tree,
  Because it is mellowed by time,
So thou hast gone out on eternity's sea,
  To abide through the ages sublime.

Kind Nature accorded thee many long years,
  With a form that was rugged and sound ;
A mind, in its prime, that encountered few peers,
  And intelligence broad and profound.

A manly deportment and frankness of speech,
  With a heart that was noble and true,
Were characteristics of thine which should teach
  The worth of true manhood anew.

As friend and companion — adviser in need —
  Few men will be missed more, I trow ;
A host in thyself, for a just cause to plead —
  No truckler to cringe or to bow.

As sturdy as would be a century's oak,
  Yet as tender at heart as a child ;
As firm as a rock, should occasion evoke —
  Sympathetic and kindly and mild.

Thy simple demeanor, devoid of pretense,
   Endeared thee to young and to old ;
For modest simplicity knows no offense,
   Nor is it intrusive or bold.

Thy early companions have all gone to rest,
   And thou, likewise, are with us no more,
But thy name shall be numbered with those who
     are blest —
On that dreamless and echoless shore.

Farewell, genial spirit, thy mem'ry we cherish,
   With all that is noble and just ;
Remembrance of thee shall still live, and not
     perish
Till we, too, are laid in the dust.

TO DR. T. H. DAVIS,

On the Return of "Looking Backward," a Reform Novel, by Edward
Bellamy.

I thank you for the book, dear sir ;
   Its words seem true and kindly ;
And now the way is made so clear,
   We need not " go it " blindly.

January 29, 1890.

THOUGHTS OF AUTUMN.

How somber and how sorrowful
  Are Autumn's dreamy days —
When Nature's life, so beautiful,
  In all its forms, decays ;

When no more flowers may dare to bloom ;
  When leaves shall fade and fall ;
When wailing winds proclaim their doom,
  And death o'ertakes them all ;

When birds, that charmed us with their strains,
  Have hied them far away ;
When cheerless, chill November rains
  Distress us, day by day ;

When frost and snow have veiled the earth,
  And hid green fields from sight —
There seems, indeed, of joy such dearth
  As when hope wings its flight. .

So those who now are young, grow old —
  The years go swiftly by —
And life's few days are soon unrolled,
  For all were born to die.

Alas ! that life should be so brief,
  Its joys so short and few ;
That hope so often ends in grief,
  To pass like morning dew.

OCTOBER 7, 1895.

DECEMBER 8, 1894.

This morning Nature seemed in tears,
  And wept a misty rain ;
Anon, great floods in torrents fell,
  In soft, melodious strain ;

For it had long withheld its stores —
  Till earth and air were dry ;
The springs beneath had ceased to flow,
  And brazen seemed the sky.

The fountains and the streams had failed :
  We neared the awful brink
Of famine — which the drouth entailed —
  Of aqua pura drink ;

But Nature — ever kind and true --
  Supplied our needs at last,
For which sincerest thanks are due,
  Since danger now is past.

THE CURFEW BELL WILL RING TO-NIGHT.

A word to the boys, and a hint to the "city fathers."

The curfew bell will ring to-night —
　Boys, heed the call and seek your homes;
The streets are schools of shame and blight,
　So do not from your firesides roam.

Be prompt to heed, be kind and true,
　Appreciate a parent's care,
Whose love would yield up all for you,
　To shield you from the tempter's snare.

The shades of night breed wickedness;
　Then vicious spirits stalk abroad,
And with their kind, in wantonness,
　Indulge in revelry or fraud.

The youthful novice launches forth
　To have a "time" in vile resorts —
Apt learner he, in crime — though young —
　Fluent of slang and foul retorts.

TO THE CITY FATHERS.

To lessen orgies on the street,
　And purge them of the ruffian brood,
Let light flood all the dark retreats —
　For light no prowler e'er withstood.

It likewise aids the moral force,
　But danger ever haunts the dark ;
All crime from light seeks sure divorce,
　To flourish far from Phœbus' spark.

TO THE BOYS.

Boys, that you may be doubly safe,
　Desert the city's streets at eve ;
And shun the doubtful play or cafe,
　For sins of youth cause age to grieve.

Be circumspect and moral now,
　And keep aloof from evil ways,
And you will make good men, I trow,
　Through lengthened years and happy days.

Farewell, remember what I say :
　Adopt the good and spurn the bad ;
The virtues should be sought alway,
　The vices only make us sad ;

Avoid the dark and seek the light ;
　Be ever armed to do the right —
For worthless boys make worthless men,
　Whom no one cares to meet again.

November 21, 1896.

I HATE THAT DRUM'S DISCORDANT SOUND.

———

" I hate that drum's discordant sound,
  Parading round and round and round."
To me it tells of war's alarms,
And none but baser spirits charms.

Employed to lead the battle's fray,
Inspire demoniac passions' play ;
Arouse the evil men possess,
Without one virtue to redress :

It is the symbol of revolt,
The horrid tocsin of assault ;
The bold and noisy thing displayed
By politics, when on parade —

To prove a weaklings's cause is strong,
Which must succumb to right ere long.
It is the shameless trickster's way
To bolster weakness, by display —

With deafening noise, parading round,
To emphasize his cause by sound.
The stilly depths of thought, below,
Far better truths assist to know.

Speech, as silver, silence golden,
Long was taught in days of olden ;
Only empty vessels ring —
Crashing sounds prove not a thing.

SATURDAY, SEPTEMBER 19, 1896.

CHARLES H. BURCHENAL.

Died December 7, 1896. Aged sixty-six years.

The mild, the scholarly, the gentle,
  The genial, intellectual friend —
Peerless 'mid " brethren " occidental,
  Who did or still Wayne's legal bar attend.

He was so kind, considerate and loving —
  Aye more — so manly and so true to all :
To home devoted, from the base removing —
  His gentleness made friends of great and small ;

Simplicity was wrought in all his being ;
  He knew no art save artlessness in art ;
The good he ever sought, the evil fleeing —
  His was a soul sincere, and kindly heart.

God created him a man, and man he was —
    An honest man — the noblest work of God :
Upright and contrite, he plead in virtue's cause —
    His soul now fled, he rests beneath the sod.

Long live his memory, for his life was just ;
    His friends were many, and they loved him well ;
He was a man whom all could truly trust ;
    Sweet be his slumbers — and a long farewell.

Tuesday, December 15, 1896.

HENRY R. DOWNING.

For twenty years an undertaker. Died December 15, 1896. Aged sixty-five years.

One more of Nature's noblemen has passed
    To that long sleep, from which no soul returns.
He wrought faithfully and long, and at the last
    Surrendered life and love, and their concerns.

His were truly arduous duties, for he led
    Thousands of his fellows to their narrow home ;
And ofttimes have his sympathetic tears been shed,
    To witness sundered ties — foreboding sorrows
        yet to come.

Sad though his calling, he had cheer for many ;
  His friends increased as years were multiplied ;
Faithful and true, he had few foes, if any ;
  His goodness was a common theme until he died.

Along the even tenor of his way,
  For many a year, stern duty kept him at his post ;
But now, alas ! his friends will never more
  Behold his well-known form amid the busy host.

Retired from duty and this life's endeavor,
  He has gone hence to seek a dreamless rest,
Where troubles never come, nor cares, forever —
  In peace supernal, to be always blest.

DECEMBER 21, 1896.

NEVER DO THOU STOOP TO CONQUER.

Never do thou stoop to conquer —
  Never cringe to mortal man :
Stand erect, in each endeavor,
  As was God's intent and plan.

Ne'er abase thyself to any ;
  Fawn not on the proud or rich :
Be a man, among earth's many,
  Though a delver in the ditch.

Men are men, however lowly,
  And the lordling is no more ;
His great goodness made all holy,
  Only some have less in store.

Pride, inflated, oft is flaunted
  In a manner most unwise,
As presuming men have vaunted
  Doubtful virtues to the skies.

Poverty is not a crime —
  Only evil-doing is ;
Works alone can make sublime
  Every being known as His.

Pay no tribute — it is weakness —
  Thou canst do thy thinking, free ;
Thou hast brains and heart and conscience,
  And hast, also, eyes to see.

Thou canst make of earth an Eden,
  For thou knowest well the right ;
Sins are not by men forgiven —
  All are equal in His sight.

See that every act is noble,
  See that every thought is high ;
Let no carnal deed cause trouble —
  Sooner yield thy breath, and die.

Ne'er surrender aught of manhood
　　To a servile act or deed :
Such abasement bodes no good,
　　Nor can there be any need.

Never do thou stoop to conquer —
　　Never bow the knee to man :
Stand erect in God's own image —
　　Such was His intent and plan.

Only servile weaklings cringe
　　In the presence of pretense,
Who might crawl to touch the fringe
　　Swaying from their garments hence.

God forbid that we should fear
　　Any form of mortal mold :
Self-respect is far too dear,
　　And our pride too great and bold.

DECEMBER 7, 1896.

POETICAL LETTERS.

TO CLAUDIUS BYLES.

ADDRESS.

To California haste thee hence,
  And speed to Claudius Byles —
In Sacramento city, dense —
  And greet my friend with smiles.

Full oft I've longed to hear from thee —
  Thou dweller on that strand
Where ''old Pacific'' rolls its waves,
  And laves its yellow sands.

Return to me an answer soon,
  And tell me how thou art —
If all those golden dreams of yore
  Are realized, at heart.

Thou hast my kind regards, old friend —
  May others prove as true —
May fortune's smiles bestow on thee
  Health, wealth, and beauty, too !

MARCH 14, 1855.

TO S. F. SMURR.

ADDRESS.

I wish this sent to S. F. Smurr,
  Brook Haven. Mississippi ;
And to that end let naught deter—
  Nor flood. nor fire, nor e'en "la grippe."

It is long since I wrote you, dear friend, and I trust
  To what I may say you will kindly give ear ;
And, though we lack eloquence, feel that we must
  Convey you our thoughts, which, though crude, are
      sincere.

We have naught to complain of, and hope this may find
  Both you and your kindred, all, happy and well,
With not a concern or care of the mind—
  A boon that is greater than language can tell.

The season just past gave us bountiful store—
  Of grasses and grain and of fruitage, the best :
Quite up to the measures of others of yore,
  And thus the glad heart of the farmer was blest ;

And yet it supplied not all needs, I confess,
  For many were idle whose hands were most willing,
And some of these bordered on want and distress,
  And could not have raised e'en a dime or a shilling ;

But such were exceptional cases with us —
  Improvident people will always be found,
Who are fluent of speech, and freely discuss
  Conditions and things, while themselves are unsound.

'Tis easy to criticise what others do,
  And expatiate largely of cause and effect —
The tariff that benefits only the few,
  Or a measure that aids all the masses, direct ;

But never so readily find we a way
  To right all the evils that wrong has produced,
For party corruption so long held its sway
  That morals, by money, were often seduced :

Thus corporate bodies bribed makers of laws,
  And used them as tools, to forward their schemes —
To the hurt of the people and honesty's cause —
  And duplicate millions beyond their own dreams.

Extravagance, too, had a hand in the trouble —
  The masses were reckless of living expense,
And did not foresee how soon the great bubble
  Must surely collapse, for the want of good sense.

To cap a fool's climax, leader Debs and his dupes
  Made a strike for their rights — as they held them
        to be —
Destroying some millions, till Government troops
  Compelled their dispersion and caused them to flee.

The hordes that were poverty-stricken before
   Are paupers, beyond peradventure, since then :
Dependent on charity — wanted no more —
   They now are both wretched and desperate men.

Experience so sad, and a lesson so dear,
   Should teach such, in future, to think for themselves:
Be led by no leader, but like men appear,
   Instead of stray sheep, who are senseless as elves.

It is now to be hoped, with the change of affairs
   The recent elections have wrought in the States,
That — doubly inspired by efforts and prayers —
   We may open to commerce prosperity's gates ;

But no more to foreigners, low-bred and vile,
   Who seek to find refuge upon our fair shores,
Nor to anarchist hordes, who assail and defile —
   To these and their allies, we must shut our doors.

Thank God for the " beacon of hope " which afar
   Gleams out through the haze and the mist of the fray!
The sun may yet shine, as did Bethlehem's star —
   To cheer and to gladden our hearts on the way.

So now, fare you well ! May all blessings be yours :
   May health and prosperity go with you ever —
The kindness of friends, and a love that endures —
   To last through a life-time of earthly endeavor !

    NOVEMBER 22, 1894.

TO MY SISTER.

——

ADDRESS.

Nebraska's fruitful plains in view,
To Brownville next thy way pursue —
Where fields are green, 'neath vernal sun —
And kindly greet Sue Jameison.

Dear Sue : — I am sad and feel lonely to-day —
Half sick and dispirited, I cannot be gay ;
The weather 's so gloomy, so scowling and cold,
'Tis enough to cause grumbling, from young and
    from old.

'Tis the sixteenth of April, and yet we 've no Spring —
E'en the birds, in their glee, dare not venture to sing.
How I long for the sunshine, as 't steals o'er the hill,
To dissolve the chill frost-work that seals up the rill ;

And the warm, gushing rains — like the tears that are
    spent —
Break forth in their pride, and be joyously spent —
Giving life, as they fall, in abundance and showers,
To all of earth's beautiful herbage and flowers !

Dear sister ! may never a care interpose,
To add one regret to thy life, till it close ;
May sorrows ne'er greet thee — like storms, dark and
dreary —
To cause thee to falter in faith, or to weary,
But, like the gay Spring-time, thy sun ever smile —
To banish each doubt, and each sorrow beguile.

APRIL 16, 1854.

THE SEASONS.

JANUARY 1, 1893.

Wet and damp, and dank and chill,
Pouring rain with might and will;
Aiding snows of yesterday
To dissolve themselves away;

Slush and moisture, all around,
Cover all the frozen ground;
Icy walk and slippery path,
Doth excite pedestrian wrath;

While with guarded steps, and slow,
All in locomotion go —
Surely, such a cheerless day,
None could ever wish to stay.

" Happy New Year," if you will,
When the elements are still;
But absurd would be the greeting,
While thus raining, snowing, sleeting.

JANUARY 1, 1893.

FEBRUARY.

This day is sadly fraught with gloom :
The sun is absent from my room,
And all without is like the tomb —
    Dark and dank and cheerless —
But since 'tis not the "day of doom,"
    We may be fearless.

To-morrow morn new joys may bring,
And Phœbus' radiant beams may fling
Athwart the world, and birds may sing
    To make us cheerful.
With glee, let all the welkin ring,
    And be not tearful.

Our lives, at best, are all too sad.
Cast care aside — strive to be glad,
And ne'er conform to every "fad,"
    But live content ;
Be true and simple — shun the bad,
    Till life is spent.

And if, perchance, we live again,
We shall go hence, without a stain,
A prick of conscience or of brain,
  To our reward —
And thus a blameless life maintain,
  In just accord.

Existence is a summer's day,
With here and there a cheerless way
Along the path we have to stray,
  From morn till eve ;
So let us live as best we may,
  And never grieve.

But cultivate the better part :
Let flowers of love bloom in the heart ;
Excel in every kindly art
  That brings us peace ;
Till we, at last, from friends must part,
  At life's surcease.

February 7, 1894.

WINDS OF MARCH.

———

I love to hear the winds of March
   Blow lustily and strong ;
They wake the dormant buds and flowers,
   And herald sun and song.

I love to hear tumultuous airs
   Wail out, in accents wild ;
For Nature thus her power declares
   To every human child.

I love to see the angry clouds
   In stormy billows rise,
Like spirits veiled in misty shrouds —
   A wonder and surprise.

I love to hear the gale, afar,
   Distinct, and loud and clear —
Like rush of coming, distant car —
   'Tis music in my ear.

I love to see the swaying trees
   Bow to the driving blast,
And toss their branches in the breeze,
   Like straws by whirlwinds cast.

I love to hear old structures creak,
  And see the wreckage fly —
When winds in sullen voices speak,
  And sweep along the sky.

A sense of awe pervades me then —
  Magnificent and grand —
I feel the puny works of men
  Can scarce a breath withstand.

The troubled airs, at His behest,
  Strike terror to our souls ;
He sends them forth, or puts to rest —
  His will, alone, controls.

FEBRUARY 20, 1893.

AN APRIL MORN.

Clouds and storms have passed away,
And Phœbus gilds the new-born day ;
The earth is bright, and flowers arise
And ope to Heaven their dewy eyes.

Across the plain, along the hill,
And bordering on each gentle rill,
These gems of beauty smile and spring —
Rejoicing every living thing.

Thrice happy, each expectant heart,
To see the boding clouds depart ;
And greet with joy the rising morn,
Whose beams unnumbered worlds adorn.

APRIL 25, 1854.

A MORNING IN MAY.

Bless the genial sunshine, speed the cheerful ray
Into every human heart — merry month of May.
Nature's voice is jubilant, brooks and birds are singing ;
Bells, on all the towers 'round, merrily are ringing :

Flowers gay and grasses green, everywhere are teeming:
Why should sad humanity sit in silence, dreaming ?
Be we, then, awake to life, smiling as the flowers —
Happy as the joyous birds, in their leafy bowers.

Life, at best, is all too sad ; we should cease repining —
Look upon the brighter side, while the sun is shining :
Earth were not so dark a place, if we were but willing
To admit some rays of light — all its niches filling.

Let us, then, with cheerfulness — faith and duty
        blending —
Make of all the rolling year, Summer, never ending.

MAY 1, 1864.

REFLECTIONS

On a morning in May.

O ! how shall I express my fond
Delight for such a morn as this —
Whose glories, if protracted to the
Span of years, would make a
Paradise of earth?
Its soft and
Mellowing influence sheds calm
Serenity around, and every
Sound of Nature seems like
Music borne upon the breeze ;
While tuneful warblers pipe aloud
His praise, rejoicing as they go.
I would that life were one
Perpetual morn like this.   My pulse
Would leap with hope renewed,
And every sense would thrill,
As nerved with newer impulse
By the gladdening current —
Bounding, joyous, through a
Thousand veins.

MAY 4, 1854.

IN THE SUNNY DAYS OF JUNE.

In the sunny days of June —
When all Nature is in tune,
  And the elements at rest —
All the sentiments of life,
With a sense of joy, are rife,
  And we feel that we are blest.

We inhale the balmy air,
And, with thankfulness, declare
  We should like to live for aye :
For the flowers and the bees,
And the birds among the trees,
  Seem so happy all the day.

The farmer now rejoices,
And we hear the merry voices
  Of the harvesters afield ;
While the clover and the grain
Make obeisance to the plain
  And the sickle, as they yield.

Soon the binders form the sheaves,
Till their labor nothing leaves
  But the stubble on the ground ;
While the rakers toss the hay,
And are happy all the day,
  Till the vesper bells resound.

Not a season lends a charm —
To the city or the farm —
  Like the cheery days of June :
For all Nature now is bright,
And existence a delight —
  But it endeth very soon.

We shall ever thank the Giver
For the gently flowing river,
  And the woods, and the vales, and the groves
For the brooks, and the lanes, and the hedges,
And all His goodly gifts and His pledges,
  And the flowers, and the birds, and their loves:

For we long to sit and muse,
Or to wander — as we choose —
  By the stream or shady wood,
Where the shadows and the sun
Ever mingle into one —
  For it seemeth very good.

Could we ask a fairer Heaven
Than to mortal man is given,
  For his dwelling here below --
When the perfect days of June,
And the silver-lighted moon,
  Their fair radiance bestow?

Let us render praise forever,
Till we go beyond the river
  Out of Time —
When we trust a change from this
Will be heralded by bliss
  More sublime.

JUNE 10, 1893.

JULY.

"July, the month of Summer's prime,
Again resumes its busy time;
Scythes tinkle in each grassy dell,
Where solitude was wont to dwell."

Such was the story told of yore,
Which time repeated o'er and o'er:
For then 't was true, but now 't is not,
For tinkling scythes are all forgot.

And as for solitude — alas !
There's little left in grain or grass —
July is still the Summer's prime,
And will continue such through time.

But when we glean our harvests now,
We do it at the reaper's prow ;
And those who bound the sheaves of old,
Are absent from the harvest fold ;

The same deft instrument that reaps,
Now binds the grain and drops in heaps,
And saves, from labor in the sun,
The toiler — for his work is done.

So, with the grass that clothes the field,
The swinging scythe the palm must yield
To newer modes — however loth —
Which cut in haste a wider swath.

The men and boys and rustic girls —
With happy hearts and sunny curls —
No longer rake the fragrant hay,
And deem the work a merry play :

For in their stead machines now toil
With equine power, their sport to spoil ;
And jocund songs, at close of day,
No longer while the hours away.

Thus, ever, in this world of change,
Utility of wider range
Supplants the primitive device
For more of speed — though great the price —
Regardless of a sacrifice.

July 13, 1893.

AUGUST.

The harvest is over, the Summer is ended,
  The season is on the decline ;
The beauty of bloom and of growth are suspended,
  The grape is matured on the vine ;

The peach and the apple, the pear and the plum,
  Are now in their glory and prime ;
The melon is ripe, and the corn is to come,
  With the blushing tomato, in time ;

The pumpkin is still immature in the field,
  But its day will be here by and by,
When its golden rotundity treasures will yield —
  For Thanksgiving and Christmas pie ;

The wealth of the walnut and hickory tree
Will add to our wonderful store,
While cider and glee will cause Winter to flee,
Till its boreal blasts are no more.

Thus, let us be jolly — for sadness is folly —
And merrily live as we go ;
For Nature, in lavish profusion, has given
Of all that she has to bestow.

The harvest is over, the Summer is ended,
The season is on the decline ;
But ne'er, for a day, to forebodings give way,
Nor e'en for a moment repine.

August 23, 1895.

AUGUST.

The Summer's heat is now supreme —
The solar rays their power declare —
And Nature all athirst is seen,
From dearth of moisture, everywhere.

The earth is parched, its fountains dry —
The warbling brooks no longer flow :
Their cooling draughts they now deny
The lowing herds, where'er they go.

The sheep lie panting in the shade,
   Oppressed with heat, and sleepy-eyed —
Dreaming, perchance, of cooling glade,
   Or pastures green, some stream beside.

The birds sit silent in the trees,
   And hushed are all their tuneful lays ;
No leaf is stirred by passing breeze,
   Through all the sultry Summer's day.

The corn is languishing afield —
   The shriveled blades attest their need,
And showers withheld have shrunk the yield
   Which Nature's lavish laws decreed.

The grass — which late was green — is dry,
   While some dead leaves begin to fall ;
A brazen aspect fills the sky,
   And heat and dust are over all.

Throughout the day the locust sings —
   At even-tide, the katydid ;
And daylight naught of comfort brings
   Till Phœbus, by the world, is hid :

Then Nature deigns to grant relief,
   Responsive to our earnest prayers ;
And for a season — glad, but brief —
   She sends her grateful, soothing airs.

In slumbers deep, profoundly blest —
　Forgetful of the weary days —
Renewed by rest, we rise with zest,
　To journey on our devious ways ;

For such is life : its joys and strife
　Are blended like the cloud and sun —
A mingled web, with changes rife,
　Of many phases wrought in one.

August 10, 1893.

SEPTEMBER.

Summer Wanes.

'T is written on the changing leaf,
　Reflected in the lifeless grass ;
Declared by absent shock and sheaf,
　As o'er the dusty field we pass ;

The downy peach, so rich and rare,
　The apple, blushing on the bough ;
The grape, in glorious clusters, fair,
　And melons fit for gods, I trow —
　All tell the year is changing now ;

While corn, in tasseled grandeur, stands,
   Adorned with silk-embellished ears,
Whose near maturity commands
   A thought of fleeting days and years.

We soon shall hear the huskers' call —
   Who gather in the golden grain —
As Summer merges into Fall,
   Or comes the cold, November rain ;

Ere long the frost will chill the vine,
   The pumpkin's cherished fruit destroy ;
And as the season's days decline,
   The frigid airs will work annoy.

Thus, from the spring-time of the year,
   To its voluptuous end and close,
The changing seasons lend their cheer,
   And lessons to mankind disclose.

The Spring gives promise, fair and bright,
   The Summer charms us everywhere ;
While Autumn's gifts the soul delight,
   And Winter's joys relieve our care.

For all these worldly blessings, given
   With life and peace and health and years,
Thank Nature's God — who wrought the
      heavens —
   For rest, at last, shall dry our tears.

September 4, 1893.

OCTOBER.

Lines suggested by a drive through the city park, Sunday, October 16, 1892.

Magnificent, in its decay,
　　Is Nature, surely, now;
Such glory crowns these Autumn days,
　　Such radiance gilds its brow.

No pen can picture all its charms,
　　No pencil paint its dyes;
To imitate these works of God,
　　All human art defies:

The leafy hosts upon the trees,
　　Ten thousand shades display;
And as they rustle in the breeze,
　　October vies with May.

Truly, no earthly scene compares
　　With this we now behold;
For all the waving forest, wide,
　　Seems one vast sea of gold;

A fairy landscape bounds the view,
　　Like visions wrought in dreams;
The sunlight streams o'er skies of blue,
　　And all with glory teems.

We thank Thee, Lord, for this fair scene,
   Thy presence, here, it brings;
This Eden types that Heaven of bliss,
   Where dwells the King of Kings.

NOVEMBER.

The sky pours rain, in a dull refrain —
That it means to be wet, is all too plain —
The clouds hang low, as they come and go,
While the chill air tells of the promised snow;

The sad winds moan, and the birds are flown;
The dead leaves fall, and around are strown;
A misty darkness pervades the air,
And the sun shines not, out of pure despair.

Alas! for the joys of the Summer past —
The gloom of November is here at last,
And all we can do is to make the most
Of what still remains of the dead year's ghost.

November 1, 1892.

DECEMBER.

Cheerless month of frost and storms —
  Fitful, gloomy, dark and drear —
Terror dwells in all thy forms,
  Monarch of the dying year.

Ruthlessly, thy chilling breath
  Smites the Summer's pride and glory —
Searing all the fields and woods —
  Telling Nature's saddest story.

Countless floral forms have bowed
  'Neath the fury of thy blast,
Seeking, in a snowy shroud,
  Peaceful shelter at the last.

Not a tendril of the vine,
  Not a leaf of shrub or tree —
If we dare except the pine —
  But has yielded all to thee.

Like some tyrant, grim and hoary,
  Heralding his fell decree,
Thou ordainest death to beauty,
  As a sacrifice to thee.

Mercilessly unrelenting,
  And remorselessly, as fate,
Fall thy frigid shafts around us,
  Sparing neither age nor state.

Would that some mysterious power
  Might consign thee to the Poles —
Where the airs of " old Æolus "
  Hie them to their gusty goals !

There, in frigid might to revel,
  In a region drear and wild ;
Where the avalanche is frowning,
  And " fair Nature " never smiled ;

Where the poor, untutored savage
  Reigns, sole tenant of the waste ;
And no perfumed breezes — wafted
  O'er his dusky cheek — are chased.

Dwellers we in regions mild,
  Warmly welcome and remember
Summer as a sunny child,
  While we shudder at December ;

Then, I prithee, stay thy bluster ;
  Lull thy raging winds to rest ;
Loth, thy frosty wrongs we suffer —
  Vengeful shafts of thy behest.

Waft thy gales to Labrador —
  Where eternal Winter reigns,
And the sun shall nevermore
  Break its everlasting chains ;

Regions where the ancient rocks —
  Rent by its intensest sting —
Sunder, as with earthquake shocks,
  Making hills and valleys ring.

DECEMBER 15, 1861.

LET EVERY TONGUE REJOICE.

Let every tongue rejoice !
  Let praise resound aloud !
Spring greets us with her voice,
  Dispelling storm and cloud.

The streams, long fettered, leap
  From crag to crag, and fling
Their rushing waters deep,
  Their joy acknowledging ;

The birds, on leafy bough,
　Or mounting high in air,
Praise their Creator, now,
　For bounties everywhere ;

Fair floral forms arise —
　By Phœbus' magic cheered —
And make a paradise
　Where lately gloom appeared ;

The garden and the field,
　That late were sere and brown,
A new enchantment yield —
　Bedecked with Nature's crown ;

The forest's giant forms —
　Whose coronal of leaves
Is bowed before the storm,
　Or the blue ether cleaves —

Attest their thankfulness
　For vernal shower and sun ;
While through their leafy dress
　Glad, laughing murmurs run.

All Nature now is rife
　With growth and gleeful sounds,
And every form of life
　With happiness abounds.

Then let us not withhold
Our meed of praise and prayer,
For blessings manifold,
And Heaven's protecting care.

FEBRUARY 25, 1891.

SUMMER SALAD.

Surely, now, the "dog-star" rages,
If by ardent heat it reign,
And mercurial upward stages
Aid in making such things plain.

Scarce a breeze is put in motion —
Silence reigns profound and long ;
And the air, a stagnant ocean,
Beareth not a sound or song.

Not a bird upon the branches
Of a tree or shrub, is seen —
Neither on the air it launches,
But has sought some shelter, green ;

Kine upon the lowlands linger,
In some shady nook or dell,
Where — and I might point my finger —
Patience and contentment dwell ;

Sheep have sought the shade of fences —
   Panting, sleepy-eyed, at ease —
Or umbrageous, cool defences,
   Under amply-spreading trees ;

Swine secure a place to wallow
   In some oozy slough or slum,
Where content of mind shall follow,
   Which may not to heat succumb ;

Every creature strives to lessen —
   By some means of its devising —
Solar ardor, so distressing —
   In a manner oft surprising :

Human nature, worn and weary —
   Not unlike the bird or beast —
Seeks seclusion, cool and cheery,
   Dreamily to muse or feast.

When the Summer days are over,
   And the torrid term is past,
We may be rejuvenated
   Back to statu quo, at last.

Tuesday, August 11, 1891.

A SUMMER'S DAY.

***

MORNING.

Softly, now, the light of day
    Dawns upon a sleeping world,
And the darkness fades away
    As its splendors are unfurled ;

Phœbus, in his golden car,
    Like a rising monarch comes —
Silently, and from afar —
    Without herald, trump or drums ;

Joyous sounds are everywhere —
    In the field and in the wood —
Wafted on the ambient air,
    To the Author of all good ;

Winged songsters trill their lays,
    And the bee goes humming by ;
Toiling mortals go their ways,
    While the day-god climbs the sky ;

Now the world is wide awake
    To its clatter, clang and rush ;
Let us each some task betake,
    Till the evening brings its hush.

EVENING.

Homeward, now, let all retire,
　To some blessed haven, near —
Worthy son and honored sire,
　Seeking comfort, peace and cheer

When the sun has sunk to rest,
　And the twilight dies away,
While the moon is still thy guest,
　And the stars reflect the day :

Seek thou, then, in sweet repose,
　Rest from worldly care and toil ;
Praying for release from woes,
　Life's contentions and turmoil ;

Dreams, if any, be they sweet —
　Only such as infants know ;
Guardian angels guide thy feet —
　Heaven above, and peace below.

So, may'st thou the hours beguile,
　Happily, till life is done,
And thy evening, like a smile,
　Beam serene as morning sun.

Sunday, January 28, 1894.

AUTUMNAL LEAVES.

Autumnal leaves are falling fast,
And soon the chill November blast
Will hurl them through the gusty air,
Like things of no concern or care.

A few days more of genial sun —
As of a heaven on earth begun ;
Of dreamy haze, with glories blent —
Too brief, alas, for our content,
Since Summer's cherished charms are spent.

Thus, youthful years merge into age,
While sober cares our lives engage,
Till hoary time, with chilling breath,
Dispels our worldly dreams in death.

So, whether leaves upon the trees,
Or creature forms of high degrees,
They all obey the laws of God —
Fulfill His purpose : '' kiss the rod '' —
And rest, at last, beneath the sod.

October 21, 1894.

TO WINTER.

Thy reign is long, and thy bonds are strong,
    And bound are the streams by thy chilling breath ;
Thy blustering song is a song of wrong —
    The story of famine, and want, and death.

FEBRUARY 22, 1895.

RELIGIOUS POEMS AND SENTIMENTS.

O, WHY SHOULD WE MOURN?

O, why should we mourn, or in sadness repine,
   To depart from a world such as this? —
Since Heaven so kindly has pointed the way
   To its mansions eternal, in bliss.

A few kindred spirits, who loved us below,
   May mourn our departure awhile,
But soon such dark shadows will pass from the brow,
   And the tear will be chased by a smile.

The world will move on as it ever has done,
   With no care for the dead or the morrow ;
The merry will laugh, and the joyous will sing,
   Regardless of sickness or sorrow.

Then why should we mourn, or in sadness repine,
   To depart from a world such as this? —
Since Heaven so kindly has pointed the way
   To its mansions eternal, in bliss.

WRITTEN IN 1850.

IN LENT.

———

When faith runs low, and cash is spent,
Then come the gloomy days of Lent —
When weak and wicked souls repent,
    And take a rest from sin.

The faithful have their faults forgiven —
To smooth the rugged road to Heaven —
And pray o'ermuch, one day in seven,
    Joy's gates to enter in.

They now refrain from pleasure's round —
Look sober, penitent, profound —
Nor utter they a happy sound
    For forty days.

With faces sad and wan with woe,
They "fast" and pray, and "go it" slow,
For that the fashion is, you know —
    They think it pays.

No fellow now can see his girl —
His faith has made him such a churl ---
Nor can she smile, or kink a curl,
    For that were awful ;

But when the Lenten time is past,
And Liberty regained, at last,
They all begin to '' go it '' fast,
For then 't is lawful.

February 16, 1893.

AT THE LAST.

Thank God for the rest that shall come to us when
The journey of life is accomplished, at last,
And we have gone out from the dwellings of men,
And the sorrows and cares of the world have been
passed.

We shall sleep a last sleep, in an unbroken spell —
To continue eternally, down through all time —
And the soul and the spirit, in silence, shall dwell
With this temple of dust, in the ages sublime.

We are born and mature, we grow old and we die —
We sport our brief day, in the sunshine of earth ;
We enjoy and we sorrow, we laugh and we cry
To the end, as we did on the day of our birth.

Like to Gods, we are men with a potency fraught ;
  We are germs of the Deity, noble and high —
The will of Almighty, the essence of thought.
  Alas ! that our frailties compel us to die.

Elder sages have taught — who professed to be wise —
  That we shall go hence to a haven of love —
Located somewhere up aloft in the skies,
  'Mid fields of Elysian, or worshipful grove ;

But what can we know of a future estate —
  No mortal has ever returned to us here,
And what lies beyond not a soul can relate —
  For never did absentee ever appear.

So when we have passed the dark river of death,
  And the rays have gone out that illumined our sight,
We shall yield up this life, as we gasp for a breath,
  While eternity shrouds us in darkness and night.

If, perchance, there be light from a beacon beyond,
  We gladly shall hail it and seek the bright shore —
To all its allurements our natures respond,
  And joyfully welcome a life evermore ;

But as to such knowledge, in truth, we have none —
  We can only be hopeful or trustful, at best —
Yet this blest assurance we have, everyone :
  That the end will bring peace and an unbroken rest.

AUGUST 8, 1893.

CHRISTMAS.

"Christmas comes but once a year,"
And when it comes it brings good cheer,
Fraught with pleasures all enjoy —
Innocence without alloy.

Life and love, serenely blent,
Lend the soul a calm content —
Marking, thus, the great event
Of Jesus' birth, so wise and good,
Even then misunderstood.

A jealous priesthood saw Him tried,
And under Pilate crucified —
Since when His teachings, just and pure,
Are destined, always, to endure.

And thus it is, with heartfelt cheer,
We celebrate from year to year —
Happy to know that what is good
In this, our day, is understood.

December 18, 1893.

THANKSGIVING DAY.

And this is called Thanksgiving day,
When people go to church and pray ;
Dress in their best, like gaudy sinners,
And gormandize their turkey dinners ;

Give thanks at morn, on bended knees,
Return at noon to take their ease —
Not only feast, but drink extremely,
Berate their neighbors, act unseemly —

Then think that they have served the Lord,
And worshipped Him with one accord,
In thankfulness for many blessings :
Plum puddings, pies and cakes and dressings.

These are the ways of " toney " people,
Whose place of worship has a steeple ;
The plainer sort give thanks at lunch,
In some low den, with beer or punch —

Where oaths pass current 'mid the revel,
And each one strives to serve the devil ;
And in this wise they make display
Of how we spend Thanksgiving day.

And thus it goes, with saint and sinner —
Our highest aim is turkey dinner —
The day is given o'er to riot,
As we well know, and scarce deny it.

Yet, 't is the fashion, and we do it,
However wrong, or long we knew it ;
We all debauch what should be pure,
And need a prompt, heroic cure.

Then let us turn a leaf to-morrow —
Renewed in grace, sans sin or sorrow —
Rejoice in what the Lord may give,
And lovingly and justly live.

Not only thank Him once a year,
For that ungrateful doth appear ;
Nor even one day out of seven,
But daily, render thanks to Heaven.

November 30, 1893.

RANDOM THOUGHTS.

We are a puny race of creatures,
   With little range of mental vision ;
And oft assume the role of teachers,
   When we deserve the world's derision.

Away with such presumptive folly —
   'T is but the self-esteem of fools,
Whose ways are evil and unholy,
   Because untaught of wisdom's schools.

Man's urgent need is common sense,
   To regulate his acts and deeds —
A love supreme, without pretense,
   And works, instead of forms and creeds.

Thus, he may hope to show mankind
   That he is what he seems to be ;
And not, with dogmas, crude and blind,
   Obscure the little light we see.

Onward and upward, let us rise,
   From fictions to a truthful goal,
And by just methods make men wise,
   With loving hearts and lofty souls.

This is, indeed, a goodly world,
  So far as Nature's God has wrought ;
But often have His creatures hurled
  His good intentions into naught.

Why not be men and brothers, all,
  And feel that tie which kindred brings? —
The ills of life by love forestall,
  Which out of every bosom springs.

Be just and true, that voice obey —
  That still, small voice, within thy breast —
Love God and man ; and every day,
  Through life and death, shalt thou be blest.

JANUARY 14, 1894.

AND THIS IS TRUE.

That man who undertakes to tell me what the
future holds in store, presumes upon my ignorance or
credulity, or both ; and as all men know such knowledge has never been imparted to any human being, he
may safely be regarded as an impostor and a fraud.

SEPTEMBER 25, 1890.

"BE JUST, AND FEAR NOT."

To be moral men and women, we must live uprightly and deal justly — doing to others as we would that they should do unto us. We are always judged according to the deeds done, and not according to our faith or profession. Hence, it follows that what we do is the thing which stamps us good or bad. "Faith without works is dead."

Tuesday, December 6, 1892.

SOME REFLECTIONS.

When we attempt to ascend to a higher degree of goodness than that prescribed by morality, we are wholly out at sea. The mind cannot grasp the invisible or the unknowable, or attain to the unattainable.

A superstition is a false faith — a belief in improbable or impossible things — the religion of ignorance.

February 6, 1885.

AS I SEE IT.

I find it impossible to believe that Deity ever
created human beings in this world that He might
punish them in a future state ; for, knowing the end
from the beginning, as an All-wise Being must, such
an act would be inconsistent with the nature and conduct of a loving, just and merciful God — impossible,
even, with a human parent.

That great, first Cause, whose supreme wisdom and
power created all things, and whose mysterious laws
sustain a universe of suns — and systems of revolving
worlds, whose numbers are infinite, and whose extent
is without bounds — is too great and glorious to be com-
prehended or understood by such puny, finite beings
as ourselves.   Yet reason teaches us (and it is our only
guide) that, from such an exalted source, good alone
can flow — only love, justice and mercy, to the least,
as to the greatest of His creatures.

MARCH 2, 1884.

JEWELS ARE JEHOVAH'S TRUST.

[The following poem was written years ago, under the inspiration
of the author's early teaching.]

It is written, it is written —
    And its truth all things disclose —
Jesus is the fount of mercy,
    Yielding balm for human woes.

Sun and moon and stars attest it ;
    Angels sanction it, above ;
And the very breezes whisper,
    " Jesus is the source of love."

Rustling brook and mighty river —
    As they course the earth's domain —
Praise Him ever and forever,
    Low or loud, in sweet refrain.

All the universe of matter,
    All the planets, as they roll ;
Blue ethereal vault of Heaven —
    Boundless as the mighty whole —

All proclaim Him Lord and Savior,
    Mediator of our race —
Only source of true redemption,
    Free contributor of grace.

Come ye, then, who seek salvation
  In the gospel of our God :
Worship Him, in truth and spirit —
  Tread the paths His chosen trod.

Prize not highly earthly gifts,
  Nor with Mammon barter gold :
Heaven's hopes are endless bliss —
  Boundless wealth of love, untold.

There no selfish miser hoardeth
  Sparkling gems, or yellow dust —
Such are toys of earthly children —
  Jewels are Jehovah's trust.

MARCH 13, 1852.

JESUS.

A Triple Acrostic.

Jesus, Thou Justly honored, grant that I
Employ my Ev'ry hour in serving TheE ;
Secure   in   Such a cause, we well may blesS
Unequalled, Unexampled love from YoU.
Surcease from Sin, we ask in our distresS,
That our sad lives be fraught with happiness.

DECEMBER 26, 1896.

"JUST AS I AM, WITHOUT ONE PLEA."

Written during severe illness.

"Just as I am, without one plea,"
  Gladly I come, dear Lord, to Thee;
  For I have longed, for many a year,
  To see Thy Face and feel Thy cheer.

This world is sad and cold, indeed,
  And of Thy presence have I need —
  I feel that Thou wilt welcome me,
  However lowly I may be.

I do not love pretentious fanes,
  Where formal superstition reigns;
  Where Jesus — Mary's Son — is first,
  And God's great Name is scarce rehearsed;

Where pomp and show and organ's peal,
  Magnificence, alone, reveal;
  Where only pride and wealth abide,
  And poverty cannot preside.

Lo! I have lived a simple life,
  Amid the world's turmoil and strife;
  Have sought to be upright and just,
  And in the right, and Thee, to trust.

I ne'er employ a mask to hide
My weaknesses, whate'er betide,
Nor feign to be a saint, when sin
Has cankered all my soul within.

Self-righteousness, which long has striven
To have its own exclusive Heaven,
May find, at last, that all mankind,
However vile, or base, or blind,

Will be as kindly welcomed there
As multitudes whose trust is prayer ;
His goodness, like a mantle, wide,
Will shelter all — protect and guide.

For God is just — He made us all :
The rich, the poor, the great and small ;
And from the first our frailties knew,
And weaknesses we might pursue.

No earthly parent, here below,
Condemns his child to endless woe —
Much less the Father of our sires
Consigns mankind to endless fires.

A shame on all such falsehoods taught —
Intelligence well knows 't is naught
But relic of some barbarous age,
A plague-spot on the '' sacred page.''

He giveth all His creatures peace —
From worldly strife a long surcease —
Where they shall be forever blest,
In one eternal, endless rest.

Friday, February 28, 1896.

ALBUM PIECES.

TO BEAUTY.

Written by request, for Mary B———.

There are moments in life
When the soul, in devotion,
Has knelt at thy shrine
In the depth of emotion —

Confessing how vainly
It strove 'gainst enrapture,
While bowed in submission
And yielding to capture.

How ardent the feelings :
The heart over-flowing —
Its fountains unsealing,
Its treasures bestowing.

O ! Who would not give
    All of earth's brightest treasures,
One moment to live
    Through such transport of pleasures.

Alas ! that this world,
    With its clouds and its sadness,
Presents us no more
    Of its sunshine and gladness.

FEBRUARY, 1851.

TO MARY MASON.

Lady, when thou seest this,
    Kindly think of me the while —
And thou wilt confer a pleasure,
    Even in thy happy smile.

Surely, thine's a fairy spirit,
    Light and free and gladsome, ever —
Chasing care away, and sadness,
    To return upon us, never.

Would that I possessed the magic
   That is sparkling in thine eyes:
I should vie with lovely Venus,
   Twinkling in the evening skies;

I should strive to be the Mistress
   Of a multitude of hearts,
With no stratagem or weapon
   Save thy artlessness in arts.

SEPTEMBER, 1853.

TO GABRIELLA NEWTON,

On the Eve of Her Marriage to Mr. J. B. Hunnicutt.

May all the joys of earth be thine,
And all the fav'ring stars combine
To swell the volume of thy bliss
In worlds to come, as well as this.

May sweet content and rosy health
Be part of thy domestic wealth,
And ne'er a care invade thy cot,
But happiness be all thy lot.

DECEMBER 7, 1851.

TO MARY FINLEY.

Written on our return from a picnic in the grove near Westville, Ohio.

The sun is now set,
And the flowers are wet
With the dew, which from Heaven descended ;
And evening appears
As the coming of years,
With night's sable curtain suspended.

Farewell to the day,
And to Phoebus' bright ray ;
We will seek, in sweet slumber, repose,
Till the dawn's early light
Shall dispel the dark night,
And Aurora shall smile as the rose.

May never a care
To thy bosom repair,
To lessen the joys of the hour ;
But, morning and even,
Fresh pleasures be given,
To lighten the clouds that may lower.

MAY 20, 1853.

TO MARY E. H———.

O ! Mary, believe me, and deem it not strange
That love is most fickle, and subject to range ;
Like the bee on the floweret, he sips and he flies
To seek some new victim — in gaudy disguise.

He pierces the delicate bud to its core,
Then leaves it to pine on the stem, evermore ;
His sting is the sharpest that mortals may know,
His pleasures so sweet that no heart can forego.

A strange, contradictive compound is this love :
It rules on earth, and it rules us above ;
It kills or it cures us, it makes sick or well,
And more than my pen or my fancy can tell.

Beware, then — O, Mary — of Cupid's sly darts,
And shield thee against his gay wiles and his arts ;
For seldom we meet with a heart that is true —
So fickle and changeful, their number is few.

MARCH 17, 1851.

TO MARY ELLEN WARD.

And thou wouldst have me write, Ella,
  Upon this spotless page ;
And write thee something eloquent —
  Witty, perchance — or sage.

But O ! I ne'er possessed the gift
  To charm with lay divine ;
To sparkle with a ready wit,
  Or eloquently shine.

Mine is an humbler muse, by far —
  Unused to lofty flights —
Preferring more familiar haunts,
  To fame's untrodden heights.

Here, then,'s a health to thee, Ella :
  May joy be ever thine,
And love and hope and faith, for thee,
  A garland, fair, entwine ;

And friendship — purest, peerless gem —
  May it be set within it ;
And thou, and I, and those we love,
  Appreciate and win it.

Wishing no care may cloud thy brow,
    Nor sorrow dim thine eyes,
I ask that thou remember me
    While youthful scenes arise.

JANUARY 27, 1853.

TO ELMIRA BASSET.

Acrostic.

Elmira, friends unknown to thee,
Long have loved the name thou bearest:
Many who were fair to see —
In death now sleeping — once the rarest,
Radiant gems of life and love —
All now gathered home above.

They, like thee, were bright and joyous:
    Naught of care had marred their pleasures;
Birds of song were not more free —
    Happiness was theirs, the treasures.

May it likewise be thy lot,
    That, through life's dull round of cares,
Sorrow — all to thee forgot —
    Ne'er may cross thee unawares.

FEBRUARY 7, 1850.

TO REBECCA D. STRATTAN.

When, in the course of after years, we shall be led to take a retrospective view of life, it will be pleasant to revert to early scenes and their associations, to home and its endearments, and the thousand happy hours we spent beneath its venerable roof. Those ties which early bind us to a parent, brother, sister, or associate, will be long in breaking, for the mind dwells fondly on the past, and reckons all the little incidents of youth as golden sands, when, in comparison, we view them and associate their glitter with the grosser and less real pleasures of maturer life.

There also is a sacredness connected with the happiness of youth which makes the vain attempt to be as light of heart and free from care, in after years, a very mockery. So I have often thought it must be pleasing to review a volume on whose leaves are written thoughts and sentiments of those we cherished as our early friends, and though they be no more, they speak a language to our hearts, the memory of which we long regret to lose.

Thus, may it please thee, '' Becca,'' when, in many a year to come, thou dost peruse these lines, to think of me as one who was, at least, thy friend.

August 28, 1852.

TO SARAH F———. ·

The flowers have ceased to bloom, dear friend—
  Their leaflets fall and fade,
And naught is seen but withered leaves,
  Through all the woodland glade.

They tell us of departed Spring,
  Of Summer's changing glow,
Of Autumn and its somber hues,
  And Winter's chilling snow ;

They tell us, too, of blighted hopes,
  Which, in the bloom of youth,
Shone brightly as the radiant sun,
  And beautiful as truth.

But now, alas ! they all are fled —
  Both faded hopes and flowers —
And naught is left us but regrets,
  For life's young, dreamy hours.

May we so live that when the close
  Of life's long year is past,
We all may join the friends we loved,
  Where joys through ages last.

NOVEMBER 10, 1852.

TO REBECCA MEEK.

———

May care never rifle thy cheek of its bloom,
  Nor dim thy bright eye with a tear ;
But freshness and beauty bloom on to the tomb,
  And love, to thy heart, lend its cheer.

WRITTEN IN 1854.

———

TO JULIA BRADY.

———

As memory often wanders back
To scenes of yore, I find, alack !
How very few,
Of all we loved, remain to cheer
Our passage through this mundane sphere,
From day to day.

Alas ! they have been called to rest —
Their dwelling is among the blest,
Beyond the sky.
Farewell, old friends — a long adieu !
We, too, expect to follow you —
At least to try.

We hope to share that higher bliss —
That joy unknown to worlds like this —
In peace divine.
O, what a rapture we shall feel,
Permitted at His feet to kneel,
And seek His shrine.

So, when the summons, dread, is given,
May we be all prepared for Heaven,
And its repose.
Then let us duly act our parts —
Perform His will with willing hearts —
Nor shun the close.

October 21, 1853.

VALENTINES.

TO MISS MARGARET McCOY.*

A Valentine.

The rose, in its beauty, has charms for the eye,
  And a sweetness, exhaled in perfume —
Which, sooner or later, must perish and die,
  For brief is its season of bloom.

So thou, fairest Margaret, beautiful now
  In all that this world can bestow,
Must also depart, like the roses, I trow,
  Though spotless and pure as the snow.

May never a care that is harsher than zephyr
  E'er ruffle thy delicate form,
But softly and lightly be fan'ed thy fair brow,
  Unapproached by life's pitiless storm.

FEBRUARY 14, 1852.

*Miss McCoy was the daughter of Daniel McCoy, one of the contractors for the stone-work of the old National road bridge, at the west end of Main street, erected between 1833 and 1835.

TO MISS PHŒBE C————,

In reply.

Lady fair, lady fair, tell me thy name —
Make thyself known to me, fearless of blame.
Suspense is unpleasant, and therefore would I,
By knowing thee better, exchange sigh for sigh.

Avoid the cold glances which flash from mine een,
And change them to love and to mildness, serene.
Perhaps, as you say, fair enchantress of love,
If I knew thee, I'd give to thy rival the glove.

But thou hast none, I trow — I am free from the
    chain —
And perhaps, if thou strivest, thy object may'st
    gain ;
'T is not beauty, alone, that I madly should prize,
Nor affectation's arts, nor a love in disguise :

But simple effusions, direct from the heart —
Spontaneous, and free from the foibles of art ;
Ad referendum, I leave it with thee,
To grant my request, or be silent, ye see.

February 14, 1851.

TO REBECCA D. S———.

A Valentine.

I love the maiden in whose heart
Nature forms the nobler part,
And whose feelings gently flow,
Unrestrained by art or show ;

In whose happy smile we see
Kindness and sincerity,
And in whose expressive eyes
Earnest thought and feeling lies ;

One who feels respect is due
A father and a mother, too,
And, with due regard and tact,
Always knows her part to act.

Such an one I long have known —
Scarcely daring to confess
How my spirit hath been moved
By her grace and loveliness.

FEBRUARY 14, 1853.

TO MISS REBECCA MEEK.

Dear " Becca," I meekly suggest it to you --
      Not wishing that others should know it —
That if you incline to dispose of your heart,
      On me you'll be pleased to bestow it.

I'll try to deserve it as much as I can,
      And love it and cherish it well ;
So do not be blushing and causing delay,
      But if you will do it, pray tell,
                  Immediately.

February 14, 1852.

TO MISS MARY R———.

Dear Mary, remember, 't is Valentine day,
      And leap-year, forsooth, is at hand ;
An' if ye'll display half yer charms as ye may,
      We will do as ye please to command.

I ne'er knew a " lassy " was handsome as yez,
      Without half a dozen spruce beaux
From whom to select, with the greatest of ease,
      A partner — at least if she chose.

Then doff the fantastical airs of yer sex —
　　Be "naturl" an' "aisy" an' free ;
And when a young "gintleman" "axes" ye nex',
　　Just answer affirmatively —
　　Say yes.

FEBRUARY 14, 1852.

Local Historical Sketches.

LOCAL HISTORICAL SKETCHES.

PAPER NO. 1.

ON the 9th day of December, 1847, the writer hereof first set foot within the precincts of this fair city, and here he has ever since remained. It was then a mere village of some 2,500 inhabitants, acknowledging John Saylor as its chief executive and head. Elected, first, in 1845, he continued in office until 1852, when he was succeeded by the late John Finley, Esq.

At that somewhat distant period the Friends, or Quakers, as they were commonly called, exercised a very marked influence over the society about them, their numbers being much greater then than now, in proportion to population. They were a thrifty, honest, intelligent people, possessed of many virtues, while their wives and daughters were the peers of any in the land. As a people, however, they were rather non-progressive, and lacking in that spirit of worldly enter-prise so remarkably manifest at the present day. They were very tenacious of their religious opinions, and rigid in regard to their teachings and observances. To one not of their faith and unaccustomed to their modes of thought, or manner of life, there seemed an ever-present feeling of restraint and repression — a sort of mental and physical embargo, by no means congenial to liberty of speech and action. Mirthfulness was rarely encouraged, and, if indulged in, was quiet and subdued ; while demonstrations of gayety were rare and guarded. Speech was as silver, but silence was golden. The brilliant hues of beautiful flowers, and the happy, gleeful songs of birds, seemed inappropriate to their surroundings. Instrumental and vocal music were but little understood or cultivated by the people of the time, and by members of *their* Society in *no* degree whatever. Such practices were regarded as sinful and as unbecoming the dignity, gravity and soberness of that peculiar people. Their speech and attire were alike of the plainest kind, and every color worn was in harmony with both. Under the shadow of their influence even pastors of other denominations discouraged the wearing of gay colors. Broad-brimmed hats and plain silk bonnets, wholly unadorned, were everywhere to be seen. A bearded face was the merest exception to a general rule, and was not unfrequently the subject of comment and criticism, while the unfortunate moustache was held in still greater disfavor, as its wearer was supposed to be of that class whose ways are dark and whose deeds are evil.

The good people of the village were generally distinguished for simplicity of habits and manners, but

little effort was made in the direction of personal adorn-
ment or display. We distinctly remember that eight
yards of material constituted a pattern for a lady's
dress, and sometimes even less would serve ; but times
have changed — both larger views and ampler garments
now hold sway. We remember, also, that the female
head-gear did not then consist of those indescribable
nondescripts now so fearfully and wonderfully formed,
but simply, and in fact, of hat or bonnet, severely
plain — *sans* fuss or feathers. The folly and extravagance of display and dress came by degrees, and were
the result of increased wealth, the war, and foreign
innovation.

At that day, good boarding could be had for $1.50
per week, and the hire of a horse and buggy was but
$1.25 per day. We had neither railroads nor turn-
pikes (excepting one to Boston), while gas and electric
lights, telephones and telegraphs were, as yet, of the
things to come. But a "coach and four" used to
carry the mail for "Uncle Sam," and the few unlucky
passengers, whose business or necessities required them
to be abroad in the land. Cattle, hogs and sheep were
then driven by thousands, along the National road, on
their way to some eastern market. The surplus products of the country commanded but a nominal price :
hauling by wagon was too expensive, and our present
facilities for transportation were not yet in existence.
At that time all the business of the village was trans-

acted on the three squares of Main street lying between Fourth and Seventh, that between Fourth and Fifth doing much the greater part. No mercantile business whatever was done anywhere off Main street.

A shabby old market-house stood in the middle of South Fourth street, about 150 yards from Main. On the present site of Reed & Vanneman's business block, corner of Noble and Fifth streets, and nearly opposite the west end of the passenger depot, was located Kenworthy's tannery, the only structure in that vicinity. Where the passenger depot now stands, with its immediate surroundings, was an inclosed field, and on the west front of it was the "Quaker walk" leading to Friends' Orthodox Meeting-house — a large, plain, two-storied brick structure, erected in 1823. The walk referred to was partly planked, and separated from the main road by a row of posts. The writer distinctly remembers seeing a horse and buggy, with two occupants, stick fast in the mud in front of where stands the "Avenue House" — immediately north of the railroad crossing, on the west side.

The brick business block now occupying the east side of Fort Wayne Avenue and covering a full square in length, and forming something of a triangle, stands upon "made ground," formerly a stagnant pool — whence came, in Spring-time, the doleful music of the frog. This was then the property of Charles W. Starr, by whom it is said to have been offered for a few hundred dollars, without finding a purchaser. On one occasion, the writer remembers, water was procured from this source to extinguish a neighboring fire. The old "Starr House," subsequently known as the "Meredith" and "Tremont," corner of Eighth and Main, was considered "away out of town," and even the Huntington House was thought to be inconveniently far from business. An old mile-stone used to stand on the north side of Main street, between Tenth and Eleventh, marked "One-Half Mile to Richmond." Between Seventh and Tenth streets there were but few buildings, and Ninth street had, as yet, no existence. All east was either orchard, open field, or wood.

Basil Brightwell, Benjamin Strattan, Thaddeus Wright, Jesse Meek, John Haines, William Blanchard, John M. Laws, William S. Watt, William Petchell, and Ralph A. Paige were our dry goods dealers, not one of whom is in the business at the present day, and only two of the ten survive, to answer to their names, to-wit: Wright and Strattan. Their companions have all gone hence, where barter and exchange are unknown and the weary are at rest.

Although not in business here at the time to which these papers refer, Daniel B. Crawford was, nevertheless, a citizen of this vicinity for years before; and from 1850 until 1896 — when he retired — has been a leading and prosperous dry goods merchant in our midst, and still survives, being nearly ninety years of age. He has also been identified with various other interests of the city and county, both secular and religious, until his name has become as familiar as household words.

Messrs. Fletcher & Benton first sold hardware, on the southeast corner of Fourth and Main, afterwards known as "Nestor's corner," now Eggemeyer's, and east of the court-house. Subsequently, Thomas Benton alone engaged in the business, in an old brick building, corner Fifth and Main.

A single member of the old Wiggins firm — Charles O. — with some added juniors, until lately held forth at the same old stand as in days of yore. William L. Brady was also a pioneer, and for many years successfully engaged in the harness trade. Samuel and William Lynde will be remembered as among our principal grocers ; neither must we omit Elijah Githens, in the same branch of trade. The former long did business where George W. Barnes, for so many years, dispensed his excellent family supplies, and where Joseph A. Knabe lately catered to the public wants.

The drug business was in the hands of Messrs. George Doxey, Irvin Reed and Dr. Joseph Howels, the former of whom died here during the prevalence of the cholera, in 1849 or 1850, and the latter, recently, in California ; while Mr. Irvin Reed, for many years subsequently, dealt in hardware, on the southwest corner of Seventh and Main. He, too, died some four years since. To him had been vouchsafed the most extended business career, in point of time, accorded any member of this community, covering a period of sixty years, and crowned with ample success. These gentlemen were succeeded by Dr. James R. Mendenhall, John T. Plummer and Lewis H. McCullough, each of whom continued in the business some years.

Hon. David P. Holloway, for many years past a resident of Washington City — who also died some dozen years ago — was in the book trade at the time of my advent to the village, and was located in an old frame building on the south side of West Main street, near the corner of Fourth. Dr. J. R. Mendenhall soon after became his successor ; and our former City Civil Engineer, Hon. Oliver Butler, was his business manager for years.

Your humble servant, the writer, first greeted the public here in the capacity of salesman for Strattan & Wright, whom he faithfully served for five long years, for the meager salary of $15 per month and board, saving therefrom, by the strictest economy, his first $500 — a result utterly out of the question in these times of increased values and multiplied temptations, from no greater pay.

It was my good fortune to find a home in the family of "Uncle" James and "Grand-mother" Hunnicutt, who kept the only boarding house of the time, which was quite liberally patronized — as well it might be, when we remember that they charged but a dollar and a quarter per week for board. Their house was headquarters for many old-time Friends, during Yearly Meeting. They were, most truly, a kindly old couple, called hence this many-a-year.

Thomas J. Bargis and Isaac L. Dickinson dealt in stoves and tinware. William Show and Isaac Paxson, senior, supplied the citizens with meats. Mark Lewis and William Mason, who soon after came to the rescue, furnished bread, cakes and crackers. John Suffrins, the hatter, then, and for many years after, took care of the cranial department of the multitude, and C. A. Dickinson and J. B. Hunnicutt supplied our wants, real or imaginative, with jewelry, watches, etc. Both have long since retired from the stage of action. J. W. Gilbert, Dan Sloan and K. Brookens catered to the public wants in the capacity of hosts. We had but one monied institution, known as the "Old Branch Bank," Elijah Coffin, cashier. The building adjoined the Richmond National Bank, on the east, and was removed, a few years since, to make room for other improvements. Our lawyers were Stephen B. Stanton, James Perry and William A. Bickle. The two former are deceased ; the latter, alone, continues in practice. The medical profession was ably represented by Doctors John T. Plummer and William B. Smith, both of whom have long since paid the debt of Nature. A. N. Newton was the only dentist of the time, and was, for several years, without a rival, until Doctor William R. Webster located in our midst. Doctor Newton has retired from the profession, and Doctor Webster has passed to that bourne, from which no traveler returns. They were both good men, and professionally equal to the requirements of the times. Milton Hollingsworth is deserving of special mention, as being one of Richmond's foremost teachers — earnest, capable and efficient. He was beloved and esteemed by his pupils, admired and respected by all. He, too, has gone to his reward. John K. Boswell was the first Daguerrean artist, of my recollection, here. His work was a credit to his profession, and specimens of his art, in the writer's possession, will bear comparison with that of the present day.

James Elder was postmaster here during 1847 and 1848, and it is my recollection that he also dealt in books and paper. He recently informed me that during his administration single letter postage ranged from five to ten cents, according to distance transmitted. Speaking of postal matters reminds me that about this time letter envelopes first made their appearance, and their utility being so manifest, were not long in gaining public favor. Not so, however, with the equally useful steel pen; for, although upon the market for years, they were just beginning to win their way to public favor and appreciation. N. S. Leeds was the first citizen of Richmond to learn the art of telegraphing, which he did at Dayton, Ohio, some time during 1848, for the purpose of serving a company who put up a line along the National Road, in that year. Their office was located on the north side of West Main street, between Fifth and Sixth, in the room afterwards owned and occupied by James J. Jordan, as a fancy grocery. L. H. McCullough soon after learned to manipulate the instrument, and became the former's successor. For lack of patronage, or some other cause unknown to the writer, the enterprise proved a failure, and the line went down. Mr. Leeds has responded to a message from the eternal world, while Mr. McCullough, for some years later, still toyed with the subtle fluid, in its various moods.

It may be of interest, in this connection, to state that the latter gentleman was the first person to introduce coal oil into this city for the purpose of illumination. This was in 1858, and the oil so used was distilled from coal, by some enterprising individual of Covington, Kentucky.

It may be said of the amusements of those days, that they were neither varied nor numerous. Picnics in Summer, and balls and parties in Winter, constituted about all the diversions of that period. Lectures, concerts and theatricals were not in vogue; the reigning influence seemed averse to anything of a happy or joyous nature. The piano, that much-tortured instrument, had but two representatives in the town ; and as for the sewing machine, alas! it was not—unless, indeed, we dared, without irreverence, apply the term to Eve's fair daughters, those blessed earthly ministers, who are ever ready to repair our garments or relieve our woes.

The press, that mighty engine, had its representatives in two weekly journals : the *Palladium* and *Jeffersonian*, republican and democratic, respectively, in politics. The former was, for many years, published by Messrs. Holloway & Davis, and since 1876 has been issued both daily and weekly. It is now under the management of Messsrs. Surface & Flickinger. The *Jeffersonian* was presided over by James Elder, Esq., but has long since ceased to greet the public.

In those "good old days" there were no women in the professions, none as teachers in the schools ; they were unknown to the editorial chair, nor had they a place at the desk, the case, or the counter. With rare exceptions, they were deemed incompetent for places of trust or responsibility. Man's estimate of woman was not creditable to his head and heart ; his bigotry and selfishness were a bar to her advancement. But, thanks to the dawn of a higher intelligence and the spread of more liberal views, the day of her deliverance has come ; the shackles of prejudice and superstition are falling about her, and she is free to pursue whatever occupation she may choose. A universal culture has

taken the place of a partial education ; a better system of
schools, the press, and the facilities for travel and inter-
course, added to a growing disposition to investigate
all subjects — taking nothing for granted — have combined to elevate, and fits her for the active duties of
life. She is freer, stronger, more self-reliant than her
sisters of any age. May the bondage of hand or brain
be hers no more, while the freedom of thought and the
freedom of speech shall continue to be the just inheritance of a free and independent people.

Referring to pioneer times, it is recorded that the
first settlers came here in 1805 ; that John Smith laid
out the town in 1816 ; that it was incorporated in 1818 ;
that a brewery and post-office came into existence the
same year ; that Robert Morrison was postmaster till
1829 ; that the first newspaper was issued in 1821 ;
that the first roads were opened in the direction of New
Paris and Eaton, Ohio, in 1806 and 1807 ; that the
National Road was located in 1828 ; that the same
became a pike, or gravel road, in 1848, about which
time several others were constructed. The railroad
first entered Richmond in 1853 ; the first grist-mill was
built in 1807 ; the first brick house, by John Smith, in
1811 ; the first tavern was opened in 1816, and the first
banking house in 1835 ; the first doctor came in 1818,
the first lawyer in 1826, and finally, the first census,
in 1824, showed a population of 453 inhabitants.

We might very properly supplement these hasty sketches, by briefly tracing the career of such early citizens as John S. Newman, David Hoover, Charles W. Starr, Robert Morrison, Albert C. Blanchard, Elijah Coffin, John Finley, and many others, whose lives have left their impress upon this community ; but such an undertaking would transcend the original purpose of these papers, as well as the needful information and ability of the writer. We trust, however, that the subject may yet receive the consideration it so justly deserves, at the hands of some one fully competent to the task.

At the period of my coming, as before stated, we had no railroad, but one turn-pike, no telegraphs and no telephones. At the present day they radiate in all directions from us, and encircle us round about. Then, communication with the outer world was slow and difficult ; now, we have almost unlimited facilities for transportation and travel, and almost instant communication with the uttermost parts of the earth.

Behold ! what a marvel has been wrought ! What wondrous change in the brief space of something more than two score years !

PAPER NO. 2.

MANY years before the writer's advent to this city, the National road was constructed, but, from the State line to Indianapolis, had never been graveled, so that travel in Winter and early Spring was almost out of the question. The older citizens will remember that during those seasons the mail was often carried on two wheels, surmounted by an open, queensware crate, which held the driver, the mail bags, and an occasional weary, mud-bespattered passenger —all drawn by four equally weary, worn and muddy horses— for the condition of the roads was simply fearful, requiring expert drivers and good teams to pull through. "The mud wagon," as it was aptly named, was used when the roads manifested signs of improvement, and consisted of a common, four-wheeled farm wagon, with board bed and canvas cover, stretched over wooden bows — having two or three plain boards placed across for seats, *sans* springs or cushions. This rude contrivance was especially designed for the accommodation of the traveling public, and it may readily be imagined what a treat it was, and what a degree of comfort it afforded. It, also, was drawn by a quartet of weary equines, who slowly trudged through mud and mire, now over some rude causeway — here of rails, and there of logs — and anon into some "slough of despond," sometimes sticking fast and requiring the united efforts of all the passengers to pry it out — they, meanwhile, receiving such a baptism of mud and water as, in these days, it would be almost impossible to conceive. As Summer approached and the roads improved, stage coaches were brought into requisition, making travel, if not absolutely comfortable, at least quite tolerable. I remember making the trip from this city to Cincinnati, one bright October day, about the year 1848, in a "coach and four," and I think I never enjoyed a day's journey so much in all my life. The time required was about twelve hours. In conversation with one of our older citizens, a short time since, he informed me that during the period in which our townsman, Joseph W. Gilbert, and a Mr. Voorhees, were each running passenger coaches to Cincinnati and intermediate points, the former, for a brief period, reduced the fare to the nominal sum of fifty cents, each way, thus hoping to discourage his rival, and induce him to withdraw, that he might have a clear field to himself. This, my informant thought, was about the year 1840. Many doubtless still remember the great droves of far-western cattle, as well as hogs and sheep, and on one occasion, turkeys, driven to market over that great highway, the National Road, and so continued until the introduction of steam and an iron outlet to the eastern world.

During these years there were also countless emigrant wagons going west with their precious human freight, seeking homes in some visionary El Dorado of the New World. Hard, indeed, was the lot of many, whether in the midst of the forest, or out upon the bosom of some boundless prairie. Hardships, privation and sickness were sure to attend them ; friends and early associations were far away, while strange, rude neighbors, for companions, dwelt about them—few and far between. Achilles Williams, who was one of Nature's noblemen, and an early pioneer, related to the writer, some twenty years ago (now 1896), the story of his first visit, in the year 1820, to the site and surroundings now occupied by the capital of the State— whose wealth, magnitude and business aggregate are approached by few inland cities on the continent. In the midst of an unbroken forest he found but two human beings to greet him — one of whom was an adventurous white man, the other his Indian wife, whose temporary hovel of bark was the only visible handiwork of man, to rear its unpretentious form amid the trees. Truly, seventy-five years (1896) have wrought a wondrous change. I recently spent some days at the city of Indianapolis, and on one occasion, when in the union depot, I beheld and counted, over and around the ticket office, fifteen clock-faced dials, each indicating the time of departure for as many trains on fifteen several roads, while a telegraph pole, standing in front of my hotel, supported, upon its out-stretched arms, one hundred and twenty wires. These things tell their own story of a progressive age. It is doubtful if any other agency on the continent of America has exerted so vast an influence in the development of the country and the education of its people, as the various systems of railroads, now ramifying and reaching out into the uttermost parts of this great republic. It is a marvel, even to ourselves, to contemplate the astonishing progress made by this nation in the past forty years. The railroads, the telegraphs, the daily press, the telephone, the sewing machine, gas, coal oil, electric light and power — all recent innovations — besides countless improvements, inventions and discoveries in mechanics, agriculture and the arts, most of which may be justly attributed to a higher and more universal education, whose magic and mighty forces have been stimulated, fostered and encouraged by our public schools. All these things have combined to lessen our labor, increase our comforts, add to our enjoyments, develop our resources, extend our knowledge, duplicate our wealth, and in many ways tend to place us in the front rank of nations.

Recently, in looking over some old-time letters and papers, I made the discovery of a card, or ticket* of invitation, which, for a matter so apparently trivial, possesses, nevertheless, more than ordinary interest as a relic of the past ; for it was nothing less than a bid to the "railroad ball," gotten up in commemoration of an event destined to be of the greatest possible moment to this city and vicinity. It ran as follows :

"The company of yourself and lady is respectfully solicited to attend a ball, to be given in honor of the commencement of the railroads of the Whitewater and Miami Valleys, at D. D. Sloan's National Hall, on Thursday evening, May 30, 1850. Managers for Richmond : D. P. Holloway, James Elder, S. E. Iredell, Irvin Reed, W. W. Lynde, and James King." Then follow many other names — thirty-five in all — as representatives of New Paris, Centerville, Hagerstown, Winchester, Cambridge City, Connersville, Eaton, Hamilton, New Castle, Muncie, Liberty, and Dayton, concluding with the name of Reece Kendall as floor manager.

Three years subsequent to this occurrence, the Indiana Central Railway was completed to this city, and James M. Brown appointed its first temporary agent — which position he held for a few months only — transacting its business in his own private office,

---

*This ticket of invitation is now preserved in the Railroad Museum of the Pennsylvania Company, at Chicago, Illinois.

near the depot. The writer became his successor, and opened the first permanent office, in the company's own building, buying the safe, copying-press and some of the books, and other needful appurtenances, of William T. Dennis — then in the hardware business, on the northeast corner of Franklin (now Seventh) and Main. It became my duty to act in the two-fold capacity of freight and ticket agent — a post involving both responsibility and labor, greatly in excess of, and out of proportion to, the meager compensation allowed. I also fitted up and furnished for the company its first ticket office in the old, original passenger depot, an insignificant, one-storied brick structure, which, I do not think, exceeded eighteen by seventy-five feet, in size, having a narrow wooden platform on either side, with a planked extension at each end, for the accommodation of baggage and express matter. I continued to. hold my position for about twelve months, when I resigned the office, to engage in more lucrative employment. Mr. John Lynch became my successor, and S. F. Fletcher his. During my brief administration, I employed, among others, one William Zeek, to assist in the handling and transfer of freight, who has most faithfully performed the same duties, at the same place, for more than forty years. Hon. John S. Newman was president, and Samuel Hanna treasurer, of the Indiana Central Railway Company at that time, the former of whom I had frequent occasion to see and consult, on business relating to the road. At this period I was a boarder with Harmon B. Payne, who was just then preparing himself for the legal profession, and many a time have I seen him deeply engaged in his studies, long before day, by the feeble light of a tallow candle.

Asking your indulgence, to go back a few years, I will state that my object in coming here was that of accepting a position tendered me, as salesman in their dry goods store, by the Messrs. Strattan & Wright, who were then, as for several subsequent seasons, also engaged in buying hogs and packing pork. And well do I remember the numberless calls for the senior proprietor, who, it seemed to me, was more in demand than any other mortal I ever knew, and at that time clearly of more consequence than any man in the community. "Strattan's corner," as it was called, was headquarters for the clamorous horde, seeking to dispose of their defunct, and often frozen, porcine carcasses. On two occasions, which I remember, hogs were brought in of very unusual size — two of which weighed, each, eight hundred pounds, net. One of them, I think, was raised by a Jesse Evans.

The firm were doing a very fair business, having many regular customers, especially among the Friends, who came long distances to make their purchases at this popular house. But, unquestionably, too much was allowed to go out on long time. It was the prevailing custom then — and a very unfortunate one — to give to the farming community, and many others, a year's credit for what should have brought them cash, and, if unable to pay at the expiration of that time, take their notes, bearing six per cent. interest, for such additional time as might be agreed upon, not infrequently running over into a second year. The pork-packing arrangement of which I have just spoken, was conducted, in great part, to facilitate collections. The debtor would bring in his hogs, and either receive or pay the difference between the value of his pork and store account, which, being cancelled, left him at liberty to begin anew, which he often did within the same hour of his settlement.

In those days merchants from this part of the country were in the habit of buying their stocks of dry goods mostly in Philadelphia — the community being composed largely of Friends, who preferred a class of merchandise known as "plain goods," not infrequently including a line of domestics or staples, such as prints, muslins and checks, of inferior make and color, supposed to have been produced exclusively by "free labor," and termed "free labor goods"— which, to make them such, often required the utmost stretch of fancy, and very great faith. All these were more readily obtained in the great City of Brotherly Love than elsewhere.

The old house of Sharpless & Sons was a favorite with the Quaker trade, as they dealt almost exclusively in the class of goods used by these people. A few years since, in one of my visits to this grand old city, whose praises I had so often heard recounted, and desirous of seeing still more of its noted places than had previously fallen to my lot, curiosity led me into this celebrated establishment, and, to my unbounded gratification, I found it all my fancy pictured it — a real treat to a relic hunter, and quite sufficiently antiquated to satisfy the most ardent searcher after old curiosity shops. Everything within and around told plainly of the past. The fashions of the day were disregarded ; the past was in its prime ; the years had gone unheeded with their change. This house, at least, was still the same ; its construction and arrangement, and its manner of display were those of years ago. This was even true of help — male and female clerks — many of whom were past their prime, and gray with age and care, having been, most likely, fixtures in the house for — lo ! these many years. This is, in all respect, strictly in accord with the spirit of old-time Friends — a disposition to be non-progressive — a desire to let well enough alone.

This once sober city of Penn, in times past, was the Quaker's chosen Mecca — his ideal shrine of worship, and his chiefest mart of trade. But, alas, for the transitory nature of human affairs ! Both the shrine and the worshipper are changed ; it is no longer either saintly or sedate ; neither is it as of yore — a beacon to the feet of the faithful ; for the youthful scion of the pious sire has departed from the faith, assumed the worldling's garb, and, in pursuit of other gods, now goeth where he listeth.

In those days, and as late as 1850, it used to take a merchant, going East from here, from four to six weeks to accomplish the journey and purchase his goods, the trip being made by three several modes of conveyance, namely : Stage-coach, steam-boat and railroad. One one occasion, about the year 1850 or 1851, Benjamin Strattan, having been East, had his goods shipped by the usual route of canal and railroad to Pittsburg, and from thence by river to Cincinnati. The water. being low, the boat, in its passage, grounded, and perhaps sunk. At all events, his goods became badly damaged by immersion, after which they were transferred to a "lighter," and brought on down the river to the Queen City. Now, although his stock had been insured against loss or damage in transit, it was made to appear that the transfer to another boat vitiated the "policy," and, if my memory serves me rightly, he was compelled to bear the entire loss sustained. When the goods finally arrived at their destination, and were opened, they presented a pitiful sight, indeed — being thoroughly wet, and apparently damaged beyond repair. Many of the finer dress fabrics were sent to the dyers to be recolored, and, if possible, restored. But in no instance did the result prove satisfactory ; they were returned in a condition resembling so many dish-rags — limp, lusterless, and without finish. Thus they remained long upon the shelves, and when sold, invariably neted a loss. The sequel proved more fortunate, however, than was anticipated. The stock was fully and freely advertised as wet goods, to be sold cheap, and it was marvelous to note how eagerly some people sought to purchase many of these goods, at a small reduction from cost, in preference to the better, and really cheaper ones, at regular prices. I remember hearing Robert Morrison once relate the story of an old lady customer of his, who was a particularly close buyer — that on one occasion, when she appeared to be more persistent than usual in her demands for a reduc-tion, she finally exclaimed : "Robert, I do really believe that thee is asking me more for thy goods than they cost thee." The older Friends used to style those of us who were members of no denomination, "the world's people," which was generally understood to be the very opposite of a compliment — little thinking how very many of their own descendants would be no less worldly in the next generation.

Scarcely a third of a century ago the make of the garment and the manner of speech were a sure index to the religious faith of a large majority of the people of this city and vicinity ; but in later years such marks of distinction have been surely and certainly passing away. And, while we sincerely trust that the principles held by Friends may ever continue to wield their benign influence with each and every one of us, yet we earnestly hope that the time is not far distant when all such peculiarities — whether of speech or dress — will be relegated to the shades of the departed past.

I believe it was some time during 1847 that Friends' Boarding School—now known as Earlham College—first opened its portals to the public — or, rather, that portion of it denominated "the Society of Friends," for it was originally designed for the education of their own children, but, finding an insufficient support from that direction, they at length determined to admit pupils from other denominations and the outside world, at large. From these, however, it was said, they demanded a considerable advance for tuition over that charged members of their own Society. This course, however proper it may have appeared to them, did not savor of that strict justice so characteristic of these people. During the earlier years of this school's history, all scholars were required to attend meeting twice a week — Sundays and Wednesdays — and all male students unable to plead some disability, were as often mustered together, formed in line, and marched in single file, from the college grounds, in West Richmond, to the old brick meeting-house, north of the railroad — a distance of some two miles — in Summer's

sun or Winter's storm, to participate in the peculiar
services of the Society, which sometimes consisted in
passing the time allotted in silent meditation and unut-
tered prayer. The pupils were usually attended by
their teachers, who kept an eye to their deportment,
and guaranteed their good behavior on the way. This
semi-weekly parade of the students always reminded
the beholder of so many "soldier boys," recently
recruited for "Uncle Sam's" service. The sight was
both novel and remarkable, as being enacted by the
sons, and instituted by the very people who, above all
others, inveighed most strenuously against every form
of ceremony, demonstration and display.

The frequent gibes and jeers of the boys, and
uncomplimentary remarks of many of their elders,
finally put an end to the show. As an institution of
learning, Earlham College can now justly be reckoned
as among the best in the land, and as richly deserving
the patronage of all good people.

Previous to the days of railroads, and to a very
limited extent since, the Friends came to "Yearly
Meeting" in their own conveyances, usually a two-
horse carriage, bringing with them, generally, the
elder members of the family, and, occasionally, the
smaller children. This was always a great week in
the history of Richmond, and not infrequently as great
an event in the lives of many of the members — whose
quiet, plodding ways and simple habits were but seldom

varied by the most ordinary pleasures and pastimes, beyond the monotonous routine of each returning day. The younger members from the rural districts were, frequently, simplicity itself. Often have I seen them — boy and girl — go hand in hand along our streets, utterly unconscious of the world about them, munching huge chunks of ginger-bread, or indulging in some other unused luxury. This was, to them, their *ultima thule* — the crowning bliss of all their former hopes — this coming to Richmond during " Yearly Meeting," with their best girls, to share in all the joys, and revel in the sights and sounds and unaccustomed luxuries of a considerable town ; but then they were profoundly happy — and that is more than can be truly said of many of the present day, although surrounded with increased wealth and countless sources of enjoyment.

Until about the year 1849 or '50, copper coins were almost unknown as a circulating medium, in this part of the world. They were first introduced with the completion of turnpikes, or toll-roads, as a matter of necessity, to make change. Either Robert Morrisson, who was president, or Benjamin Strattan, for a time treasurer of the Wayne County Turnpike Company, ordered the first installment of a hundred dollars' worth, or ten thousand pieces, from the Philadelphia mint. They were of the large, old-fashioned variety, and made a package somewhat resembling a keg of nails, for size. These coins were doled out to the "gates" as needed, and thus found their way into general circulation.

It may still be remembered by some that the first line of telegraph known to this vicinity was that put up along the National road, some time during the Summer of 1848, but which, for want of sufficient patronage, was, within a year or two, transferred to some more appreciative locality. In fact, the people upon whom it depended for its patronage and profit had not yet attained to the commercial and personal needs of such an institution ; they had not learned to appreciate the advantages of rapid transit and travel, and, much less, those of instantaneous communication by telegraph.

While writing of this subject, I am reminded that some time during this same year of 1848 a gentleman — William Unthank — came to this city and announced a lecture, to be delivered in the lower room of the old "Warner building," on the subject of "Electricity as a Motive Power." The interest manifested by the public was not commensurate with the importance of the subject, and comparatively few persons came out to hear what the lecturer had to say. Models were exhibited and their operations explained. He desired to enlist the sympathies of capitalists, in behalf of the enterprise, who might be willing to advance the means necessary to test the merit and practical working of his theories. However, he met with no encouragement here : the subject was too new and illy understood by most people ; and such apparently visionary schemes did not readily command the confidence, much less the cash, of the general public, and, at that day, not even its curiosity. This circumstance is cited to show the lack of interest and appreciation in the public mind, too often apparent on similar occasions when matters of the utmost importance are presented for its serious consideration, as well as to illustrate the possibilities of the human understanding in the direction of growth and development ; and·also to prove that the persevering delver in divine thought will not fail, at length, to bring up priceless pearls from the hidden recesses of the intellectual treasury — whose varied stores and collective resources are almost without limit ; how an idea, once conceived, may grow, by slow degrees, from germ to bud, and, in due season, blossom into the full-blown glory and realization of the perfect and complete ideal. Such, in his day, was not the good fortune of this hapless theorist and thinker — he did not live to realize the final consummation of his dream, for he sought aid and sympathy in vain. But others, following in his wake, took up the current of his thoughts and crystallized them into form, and the seeming fancy, of a generation since, became an accomplished fact.

Thus feeble thoughts, at length, the mightiest things evolve — as towering oaks from tiny acorns grow ; as wind-strewn seeds suggest the forest, wide ; or, as chaotic atoms formed the universe — developed in the lapse of time, through ages past, of long-forgotten years.

PAPER NO. 3.

THERE is, perhaps, no other delusion so far-reach-ing, or so fondly cherished by the human race, as the popular belief which attributes to our youthful days the doubtful merit of being, in all things, better than aught of these "degenerate times." With the middle-aged and the elderly the feeling is almost univer-sal that men were more moral, more virtuous, and more upright ; and that they were less given to sensuality and dissipation ; that peace, order and sobriety reigned supreme — in short, that the world was one grand, moral paradise, as compared with the present ; whereas, in point of fact, nothing could be farther from the truth. Life was just as real, earnest and exacting in the past as in the present ; love, hatred, jealousy — all held sway over men's minds then, as now, for human nature has doubtless been much the same in all ages. Into each human history is woven more or less of the good and the bad, the false and the true. Many an airy castle, which we builded in our youth, was a mere vagary of the imagination — a mere fiction of the fancy — created out of nothing, and to nothing soon returned. Thoughtfulness and sobriety belong only to maturity of years, and follow in the footsteps of age. Youth is indeed the spring-time of life, and is glorious in its strength and beauty. But age should be no less glorious, in its dignity, serenity and wisdom. Love, virtue and goodness, with their kindred attributes, were man's inheritance from his Maker, and will continue to bless and to comfort him to the end of time. So, also, were his sins and his weaknesses a part and parcel of his human nature. If it be admitted that man has not degenerated, as I think it must, the theory that the world has grown worse than formerly can be nothing short of a fallacy. The progress of recent times, not only in the arts and sciences, but in morality and religion, as well, is indeed too evident to be mistaken, and is quite sufficient to prove the very contrary of the proposition. It may be truly said that the good that men do lives after them, the evil is interred with their bones ; for, do we not, in our contemplation of the past, remember only the virtues, the friendships and the loves of the long ago — forgetful of the sins and the weak-nesses and the human frailties, which beset us then, as now? And thus it is, we dwell so fondly on the past, and think the elder days were better than the new.

Nothing can be truer than that the world has always been wicked. Vice and immorality have been the inheritance of all peoples and all times ; and, for at least a partial illustration of this truth, we need not go from home. The writer distinctly remembers that in our own moral (?) little city, with but a tithe of its present population, and comparatively few of the influences now so conspicuous for evil, we were yet far from being altogether good. Mischief often held high carnival in our midst ; pugilistic contests were not uncommon, and the baser passions were by no means always in abeyance, even surrounded, as we were, by a people so remarkable for piety, good order and peace principles, as were the Friends, who were dominant at the time. The unruly element was rarely ever traceable to their ranks, yet these baser spirits lived and flourished here, as elsewhere, and as they ever will, in all communities, to a greater or less degree. I occasionally meet one of these old-time " Pariahs " upon our streets —" lonewandering, yet not lost "— who, in earlier days, was wont to make night hideous in his cups. His companions have mostly found shelter in their graves, while he, illy clad, neglected and alone, a wreck in morals, character and health, will soon descend in sorrow to his own.

It used to be the delight of the " hoodlums " of those days to appoint a meeting somewhere on Main street — usually selecting a moonlight evening — and after the villagers had retired for the night, to either build a fire upon the ground, or procure an old stove from the premises of some dealer, gravely set up the pipe and put on a kettle of water, and, after all was in order and the steam and smoke ascending, hot drinks would be prepared and passed around, to add fresh fuel to the flagging fires within. They would then join hands all around, and shout and dance and sing till the welkin fairly rung, conducting themselves like a company of savages, far into the "wee small hours," unmolested by officers or citizens.

At times the dry goods boxes from the four quarters of the town would be collected during the night and piled many feet high, across the principal thoroughfare, completely barricading it against the traffic and travel of the following morning, when, at a late hour, the obstruction was generally removed by the owners of the property appropriated — the guilty parties meanwhile chuckling at the annoyance and vexation thus created. Sometimes the signs would be taken down all over the village, and so changed around that the dry goods merchant got the grocer's sign, and the grocer the dry goods dealer's; the banker became a bookseller, and the book-seller a banker; or it sometimes chanced that the doctor's front door would be ornamented by the dressmaker's tin sign, and she, in turn, would rejoice in the professional insignia of the disciple of Esculapeus. On one occasion a monied institution was made to represent a shaving shop, by setting up a barber's striped pole in front of it. Once, upon a Sunday morning, after the "boys" had indulged in their customary Saturday night's revel, a new farm wagon was to be seen drawn up by the side-walk, on East Main street, having placed upon it a delapidated out-building, ornamented with the gaudy sign of a well-known tonsorial artist, looking, "for all the world," like some bona fide establishment on wheels, quietly awaiting its share of the public patronage. On some occasions the gates would be taken from their hinges and carried off to some secure hiding place, to be returned at will, or perhaps never. Again, it might be the wheel of some carriage or buggy that was missing, subjecting the owner to untold annoyance, and a fruitless search of days, or even weeks, when at last some one would fish it from the bottom of the river, where it had been sunk, or, perchance, recover it from the roof of some distant barn, or out-building, where it had been placed by the authors of the mischief.

During the period from 1848 to 1852, Richmond had nothing better than a couple of old "hand engines" with which to protect her property from fire. The companies in charge were poorly organized, and consisted largely of young men and boys, few of whom had any interests at stake. Many were reckless and irresponsible, and, in the writer's opinion, frequently guilty of firing old buildings, and possibly, also, some of the better sort — solely to get out the engines and see which could get on first water. The excitement often ran high, and sometimes the ill-feeling engendered would culminate in a row, or a personal combat, between the contestants of the rival companies. There is little doubt that these organizations were responsible for a vast deal of mischief, since, immediately after the adoption of a paid fire department, the alarms, both true and false, fell off at least one-half. There used to be two brothers here, named, respectively, Dave and Sam Edwards — both blacksmiths — and one Joshua Horner — also a son of Vulcan — besides other kindred spirits, either dead or retired, by reason of age or infirmity, from their wonted occupations, who never failed to participate in every fray which ingenuity or insult could bring about ; and, as they wielded fists like sledge-hammers, they rarely failed to be the victors. At times these contests would seem to become contagious, and a perfect row would result, involving many individuals. The writer has seen a whole square in commotion, at the same time densely packed with a swaying, surging mass of humanity. These disgraceful occurrences took place mostly on some public occasion — such as election or show days — when the streets would be thronged by our own citizens, or people from the country. At such times many became intoxicated, consequently excitable, and ready for anything that might offer, however foolish, daring or desperate.

The recollection of one of these old-time roughs occurs to me, who was never absent from a fire, who was rarely ever sober, and who was sure to do more harm than good in his possibly well-meant endeavors. I have seen him break down doors, cut down hand-railing, and knock out window-frames and sash, throw out mirrors, and carry down feather-beds, in his drunken and insane excitement, and all this in a part of the house wholly free from danger. This same individual, when in liquor, was the terror of his neighborhood. He became furious as a wild beast, fearless as a savage, and reckless as only bad whisky can make a man. In this condition he would be extremely uncivil and abusive, and thereby get himself into numerous difficulties. At such times few men would have deemed it safe to interpose as peace-makers, yet his wife — who was but a frail woman — could approach him and, placing her hand upon his arm, would quietly lead him away, utterly subdued and without a murmur — just as a loving mother might lead away a little child.

It is scarcely necessary to remind the reader that, at the period to which these sketches refer, we were not yet blessed (?) with an efficient (?) police force, as now ; but, if my memory serves me, we had but two peace officers, whose jurisdiction pertained to the village proper — namely, the mayor and town marshal. The latter was himself too often under the influence of

the "flowing bowl" to fully comprehend the failings
and offenses of his fellows ; while the former, although
a worthy and upright gentleman, was neither aggres-
sive nor progressive.

These pictures have been drawn from real life, in
our own midst, as it existed here some forty years ago,
mainly for the writer's own gratification and amusement, as well as to wrest from oblivion some of the
valorous (?) deeds and pastimes of our early contem-
poraries ; and, secondly, to in some measure dispel the
oft-cherished delusion that the past was better than the
present.

BIOGRAPHICAL.

GENERAL SOL MEREDITH.

A gallant soldier and just man — Major-General
Solomon Meredith. Born in Guilford county, North
Carolina, May 29th, 1810; died at Oakland farm, near
Cambridge City, Indiana, October 21st, 1875. A man
of good heart, pure patriotism and generous hospitality ;
distinguished for energy of character, in the promotion
of public improvement, liberal education, and progress
in agriculture. He was a member of the Legislature,
and held, with honor, many offices of public trust,
under both general and state governments. In the
war for the Union, he commanded the Nineteenth
Regiment, Indiana Volunteers, in the battles of Gains-
ville, South Mountain and Antietam, and on other
well-fought fields. He was promoted for gallantry,
and led the " Iron Brigade " through all its marches
and battles until severely wounded at Gettysburg.
He then commanded the Western District of Kentucky
until the close of the war.

ALFRED KAYNE.

———

The subject of the following brief sketch was a native of this vicinity, born of parents, poor, illiterate, and of low degree. For some years, during his boyhood, he worked as a farm hand for Benjamin Strattan, then the principal merchant of this city, and who resided on his farm, three miles east, near the National Road, and now the property of a Mr. Garwood.

Our subject's education was very limited, and was mostly acquired in the village schools of Liberty, Indiana, under the tuition of one William Houghton, an early teacher and member of the Society of Friends. He was earnest, honest and ambitious, and desiring to advance himself, obtained a position as clerk in the dry goods store of Mr. Ralph A. Paige, of this city. After a few years spent in that capacity, here, he sought and obtained a place as salesman with Acton & Woodnutt, of Cincinnati, with whom he remained some time. But, being desirous of going another round higher, he went to the city of New York, where he procured employment in a wholesale dry goods establishment, and while there made himself master of three languages besides his own, viz: French, German and Italian. This he did by obtaining board with families of culture, who spoke only their native tongues — remaining with

each long enough to speak their language fluently.
Being thus equipped, with a knowledge of four languages
at his command, success, to one of his energy and indom-
itable will, seemed almost certainly assured. He had not
long to wait. The proprietors of the house of S. B.
Chittenden & Co., 350 Broadway, who were extensive
importers and jobbers of dry goods and notions, made
him an advantageous offer, which he readily accepted.
At his first introduction to his fellow associates and
clerks, he was often ridiculed and guyed for his seeming verdancy and awkwardness. He soon, however,
proved himself not only their equal, but, as a salesman,
greatly superior to the hundred or more employees of
the house, while, at the same time, the unusual interest
he manifested in his employers' affairs did not long go
unnoticed, nor unrewarded. During the second year
of his stay he had the general management of all the
departments, was soon after sent to Paris as resident
buyer, remaining abroad for several years, and finally
given an interest in their very lucrative business. This
occurred some time during the year 1860, after which,
with very good reason, he could regard his future fortune as pretty certainly assured. The sequel to this
great, good luck was the fact that in a few years he
was enabled to buy out the old firm and re-establish
himself at its head, under the style of Kayne, Spring,
Dale & Co., his associates having been men of experience and employees of the old house. His success was,

from the first, most extraordinary, with apparently every prospect of a long and prosperous career. But, unfortunately for us all in this world, there is nothing absolutely certain but death. We may plan, speculate, and prosper for a time, but the final result is in the unseen hands of a higher power than ours, and so it proved in this particular instance. Sickness and death will ever intrude, in this unhappy world, and that, too, when we least expect or desire their most unwelcome presence. Wealth, prosperity and ambitious hopes will not avert the inevitable. On his last return from Europe he was taken ill with pneumonia, which, in its violence, baffled the skill of his physicians, and his remarkable career was brought to an untimely close on the 13th day of February, 1879 — in the very prime of life — being under forty-five years of age. His estate exceeded $500,000. He left but a single heir — a son, of twelve years, then at school in Paris — his wife having preceded him to that " better land " some years before.

Considering his lowly origin, he was a most remarkable man—simple, kindly and noble. His example stands boldly out, and clearly indicates that where there is a will, there is a way. Without friends, money or influence, he yet bravely and successfully fought the difficult " battle of life." He was energy, honesty and veracity, personified. Intelligence and a hopeful disposition led him, as a guiding star, to the goal of his ambition. He readily achieved both culture and education. Such an example as his is worthy of the very highest praise. Yet, how many there are, who, with all the appliances of wealth, friends, and great natural ability, still drift on down upon the stream of time, to become utter wrecks on the great ocean of life. Alas! How few of all his early friends ever remember him in his old home! Fame and notoriety he never sought, and this poor tribute is the only notice of his splendid and noteworthy career I have ever seen. Men are too much occupied with their own concerns to be greatly interested about even their nearest and dearest friends. And then, too, not unfrequently, envy plays its miserable part in the suppression of a noble name, because of the jealousy success engenders. Be that as it may, Alfred Kayne was one of Nature's proudest noblemen. Artificiality and pretense were wholly unknown to his simple nature. He could not play deception's part. Such men as he could only bless mankind.

Farewell, dear friend, thy like is rarely seen.

WEDNESDAY, MARCH 25, 1896.

JUDGE JAMES PERRY.

Remarks at the Funeral of His Life-Long Friend, by John Yaryan,
Esq.— A Merited Tribute, Eloquently Expressed.

There is a lesson to be learned no less in the death
than in the life of every man, and eminently so in the
case of one who has been distinguished in thought and
position, like him whose death we are commemorating.
Judge Perry was more than an ordinary man. Born
in Madisonville, Ohio, in January, 1799, he at an early
age selected the medical profession as a livelihood.
After spending about two years reading the profession
with Dr. Duncan, then an eminent physician, he
became satisfied he never would be pleased with the
practice of medicine, abandoned the profession and
went into the profession of the law. While yet a
student he came to Indiana, and in 1824, when the
county-seat was removed from Brownsville, he located
in Liberty and was admitted to the bar. His library
consisted of Blackstone's Commentaries, Chitty's
Pleadings and Tidd's Practice, but these he had mas-
tered perfectly. How different the state of affairs
now! Neither Kent's Commentaries nor Story's
Equity had then been written, and since the date of

his license we have one hundred and fourteen volumes of Indiana reports alone, to say nothing of the statutes and other law-books.

At that time the Whitewater bar was Daniel J. Caswell, William R. Morris, John Test, James B. Ray, John T. McKinney, Amos Lane, James Rariden, David Wallace and Oliver H. Smith, all eminent lawyers, statesmen and orators. With his meagre library, young Perry went into forensic combat. For dash and powers of eloquence in debate he was not remarkable, but philosophically and logically he soon became their peer. Later on came Caleb B. Smith, Parker, Ryman, Holland, Newman, Morton and Charles H. Test, with whom he traveled and practiced through the almost roadless regions of eastern Indiana. In 1828 he was elected prosecuting attorney, and well were the duties of the office performed.

In 1840 Samuel Bigger, then judge of the circuit court, was elected Governor, by which his office became vacant. By an almost unanimous petition of the board, the retiring Governor appointed Judge Perry to fill the vacancy, and he occupied the bench till 1841, when he located in Wayne county and resumed practice. In all these relations of life he proved himself equal to the duties of the trusts. One of his most distinguished characteristics, as a public man, was his loyalty to candor and truth — he deceived no one; his single inquiry was, "Is it right?" This determined on, he sometimes became opinionated, but in no instance have I ever heard any one doubt his word or integrity at the bar or on the bench.

Consumption was hereditary in the family of his father. The judge was the survivor of the family. A knowledge of this physical infirmity caused him to adopt daily sanitary rules in early life, which sometimes became amusing to his more robust but less informed professional associates. He, however, adhered to his rules and survived the whole circle enumerated.

I was often with him during his last illness. He knew better than we at his bed-side that the golden bowl was breaking at the fountain, and that the silver cord was being loosened. But his mind was an exception to the general rule of physical infirmities — apparently unclouded to the last. A single instance to illustrate: He was in charge of a perpetual trust fund. He had several times, within the last few years, used small amounts of the funds, but in every instance executed his note, payable to the beneficiary, drawing the highest rate of interest allowed by law. On the morning of the day he died, he directed me to make him an abstract of principal and interest of all the notes, that he might supersede the old notes by a new one, and to do it at once. His direction was complied with. The abstract being presented, he remarked he felt too bad to examine it, and to lay it aside till he should feel better. At 2 o'clock he called for it, examined and approved it, and then signed the new note in a legible hand. About 10 o'clock he called his daughter-in-law to his bed-side, told her he was dying and desired her to remain with him till it was over, and in thirty minutes life faded away so gently that she was at a loss, for several moments, to know whether he had dropped asleep or was dead.

On the eightieth annual birthday of the Judge, the bar presented him with a full set of the lives of all the Chief Justices of England. Yesterday they held a meeting and adopted a memorial of respect to him, to be spread on the Order Book of Court. Not content with these demonstrations of respect, to-day they are here in a body, intending to accompany the corpse to its final resting-place and mingle their sorrow with griefs of relatives, in the loss of one so venerable and by them so highly esteemed.

APRIL 30, 1887.

IRVIN REED.

———

Irvin Reed died at 9 : 30 o'clock this morning, from sheer exhaustion of vital forces, and when his lamp went out there was ended the long career of one of Richmond's oldest citizens, who, during her transition from a hamlet to a city, was identified with most of those enterprises that mark the strides in her prosperity.

He possessed those elements of success that gained for himself a sufficiency of this world's goods, and made him prominent as a public spirited citizen. Of later years he has been, in a manner, retired from active business, leaving that to his sons, one after the other, until Frank is the only one at home. But he was generally found at the store, and seemingly never lost interest in either private or public affairs. Recently he had to be helped on his way to and fro, between his residence and the store, but he insisted on going until a week ago to-day. Since then he has been confined to the house, but not to his bed, entirely, until since Wednesday. Then he was up for the last time, and he said that he would rather die than make the effort again. Last night, however, he said he was feeling better, and up to within a quarter of an hour of his demise he talked to his son, Frank, of business and "mother," saying he wanted Frank to look after her, and he guessed all else was all right. Then, conscious of the fact that the final hour was near, he resigned himself to the short wait for the dark messenger's coming, and answered the summons without a struggle.

The deceased was eighty-one years of age, having been born at Zanesville, Ohio, January 9, 1810. While yet a very young man, in 1832, he came to Richmond, and was a charter member of the town council, as well as the pioneer druggist, he and Charley Sturgess embarking in the business that year. Within about a year, however, Sturgess left, and then his brother, the late General Hugh B. Reed, of New Jersey, came here and clerked for him, as did the late J. J. Jordan, L. H. McCullough and William Schwartz. Two years later, December 18, 1834, he was married to Mary Evans, daughter of Edmund and Elizabeth Evans, who survives him. His health failing, he sold his drug store, late in the forties, and embarked in the hardware business, while he was also in the saddlery business, temporarily, before he went to Cincinnati, in 1853, to engage in the wholesale drug business, the firm being Irvin Reed & Co., Nos. 16 and 18 Main street. In 1857 he returned to Richmond and embarked in the hardware business, E. H. Swayne being a partner for some time, and he has been in it ever since, in his present location, for about twenty-five years. During this latter period he lived on what had been his father-in-law's farm, which he got in a trade with Edward

Potts — where John Fihe lives, part of it being now within the city limits, the house being No. 1413 South I street — but about the close of the war he bought and removed to his late residence, southwest corner North Eighth and A streets.

No arrangements for the funeral will be made until a response is heard from the children. Of ten children, six survive him — Arthur, of Paducah, Kentucky ; Albert, of Baltimore ; Charley, of San Francisco ; Horace, of Portland, Oregon ; Hugh, of Chicago, and Frank, of this city.

By request of Mrs. Reed, the friends will send no flowers.

APRIL 25, 1891.

SENATOR JOHN YARYAN.

Special to the Cincinnati *Enquirer:*

RICHMOND, IND., Jan. 27, 1894.— Senator John Yaryan died this afternoon, at his home in this city, at the advanced age of ninety-two years. Mr. Yaryan served in the last State Senate and was probably the oldest legislator in the country. He was born in Tennessee and came to Wayne county, Indiana, in 1859. He served many terms in the State Legislature, in the early days of the State, and was the author, in Indiana, of the law which gave the women the right to own property and to make a will. Mr. Yaryan's illness was brief.

[From the Indianapolis *Journal,* Jan. 15, 1893.]

Hon. John Yaryan, Senator from the county of Wayne, in the Indiana Legislature, is, without doubt, the oldest legislator in the world. He passed his ninetieth birthday on November 27, 1892, having been born in the second year of the century. He is fourteen years older than the State and is older than its present boundary line. At the time of his birth his parents were living in Blount county, Tennessee, of which Marysville is the seat. His ancestors were German, as the name would indicate. Mr. Yaryan's educational opportunities were fair, for those early times. A Mr. John Bigger was the first teacher of his recollection, who taught in a school-house located on his father's farm — this was in Union county, Indiana, in the vicinity of Liberty, the county-seat, which was, at that time, not yet thought of. His second teacher was William Bennett, an uncle of General Tom Bennett. The amusements of those days were corn-huskings, singing-schools and dances.

Senator Yaryan was unusually ambitious, in his boyhood, for an education, and pursued the opportunities at hand so assiduously that, at twenty-one years of age, he was able to teach in the schools of the settlement. His earnings as teacher were about ten dollars per month. The first office he ever held was that of Justice of the Peace — this was before he was admitted to the bar. Senator Yaryan began his legal studies in 1831, and was not admitted to the bar until 1839. "I was required," said he, "to pass two very rigid examinations, before two Circuit Judges. Our Constitution, which was formed in 1851, changed the requirements, so that they have ever since amounted, practically, to nothing — any citizen may become a member of the bar, on proof of moral character."

The bar of eastern Indiana had some noted lawyers in the forties: Caleb B. Smith — the friend of Lincoln — and his talented brother, Oliver H., both learned and eloquent, practiced at the Union county bar. Samuel Parke — also an orator and a noted Congressman in his day — was a compeer of the Smiths. Senator Yaryan was the partner of Caleb B. Smith, in Union county, during the decade from 1840 to 1850. Senator Yaryan's interest in politics began at an early day. He lived to vote for eighteen Presidents — from 1824 to 1892. It has only been two years since he retired from the practice of law, but he keeps busy as the executor of estates, etc., and as the secretary of the Odd Fellows' Provident Association. He has no bad habits, and is regular in everything. His present wife is his second wife, to whom he was married in 1847. He is by no means antiquated in his ideas. His faculties serve him admirably, and he keeps posted about all that is going on. His life has been a useful and an honorable one. C. R. LANE.

[From the Richmond *Item*, Jan. 30, 1894.]

During the time that the remains of the late John Yaryan lay in state, at his residence, on North Tenth street, a large number called to look upon his form once more. As he lay, surrounded by flowers, he looked more as if fallen asleep than that death had claimed him.

At the Wayne county bar meeting, following his death, there were present Judge Comstock, C. C.

Binkley, H. B. Payne, John L. Rupe, C. E. Shiveley, J. W. Henderson, Judge Abbott, F. C. Roberts, Judge Henry C. Fox, Judge Kibbey, Judge William A. Bickle, Lewis D. Stubbs, A. L. Study, Jonathan Newman, I. Ben Morris, Thomas J. Study, Charles H. Burchenal, and Judge Bundy, of New Castle. Judge Bickle said, ''I never knew Mr. Yaryan, in all the forty years of my acquaintance with him, to do a mean or dishonest act, or utter a falsehood.'' Mr. Burchenal said, ''He lived out his life well, and did his duty as he saw it.'' I. Ben Morris said, ''For fifty years he has stood a prominent land-mark among the men of eastern Indiana. His fall was like the giant oak. I consider him one of the big Americans who constitute the bulwark of society.'' L. D. Stubbs said, ''He was entirely incorruptible and thoroughly moral.''

The final services were held at St. Paul's Episcopal Church, Rev. J. E. Cathell officiating. When concluded, the cortege formed in line and proceeded to Earlham cemetery, where interment took place.

WILLIAM PARRY.

William Parry is dead. The news of the sad occurrence spread with great rapidity about the city this afternoon, and people could scarcely believe that such a familiar character as William Parry had gone forever. Without a particle of exaggeration, it can be said that no citizen, either of Richmond or Wayne county, was more extensively known, and he held a friendship enviable for its proportions. Some months ago Mr. Parry was taken ill, but he was not dangerously so, and there was no fear entertained for his recovery. He was always possessed of a robust constitution, and scarcely ever before experienced a sick day. During the last month his condition has at several times become alarming, and it had been regarded by his physicians as very doubtful if he would recover. Yesterday he showed signs of being much worse, and this morning, close to noon, he died.

William Parry was born July 20, 1810, in Montgomery county, Pennsylvania, and was a son of Joseph and Sarah (Webster) Parry, both natives of Montgomery county, his father being born in 1788, and his mother in 1789. William received a country school education at his birth-place, and at the age of 17 years came west with his parents, settling in Wayne county.

After arriving here, William came to Richmond and devoted several years in learning the plasterers' trade, after which he became a contractor in the plastering business. In 1844 his father had become so enfeebled with age that William gave up his business labors in Richmond and took charge of the farm, located northeast of the city. His peculiar knack for operating any business successfully, showed itself after he had taken charge of the farm, and he was soon managing a paying piece of property. In 1850 he purchased the farm from his father, and conducted the same with flattering success, realizing a great amount of money from the products. His great ability and decidedly honest methods in business affairs, soon placed him at the front in all movements of either city or county. In 1849, when the Williamsburg and Richmond Turnpike company was talked of, he became the chief of the project, and saw it pushed to completion in 1851. He became the heaviest stockholder, and in those times the road was a paying investment. Mr. Parry also became interested in the Wayne County Turnpike company, and from 1858 to 1871 served as president. When the Grand Rapids & Indiana Railroad company built a line from Ft. Wayne to Richmond, he, with other Richmond citizens, became financially interested, and in 1868 he was elected president of the southern end of the G. R. & I., known as the Cincinnati, Richmond & Ft. Wayne road, and has served continually, as its head officer, since that time, only last Friday he being again elected to the position. Among Mr. Parry's other offices, he has been both city councilman and township trustee, filling both positions with marked success. He was married, in 1833, to Mary Hill, daughter of Robert Hill.

The funeral will occur at 10 : 30 o'clock, Fifth-day morning, from the North A Street Friends' meeting house, and the time for meeting at the residence is 8 :.45. Interment will be at the Ridge cemetery.

APRIL 9, 1894.

WILLIAM L. JOHN.

On Friday, September 6, 1895, Major William L. John was ninety years old. He is the oldest man in Richmond : that of itself is enough to make him an interesting personage ; but that, taken in connection with the fact that he is still a comparatively active man, physically, and that his mind is as fresh and clear as in his youth, makes him all the more interesting. Then, when you find a man of that sort who, for seventy years, has been at the fore-front of all the movements for the good of the country ; who has been over the most of the United States — from Massachusetts Bay to the Rocky Mountains — and who has known all the public men of his time, most of them personally, and has worked side by side with them, the mere fact of his being the oldest man in Richmond does not impress one so much as do his character and personality. It is certain that you will seldom find a man of more marked personality than Major John. His conversation is interesting because he always says something when he talks. This is so unusual with men, whether they be ninety years old or fifty, that it is all the more noticeable and refreshing. Probably no man's talk is fuller of anecdote or of keen every-day philosophy — gotten not from books but from experience ; and the things he has seen, and the things he has helped to do, would go to make one of the most interesting biographies that has ever been written of the men of the Middle States.

Major John was born on the 6th day of September, 1805, in Butler county, Ohio. His parents, who were of English, Scotch and Welsh extraction, emigrated from Fayette county, Pennsylvania, in the Spring of 1802, and built a little cabin on the edge of the wilderness, which stretched from the Miami river to the Pacific ocean, and which was inhabited only by the wolf, the bear, the beaver and the red man. In this cabin their son was born — the third in a family of ten children — and here he grew up, in the midst of wild neighbors, with the deer pasturing in the door-yard, and the smoke of the Indian's camp-fire mingling with the smoke from the cabin's chimney. When he was five years old his parents removed to Warren county, Ohio, and there he spent all of his early life, working by day on the farm, getting a little schooling in winter, but learning for himself, most, in the great school of life. When he was twenty-one he began to read law — not because he expected to be a lawyer, but from pure love of it. He traded corn, at 12½ cents a bushel, for second-hand volumes of Blackstone and for Story on the Constitution, and he used to read these on rainy days, or at night by the aid of a hickory torch or a candle. And it may be said right here, that, though Major John was never admitted to the bar and never practiced law, in the strict sense of the term, he nevertheless is as thoroughly grounded on matters legal as many another man who has put out a shingle. The few other books that he had access to — among which were Goldsmith's " Animated Nature " and the poems of Robert Burns — he read with such understanding and so thoroughly that he got more from them than most boys to-day will get out of a whole library.

He lived on the home place till he was forty years old, when he settled in Liberty, Union county, this State, where he was one of the leading men till he moved to Richmond, in 1868.

All his life he has been an active politician, being first a Whig, and afterward a Republican. Since he was twenty-one years old he has never missed voting at an election — national, state, or municipal — and he has always been a leader in all matters pertaining to the good of eastern Indiana. His part in politics brought him in contact with most of the men who helped make the country, and he was a personal friend of John Quincy Adams, William Henry Harrison, Oliver P. Morton, Hayes, John Sherman, Tom Corwin, Joe Wright, besides a whole host of Governors and Senators. He was a member of the State convention which helped nominate Harrison for the Presidency in 1836. He built the first turnpike in Indiana, and he was a prime mover in first getting railroads into the State from the East.

Despite the fact that he has had such a part in public affairs, he has never held an office, preferring, rather, to see to getting other good men in than to get in himself.

During the war of the Rebellion he was sent West by the Government as a special agent, partly to look after Indian affairs and to watch Southern sympathizers in the posts of the Rockies ; partly to look out for a pass in the mountains where it would be practicable to put a railroad through. He traveled across the plains to Ft. Laramie, in the dead of winter, with six companions, and from there made excursions through the mountains, visiting seven different tribes of Indians, and exploring much of what is now Montana, Wyoming, Idaho and Colorado.

The honor of locating the path of the first railroad across the American continent has been claimed by many men, but there is no doubt that it properly belongs to Major John. Previous to his expedition, several corps of engineers had tried to find a route through the mountains, and without exception had reported that the plan was not possible. Not deterred by this, Major John made himself familiar with the country by his own observation and by gathering information from the Indians and from wandering trappers, and it was on a certain very memorable day in March that he lay down on the grass in Cheyenne Pass and wrote to the Secretary of the Interior, describing what he believed to be a practicable pass in the Rockies. Following his instructions, engineers were sent out the next year, and to-day the whistle of the locomotive wakes the echoes in that very pass, and the steel rails of the path of commerce gleam within fifty rods of the spot where he lay on the ground and wrote his dispatches to the department, seeing, perhaps, with a prophetic eye, the wonderful development of the country, at whose gates he was one of the first to knock.

It is impossible, in the limits of a newspaper article, to do justice to, or even give an idea of, the fullness of his life of activity. To know that, you must talk to him personally. Writing a sketch of him is not like writing of some young man who is just beginning to make marks on the page of life, and of whom you can prophesy and wonder about: here is a man whose word is spoken, and it has been a very good word. To have fronted life for ninety years ; to have assumed, without shrinking, all the responsibilities of a citizen ; to have made life happier for his friends ; to have aided young men, by his advice and his example ; to have tried always to live honestly with God and man, that is to have lived well and wisely. And, in the respect and love of everybody who knows him, such a man has his reward.

NOTE.—William L. John died October 17, 1896, aged ninety-one years, one month and eleven days.

OLD LETTERS

OF PIONEER TIMES.

RICHMOND, IND., SEPT. 28, 1834.

Dear Father :

It has been some time since I wrote you last. I will
now let you know, pretty generally, all that is interesting. John (Finley) wrote you not long since, informing you that Mr. Fleming was ill. He is not yet any
better, and his condition is very serious. I am now
sitting up with him, and employ a part of the night in
writing this letter. His condition is the result of a very
bad cold, taken some three weeks since, from getting
wet in a shower of rain. His recovery is indeed very
doubtful. Doctor Ithamer Warner is his physician.

Fever and ague has been very prevalent here this
fall, and also over a greater part of the western country.
It is now, however, beginning to disappear, on the
approach of cooler weather. The family with whom I
live have all been very sick, and nearly all at the same
time, excepting the oldest girl, who yet has a shake
every other day. As for myself, I have as yet escaped,
and am now very hearty, although for a month past I

was a good deal indisposed, but was still able to work. The time for which I engaged myself has just expired. I have made a little over two hundred dollars. My prospects for another year are better than they were last, at the same place. The people are pleased with me — much pleased with the leather I turn out — and desire me to stay. Where to go, I know not, that I might do better ; yet I am not wholly satisfied with my way of living. The people with whom I make my home, though very clever, do not live in accordance with my notions of life, in consequence of which I am restrained from every advantage of improving or enjoying myself as I could wish. What I shall finally do, I have not determined, but will shortly. I expect to pay you a visit this fall. Just now I am very busy, and find it difficult to finish leather fast enough to meet the demand. I expect, in about two weeks, to go with a company on a hunting expedition, thirty or forty miles from here, to be gone ten or twelve days. This, and my visit to the Springs — Yellow Springs, Ohio — will be all the time I can possibly spare, much as I would like to take a tour out West, to look for a better location. John expects to start, with a few horses, to Kentucky, in about two weeks ; or; he may postpone till December and enlarge his drove, and go to Carolina or Virginia.

To-day has been a great day for meetings in town. The Seceders (who are now known as United Presbyterians) held a "sacrament," the Methodists a Quarterly Meeting, and the Hicksite Friends a Yearly Meeting.　On next Sunday will be the Orthodox great day of Yearly Meeting.　You will see by the *Palladium* that the branch of the State Bank, at this place, will soon go into operation.　John expects to be a candidate for cashier, and with as good prospects of success as any other candidate.　(Elijah Coffin, however, was the successful applicant.)　I wrote to William Van Meter, some time ago, and expected on answer, soon, but I suppose he thinks he will do as I have done with him — wait a long time before replying.　I wonder why Flora (Finley) or some of the rest of the girls don't write to me?　I get no letters at all, nowadays, from home or any other source.　I will confidently look for one, soon, from some of you.　In your last letter to John, you complain you cannot write ; John says you can write better than either of us.　It is half past twelve o'clock, at night, and I believe I cannot think of anything more at present ; but let us hear from you soon, and send us such matters of interest, concerning Uncle Lyle's and Mr. Knott's families, as you may be able to procure, and give my kind regards to all, while I remain, as ever,　　　·　Your affectionate son,

ANDREW FINLEY, JR.

TO ANDREW FINLEY, SR.,

　　　　Springfield, Ohio.

AT HOME, JUNE 28, 1838.

(On the Elkhorn creek, six miles south of Richmond.)

Sister Flora :

I received your letter of the 16th inst., yesterday, and yours of March in due time, and would have answered it sooner, but I expected, at that time, each week, to know the next, when I should visit you, and then would write ; but the time I expected to go was such bad weather and roads, I could not venture out ; when the road was better, I could not leave my work. Now, it is so far advanced in the season, so hot and sultry, that traveling is unpleasant ; so that I prefer to postpone my visit until after harvest. You give us flattering accounts of religious revival in your region of country, which I am glad to hear. I cannot give so good an account for ours, although at Abington, three or four miles below us, the Methodists and United Brethren held a protracted meeting, of ten or twelve days' duration, during which time some fifty or sixty persons were added to their churches.

The Baptists have prayer meeting once a week, and preaching only once a month. As to my own feelings, in regard to religion, I feel at a loss to describe them, and am loth to communicate, for fear I might create hopes in others, only to be deceived, and also to deceive myself. But I hope for better things — yea, sometimes

I almost know it. I am certain of a great moral change taking place in my mind, and at times I have great reason to hope it is a spiritual one, as well. I know that of myself I can do nothing ; but self is mostly in the road.

As Mr. Bradbury is waiting on me to take my letter to the post-office (at Richmond), I must conclude in a hurry, without expressing myself as clearly as I could wish. Mr. Bradbury has sold some land to Mr. Fleming, which adjoins the latter's property, for about twenty-eight hundred dollars, and has purchased some lots in town — Richmond — and intends to put up a frame house this summer, into which he thinks he will move this fall, so as to be convenient to a good school. I will write to you before I see you — I may go in two or three weeks. We are hardly ever quite well ; at least I am always complaining. Little Martha is doing pretty well, but is more or less feverish every day, in consequence of cutting teeth. She has one tooth through ; she can run about everywhere, and is uncommonly active and alert ; she walked before she was nine months old, and is quite interesting and notedly smart. John (Finley) called at our house last Saturday, and said all was well. I expect to be at Centerville one day next week.   Your sincere brother,

ANDREW FINLEY, JR.

TO FLORA FINLEY,

    Springfield, Clark Co., O.

ELKHORN, WAYNE CO., IND., FEB. 2, 1839.

(Six miles south of Richmond.)

Dear Friend :

I received your kind letter, and to let you know that I am greatly pleased that you have not forgotten me, I embrace the first opportunity to answer it. You wish me to inform you how I have spent my time since you left us. That will not be difficult, for my employment has been much the same as when you were here, except that I have been studying at home, some, this winter. We expect to move to Richmond in about two months, where we will have a better opportunity of attending school than is possible in the country. There have been several changes in the neighborhood during the past year. Some of your acquaintances have been married, some have moved away, and several have died. Minerva Larsh died the latter part of August, and her sister, Miranda, died in December, following. Mrs. Larsh has none of her daughters living with her, now, but Mercey. Miss Jane Hunt was married this winter, and also Miss Francina Sedgwick. Andrew and Mary (Finley) have been living with us this winter. Andrew's health has been somewhat better this winter than it was last. Little Martha Agnes is learning to talk, and I think will make as smart a girl as her Aunt Agnes. But I must come to a close, and leave some room for Susan to write. I hope your present letter will not be the last you will write me, if it was the first. All our family, and mother, in particular, join with me in sending their sincerest love and kindly greeting. I remain, as ever,

Your sincere friend,

REBECCA BRADBURY.

Dear Sister Agnes:

Rebecca and I have adopted your plan of writing two letters on one sheet. I must first — as it has been our usual custom — apologize for not writing sooner. This was owing to the delay of your letter, dated December 19th, which I did not receive for at least three or four weeks after it was written. (This letter was mailed at Springfield, Ohio.) I have heard, however, that John (Finley) has written one or two letters to " Pa," since, so that you cannot complain of not hearing, frequently, from us. Andrew received a letter from " Pa " a few weeks since, from which we were sorry to learn that he is obliged to relinquish his business. We were glad, notwithstanding, to hear that you have got a school in town, and hope that you will all try to do something towards helping to support the family. I have been trying to get a school ever since I came here, and have at last succeeded in getting a small school, of fourteen or fifteen scholars, at two dollars per scholar, which I expect to commence next week. I expect to teach in an old house on Mr. John Hunt's farm. Though the school will be quite small, yet it will be better than doing nothing. I hope that Jane or May, or both, are going to school and endeavoring to qualify themselves for teaching. I wish that they would pay particular attention to the study of arithmetic, for I find that a knowledge of that branch is of more use to a teacher than almost any other. Flora has been staying at John's for several weeks, and will probably remain there till spring. John's family were well the last time we heard from them. But it is time that I stop writing, for it is almost nine o'clock, at night. I believe Rebecca has told you all the news. Tell Caroline that she and William must write me a letter, that I may see how much they have improved in writing and composition. Give my love to "Pa" and "Ma," and the rest of the family. I remain,

Your sincere sister,

SUSAN FINLEY.

To AGNES FINLEY,
      Springfield, Ohio.

MISCELLANEOUS SKETCHES.

COURT-HOUSE REMOVAL.

On the 14th day of August, 1873, the records of the county were removed from Centerville to this city, after having reposed there — the major part of them, at least — since the year 1822 : so says Norris Jones, who, when a boy, assisted in their removal from Salisbury (the first county-seat, and which has long since ceased to have an existence), and to-day, at the age of sixty-two, brought over the first load to Richmond. Henceforth this city will be the county-seat, if not the seat of justice. The loss to Centerville is a serious one — to us, a material gain. Here may it rest in peace.

During the early days of November the material composing the new jail at Centerville, and likewise the iron fence surrounding the county buildings, were transferred to this city, to be re-constructed here. The removal was not effected without considerable opposition by the people of Centerville, who, on several occasions, threatened, and did use, violence, in order to stay the removal, firing a six-pounder cannon, and other smaller fire-arms, at the men employed in taking down the buildings, etc.

HOW RICHMOND MET A CRISIS.

For the past ten days, or over, a singular malady has afflicted the equine family, as well as their long-eared brothers — not only here, but in every region of the United States and Canada — styled the epizootic, producing copious discharges from the nostrils, with enlarged sore throat, and other symptoms with which the writer is not familiar. The complaint usually lasts about two weeks, and does not very often prove fatal when the animal has been relieved from labor and properly cared for; many have, however, died from the disease when the owner has continued to exact the customary service, after an attack. At the present date — November 30, 1872 — scarcely a horse in the city is entirely well, while some are convalescing, others are suffering from premonitory symptoms of the disease. Of course, much serious inconvenience is experienced at the absence of so much useful motive power, and every conceivable device is resorted to, to

supply its place. The milk-man, the grocer, the
baker and expressman, as well as the drayman and
merchant, are alike sufferers. Some yoke or harness
yearling calves, cows, or sturdy oxen; while many,
lacking these, take truck, barrow or wagon in hand
and manfully furnish their own motive power. Buggies
and carriages are, of course, but seldom seen, and
those who, lately, were too delicate to walk, now walk
quite well.

RICHMOND POSTMASTERS.

A COMPLETE LIST OF ALL RICHMOND POSTMASTERS
FROM 1818 TO 1897.

The first postoffice in Richmond was established in
1818, and Robert Morrisson was commissioned as
postmaster, the office being opened in a frame building
at the southwest corner of Main and Fourth streets. It
was next kept in a frame building on the northeast
corner of Main and Fifth streets. The first regular
arrival of mail in 1818 was once every two weeks, but
as it had to be carried on horseback, and high water
was frequent and bad roads a draw-back, it often
failed to get in oftener than once a month. The
yearly receipts amounted to from ten to twelve dollars,

and the postmaster's salary for the first three months of his term was just seventy-five cents. It must be remembered that postage then was more than ten times the rate it now is.

Daniel Reid, appointed by Jackson, served from 1829 to 1836. The office was then on Fifth street, south of Main street, on the east side.

James W. Borden, appointed by Jackson, served from 1836 to 1839. For a while the office was on the north side of Main street, between Fifth and Fourth.

John C. Merrick, appointed by Van Buren, in 1839, served one year. Office in the same place.

Lynde Elliott, appointed by Van Buren, in 1840, only served one year. His office was on the northeast corner of Main and Fourth streets.

In 1841, President Harrison appointed Achilles Williams postmaster. He served two years, and his office was on Main street, opposite the Grand Hotel.

Under Tyler's administration, Daniel D. Sloan was postmaster, from 1843 to 1846, with office in same room that his predecessor had.

James Elder was appointed postmaster, by Polk, in 1846, and served three years, with his office just east of where the Richmond National Bank stood.

President Taylor commissioned Caleb R. Williams postmaster in 1849, and he served four years. The office during this time was on Main street, between Sixth and Seventh.

James Elder was again commissioned, by Pierce, in 1853, and served eight years. Part of this time the office was on the southwest corner of Sixth and Main.

For the second time, in 1861, Achilles Williams was commissioned, by Lincoln. His office was on Main street, near Sixth, and he served until 1866.

In 1866 Edwin A. Jones was appointed. He served three years, with his office on the southeast corner of Fifth and Main.

Isaac H. Julian served two years, under Grant, from 1869 to 1871, with the office in the same place.

It was in 1871 that Benjamin W. Davis was appointed postmaster, by Grant. He served until 1878, and about the first year of this time, or in 1871, he moved the office to the building where now stands the Bradley Opera House.

Almon Samson was appointed, by Hayes, in 1878, and served four years.

E. D. Palmer was appointed, by Arthur, in 1882, and served three years.

James Elder was commissioned, for the third time, in 1885, and died after serving one month.

J. F. Elder took charge of the Richmond postoffice on January 1st, 1886, and Isaac Jenkinson took charge of same on June 1st, 1890.

John G. Schwegman took charge February 1st, 1894.

DAVID HOOVER'S MEMOIR.

I think it is Laurence Sterne, who says, that — among other things which he mentions — every person should write a book ; and as I have not yet done that, I am now going to write one. As it has always been interesting to me to read biographical sketches, and historical reminiscences of by-gone days, I have concluded that some information concerning myself and family, might, perhaps, amuse some of my descendants, at least. The name is pretty extensively scattered throughout this country ; such information may therefore be of some interest to them, as it may enable them to trace back their genealogy to the original stock.

I was born on a small water-course, called Huwaree, a branch of the Yadkin river, in Randolph county, North Carolina, on the 14th day of April, 1781 ; and am now* in the seventy-third year of my age. It is customary, in personal sketches of this kind, to say something of one's parentage and education. I can only say that my parents were always considered very exemplary in all their walk through life. As to education, my opportunities were exceedingly limited ; and had it not been for my inclination and perseverance, I

---

* This appears to have been written in 1854.

should, in all probability, at this day be numbered among those who can scarcely write their names, or perhaps should only be able to make a $\times$ in placing my signature to a written instrument. In order to show the state of society in my early youth, and as an evidence of the intelligence of the circle in which I was raised, I can say of a truth that I never had an opportunity of reading a newspaper, nor did I ever see a bank-note, until after I was a man grown.

As to my ancestors, I know but little. If my information is correct, my grandfather, Andrew Hoover, left Germany when a boy ; married Margaret Fouts, in Pennsylvania, and settled on Pipe Creek, in Maryland. There my father was born ; and from thence, now about one hundred years ago, he removed to North Carolina, then a new country. He left eight sons and five daughters, all of whom had large families. Their descendants are mostly scattered through what we call the Western country. Rudolph Waymire, my grandfather on my mother's side, emigrated from Hanover, in Germany, after he had several children. He used to brag that he had been a soldier under His Britannic Majesty, and that he was at the battle of Dettingen, in 1743.* He left one son and seven daughters by his first wife, and seven sons by a second wife. Their descendants are also mostly to be found in this country.

---

* He also, it is said, served under Frederick the Great, of Prussia, in a certain company into which no man was admitted, who was not some seven feet in height.

My father had a family of ten children, four sons six daughters.* In order to better our circumstances, he came to the conclusion of moving to a new country, and sold his possessions accordingly. He was then worth rising of two thousand dollars, which, at that time, and in that country, was considered very considerably over an average, in point of wealth. On the 19th of September, 1802, we loaded our wagon and wended our way toward that portion of what was then called the Northwestern Territory, which constitutes the present State of Ohio.

Here permit me to make a passing remark. I was then in the twenty-second year of my age. I had formed an acquaintance and brought myself into notice perhaps rather more extensively than falls to the lot of most country boys. Did language afford terms adequate to describe my sensations on shaking hands with my youthful compeers, and giving them a final farewell, I would gladly do so. Suffice it to say, that those only who have been placed in like circumstances can appreciate my feelings on that occasion. And although I have lived to be an old man, and experienced the various vicissitudes attendant on a journey through life thus

---

*Andrew Hoover, Judge Hoover's father, died about the close of the year 1834, aged about eighty-three years. It was stated in his obituary notice, that he had then over one hundred descendants. Except the eldest, who died young, his children were all living until March, 1857, the oldest survivor being seventy-eight, and the youngest fifty-eight years of age. In December, 1854, an interesting reunion of these brothers and sisters was had, at the house of one of their number, in Richmond.

far, I yet look back to that time as the most interesting scene through which I have passed. My mind, at this day, is often carried back to my early associations and school-boy days, to my native hills and pine forests; and I can truly say that there is a kind of indescribable charm in the very name of my natal spot, very different from aught that pertains to any other place on the globe.

After about five weeks' journeying, we crossed the Ohio river at Cincinnati, then a mere village, composed mostly of log houses. I think it was the day after an election had been held at that place, for delegates to the convention to form a constitution; at any rate, a constitution was formed the following winter, which was amended only within the last few years. After crossing the river, we pushed on to Stillwater, about twelve miles north of Dayton, in what is now the county of Montgomery. A number of our acquaintances had located themselves there the previous spring. There we encamped in the woods the first winter. The place had proved so unhealthy that we felt discouraged and much dissatisfied, and concluded not to locate there. My father then purchased two hundred acres of land, not far from Lebanon, in Warren county, as a home, until we could make further examinations. John Smith, afterward one of the proprietors of Richmond, purchased one hundred acres in the same neighborhood, with similar views. Our object was to find a suitable place for making a settlement, and where but few or no entries had been made. But a small portion of the land lying west of the Great Miami, or east of the Little Miami, was settled at that time. We were hard to please. We Carolinians would scarcely look at the best land, where spring water was lacking. Among other considerations, we wished to get further south. We examined divers sections of the unsettled parts of Ohio, without finding any location that would please us. John Smith, Robert Hill, and myself, partially examined the country between the Falls of the Ohio and Vincennes, before there was a line run in that part of the Territory, and returned much discouraged, as we found nothing inviting in that quarter.

Thus, time passed on until the spring of 1806, when myself and four others, rather accidentally, took a section line some eight or ten miles north of Dayton, and traced it a distance of more than thirty miles, through an unbroken forest, to where I am now writing. It was the last of February, or first of March, when I first saw Whitewater. On my return to my father's, I informed him that I thought I had found the country we had been in search of. Spring water, timber, and building-rock appeared to be abundant, and the face of the country looked delightful. In about three weeks after this, my father, with several others, accompanied me to this "land of promise." As a military man would say, we made a *reconnoissance*, but returned rather discouraged, as it appeared, at that time, too far from home. Were it necessary, I might here state some of our views at that time, which would show up our extreme ignorance of what has since taken place. On returning from this trip, we saw stakes sticking among the beech trees where Eaton now stands, which was among the nearest approaches of the white man to this place. With the exception of George Holman and a few others, who settled some miles south of this, in the spring of 1805, there were but few families within twenty miles of this place. ·

It was not until the last of May, or first of June, that the first entries were made. John Smith then entered south of Main street, where Richmond now stands, and several other tracts. My father entered the land upon which I now live, I having selected it on my first trip, and several other quarter sections. About harvest, of this same year, Jeremiah Cox reached here from good old North Carolina, and purchased where the north part of Richmond now stands. If I mistake not, it had been previously entered by John Meek, the father of Jesse Meek, and had been transferred to Joseph Woodkirk, of whom Jeremiah Cox made the purchase. Said Cox also entered several other tracts. Jeremiah Cox, John Smith, and my father, were then looked upon as rather leaders in the Society of Friends. Their location here had a tendency of drawing others, and soon caused a great rush to Whitewater ; and land that I thought would hardly ever be settled, was rapidly taken up and improved. Had I a little more vanity, I might almost claim the credit (if credit it be)* of having been the pioneer of the great body of Friends now to be found in this region ; as I think it very doubtful whether three Yearly Meetings would convene in this county, had I not traced the line before mentioned.

I was now in the twenty-fifth year of my age, and thus far had been rather a way-faring disciple, not doing much for myself or any other person. Having now selected a spot for a home, I thought the time had come to be up and doing. I therefore married a girl named Catharine Yount, near the Great Miami, and on the last day of March, 1807, reached, with our little plunder, the hill where I am now living. It may not be uninteresting here to name some of the first settlers in the different neighborhoods. On the East Fork were the Flemings, Irelands, Hills, Wassons, and Maxwells. At the mouth of Elkhorn were the Hunts, Whiteheads, and Endsleys. In this neighborhood were the Smiths, Coxes, Wrights, and Hoovers, several of whom commenced operations in the woods, in the spring and summer of 1806. This may emphatically be said to have been the day of " log cabins " and log rollings ; and, although we were in an unbroken forest, without even a blazed pathway from one settlement to another, we yet enjoyed a friendship and a neighborly interchange of kind offices, which are unknown at this time.

____

* I presume Judge Hoover would not seriously question the fact.

Although we had to step on puncheon floors, and eat our corn bread and venison, or turkey, off of broad pieces of split timber, and drive forks in one corner of our cabins, with cross timbers driven into the walls, for bedsteads, there was no grumbling or complaining of low markets and hard times. The questions of Tariff and National Bank were truly "obsolete ideas"* in those days. It was the first week in April before some of us commenced operations in the woods; but we mostly raised corn enough to do us. There was, however, no mill to grind it, and for some weeks we grated† all the meal we made use of. About Christmas, Charles Hunt started a mill, on a cheap scale, near the mouth of Elkhorn, which did our grinding until J. Cox established one near to where Richmond stands, and which now belongs to the Starr Piano Company.

The Indian boundary was at this time about three miles west of us. The Indians lived on White river, and were frequently among us. They at one time packed off 400 bushels of shelled corn, which they purchased of John Smith. In 1810 a purchase was made,

---

* Or rather, unoriginated ideas.

† Many persons at the present day may perhaps not comprehend the process referred to in the text. A grater was a sheet of tin, thickly perforated, bent in a semi-circular form, and nailed to a piece of board, the rough side outward. On this the ears of corn, before becoming thoroughly hardened, were grated. The meal thus produced escaped down the board into the receptacle provided for it.

called the " Twelve-mile Purchase," * and a goodly number settled on it before it was surveyed ; but the war of 1812 coming on, the settlers mostly left their locations, and moved to places of more security. Those who remained built forts and " block-houses." The settlers in this neighborhood mostly stood their ground, but suffered considerably with fever. George Shugart then lived where Newport now stands, some miles from any other inhabitant. In the language of the Friends, he " did not feel clear " in leaving his home, and he manfully stood his ground, unmolested,† except by those whom we then styled the " Rangers," from whom he received some abuse for his boldness. The Indians took three scalps out of this county, and stole a number of horses. Candor, however, compels me to say, that, as is usually the case, we Christians were the aggressors. After peace was made, in 1814, the twelve-mile purchase settled very rapidly.

It will not be amiss, at this stage of our narrative, to state that when we first settled here, the now State of Indiana was called Indiana Territory, and we belonged to Dearborn county, which embraced all the territory purchased from the Indians at the treaty of

---

* Among the first settlers of the twelve-mile purchase, rather in the vicinity of Centerville, were Daniel Noland, Henry Bryan, Isaac Julian, William Harvey, Nathan Overman, and George Grimes. Other pioneers, whose names I can not now recall, were thinly scattered over other portions of the " purchase."

† The same course was pursued, safely, by Louis Hosier, another pioneer of the " new purchase."

Greenville, extending from the mouth of Kentucky river to Fort Recovery. The counties of Wayne and Franklin were afterward formed out of the northern part of this territory.* Although Governor Harrison had the appointing power, he gave the people the privilege of choosing their own officers. An election was accordingly held, when it was found that Peter Fleming, Jeremiah Meek and Aaron Martin were elected Judges; George Hunt, Clerk; and John Turner, Sheriff. County courts were then held by three associate judges, and county business done before them. One of the first courts† held in this county, under the Territorial government, convened under the shade of a tree, on the premises then belonging to Richard Rue, Esq., Judge Park presiding, and James Noble, Prosecutor. In order to show the legal knowledge we backwoodsmen were then in possession of, I will relate the following case: A boy was indicted for stealing a knife, a traverse jury was impanelled, and took their seats upon a log. The indictment was read, and, as usual, set out that the offender, with *force and arms*, did feloniously steal, take, and carry away, etc. After hearing the case, the jury retired to another log to make up their verdict. Jeremiah Cox,‡ one of the

---

* Wayne county was organized in November, 1810.

† The first court held in Wayne county, as appears from the records, met at the house of Richard Rue, February, 1811.

‡ Many anecdotes are in circulation of the simplicity of mind and character of friend Cox; but he has left the highest character: that of having been a genuine. practical Christian.

jurors, and afterward a member of the convention to frame a constitution, and of the legislature, concluded they must find the defendant guilty, but he thought the indictment "was rather *too bad* for so small an offense." I suppose he thought the words "with force and arms" uncalled for, and thought rightly enough, too.

Some further illustration of our legal knowledge, and the spirit of our legislation at this time, may be interesting. Although the Friends constituted a large portion of the inhabitants in this quarter, there were, in other parts of the county, men in whose craniums the military spirit was pretty strongly developed, before the war of 1812 was declared. When that came on, this spirit manifested itself in all its vigor. The Friends were much harassed on account of their refusal to do military duty. Some were drafted and had their property sacrificed, and at the next call were again drafted and fined. Four young men were thrown into the county jail, during the most inclement cold weather ; fire was denied them until they should comply ; and had it not been for the humane feelings of David F. Sackett,* who handed them hot bricks through the grates, they must have suffered severely. Suits were subsequently brought against the officers, for false imprisonment. The trials were had at Brookville, in Franklin county. They all recovered damages,

* For several years Recorder of Wayne county.

but I have every reason to believe that the whole of the damages and costs was paid out of moneys extorted from others of the Friends. To cap the climax of absurdity and outrage, the gentlemen officers arrested an old man named Jacob Elliott, and tried him by a court-martial, for treason, found him guilty, and sentenced him to be shot ! but gave him a chance to run away in the dark, they firing off their guns at the same time. It would fill a considerable volume to give a detailed history of the *noble patriots* of those days, and of their wisdom and valorous exploits ; but this must suffice.

Connected with this subject, permit me a word respecting my own course. I think it is well known that, from first to last, I stood by the Friends like a brother (as I would again do under similar circumstances), and used my influence in their favor ; yet from some cause, best known to themselves, I have apparently lost the confidence and friendship of a good number of them. The most serious charge which has yet reached me is that I have not got "the true faith," and not that I have done anything wrong. Of this I do not complain, but must be permitted to say that their course towards me is rather gratuitous. I feel confident that they cannot, in truth, say that they have at any time received aught but disinterested friendship from me ; and if some of them can reconcile their course toward me with a sense of duty, and of doing by me as I have, at all times, done by them, I shall therewith be content.

In 1816 we elected delegates to the convention which formed our late Constitution and named the State Indiana. On the third day of February following, I was elected Clerk of the Wayne Circuit Court, and, by favor of the voters of the county, held the office nearly fourteen years. I was prevented from serving out my full constitutional term of office, by a deceptive ruling of the court, which I have no fears will ever be hunted up as a precedent in a similar or any other case.

I was almost the first man who set foot in this part of Wayne county, and have been an actor in it for more than forty years. It may not be out of place here for me to say that I feel conscious that I often erred through ignorance, and perhaps through willfulness. Yet (and with gratitude be it spoken), it has fallen to the lot of few men to retain so long the standing which I think I still have among all classes of my fellow-citizens. I believe it is a privilege conceded to old men to boast of what they have been and what they have done. I shall therefore take the liberty of saying that I have now seven commissions by me, for offices which I have held, besides having had a seat in the Senate of this State for six years.

I will add, that in the employ and under the direction of John Smith and Jeremiah Cox, I laid off the city of Richmond, did all their clerking, wrote their deeds, etc. If I recollect rightly, it was first named Smithville, after one of the proprietors ; but that name did not give general satisfaction. Thomas Robbards, James Pegg and myself were then chosen to select a name for the place. Robbards proposed "Waterford;" Pegg, "Plainfield," and I made choice of "Richmond," which latter name received the preference of the lot-holders.

I have some fears that the preceding remarks may be looked upon as betraying the vanity of an old man ; but I wish it distinctly understood that I ascribe the little favors which I have received more to surrounding circumstances, and the partiality of my friends, than to any qualifications or merits in myself.

There are several other subjects connected with the early history of Wayne county on which I could dwell at some length. I could refer to the first dominant party, their arbitrary proceeding in fixing the county-seat at Salisbury, the seven years' war and contention which followed, ending with the final location of the shire-town at Centerville.* But as the rival parties in that contest have mostly left the stage, and the subject is almost forgotten, I think it unnecessary to disturb it.

---

*The county-seat was finally established at Centerville, in April, 1820.

A lengthy chapter might be written on the improvements which have been made within the last fifty years in Wayne county (to say nothing of the rest of the world), in the arts and sciences generally, but as I do not feel myself competent to the task, I shall not attempt it.

And now, in bringing this crude and undigested account of my experience to a close, short as it is, it gives rise to many serious reflections. When I look back upon the number of those who set out in life with me, full of hope, and who have fallen by the way, and gone to that bourne from whence there is no returning, with not even a rude stone to mark the spot where their mortal remains are deposited, language fails me, and indeed there is no language adequate to the expression of my feelings. I shall therefore drop the subject, leaving the reader to fill up the blank in his own way.

In conclusion, let me say a word about my politics and religion. In politics, I profess to belong to the Jeffersonian school. I view Thomas Jefferson as decidedly the greatest statesman that America has yet produced. He was the chief apostle of both political and religious liberty. My motto is taken from his first inaugural: "Equal and exact justice to all men"— and I will add: without calling in question their political or religious faith, country, or color.

And here I wish it distinctly understood and remembered, that I stood almost alone in this section of the State, in opposition to our ruinous system of internal improvements, concocted and brought about at the sessions of the Legislature in the years 1835 and 1836, which resulted in the creation of a State debt which the present generation will not see paid, and which has verified that text in the old Book to the very letter, which says that the iniquities of the fathers are visited upon their children to the third and fourth generations.

As to religion :

> Happy is he — the only happy man —
> Who, from *choice*, does all the good he can.

"The world is my country, and my religion is to do right." I am a firm believer in the Christian religion, though not as lived up to by most of its professors of the present day. In the language of Jefferson, I look upon the "Christian philosophy as the most sublime and benevolent, but most perverted system that ever shone on man." I have no use for the priesthood, nor can I abide the shackles of sectarian dogmas. I see no necessity for confessions of faith, creeds, forms and ceremonies. In the most comprehensive sense of the word, I am opposed to all wars and to slavery, and trust the time is not far distant when they will be numbered among the things that

were, and viewed as we now look back upon some of
the doings of what we are pleased to style the dark
ages. In the language of Burns:

> "Then let us pray that come it may —
>   As come it will, for a' that —
> That sense and worth, o'er a' the earth,
>   May bear the gree, and a' that.
> For a' that, and a' that,
>   It's coming yet, for a' that,
> That man to man, the world o'er,
>   Shall brothers be, for a' that."

A RELIC OF WAR TIMES.

CARRIER'S ADDRESS OF 1864. — ITS REFERENCES
EXPLAINED.

To the Editor of the *Palladium:*

The sheet of poetry which comes to you with this
letter is somewhat of a relic, serving as a reminder of
war times, and as an illustration of one phase of country
"newspaperism," a quarter of a century ago.

I believe it was the last Carrier's New Year's
Address issued in Richmond. It belonged to the customs of the newspaper business before the advent of
the modern and metropolitan science of "journalism."

The poem was written by a lady residing in this
city (then and now), but before she had attained even

State reputation as a writer of verse. Within the years since the date of that Address, she has produced many beautiful things, and her name is oftenest spoken first whenever the attempt is made to give a list of Indiana poetesses.

Her best poems — for we only do her justice when we say that the lines under consideration are not her best — come when the heart is moved. This poem was written "to order," to supply a demand. Yet, even in this, the heart shows itself, for it reflects the prevailing feelings of the hour — patriotism, self-denial, patience, anxiety, sorrow. Everything written in those days must have a patriotic avowal. These lines meet that expectation. It was far into the third year of the war, and the continuation and the result were still problematic.

The situation was contemplated with all seriousness, and seriousness is the plainest characteristic of the poem. Its writer had no place for mirth, nor any desire to be merely amusing. The over-ruling thought, in this particular, is aptly expressed in the opening lines of an address written by Forceythe Willson, and published one year before, in the Louisville *Journal:*

> The carrier can not sing, to-day, the ballads
> With which he used to go,
> Rhyming the grand rounds of the Happy New Years
> That are now beneath the snow.

For the same awful and portentous shadow
That overcast the earth,
And smote the land, last year, with desolation,
Still darkens every hearth.

The address was carried and sold by your correspondent, who took the contract to assist the regular carrier in that enterprise. At sundown, the night previous, a heavy snow storm blew up, and next morning there was a foot of snow on the ground, and the thermometer registered twenty degrees below zero at sunrise.

"The improvements, vast, on every side," were very insignificant, compared with improvements since made. The west corners of Eighth and Main streets were occupied by one-story shanties. Other localities, with similar structures, and the whole town in proportion. The town was much smaller than now, as may be supposed, for the Roberts farm and the eastern part of the Starr farm had not then been platted into lots. The regular route of the carrier, for the delivery of the weekly (there was no daily in town then), extended to Eleventh and North D, in that direction; to the park, on South Tenth; to South E, on Fifth street (then called Pearl); and the "Spring Foundry" (Gaar, Scott & Co.'s), on the northwest. Subscribers residing outside these limits must call at the printing office, or receive their copies through the mail. The office of the *Palladium* was, that winter, at No. 404 Main street, near Fourth. In the spring of 1864 it was removed to "Warner Hall," over the Mayor's office. Crossings of Main with Fifth and Sixth streets (old Pearl and Marion) were regarded as the "centers" of town.

The reference to the "Farmers of Wayne," in the eleventh stanza, and again in the fifteenth, deserves an explanation. Read the tenth stanza:

> "But while we tell of brave men on the field,
> We'll not forget the kind and true at home —
> Whose generous gifts, to all the needy poor,
> You'll not find equaled, wheresoe'er you roam."

The winter that preceded the one in which this Address was written — the winter of 1862–63 — was a severe one upon many families whose supporters and providers were away, fighting for the Union. Many families of soldiers, residing in the country and in smaller towns, had moved into Richmond for the sake of company and safety, and to be within the reach of relief, if it should be needed. Hundreds of the wives, children, and other dependents of the soldiers, made Richmond their home during the period of their husbands' and fathers' enlistments. The organized aid societies could not meet all the demands. Nor was the public fund, disbursed by the township trustee, equal to the deficiency. When the winters threatened to be long and severe, our town was likely to be the scene of extended and serious suffering. The winter of 1862–63 was of that character. Much anxiety was felt and expressed. It must not be thought that the relief extended to soldiers' families was, in any sense, akin to the common charity extended to the ordinary indigent. It was in no sense a pauper relief. The obligation to see that the families of the soldiers were not allowed to suffer, was as much a part of the compensation of the volunteers as the bounty paid them for enlisting. It was clearly understood, by those who volunteered, that their wives, children and dependants were to be cared for, in case of necessity, by those who remained at home. Hence, any aid rendered could be accepted by the families of soldiers without any feelings of humiliation. This manner of part compensation was as clearly understood by the volunteers, as if named in the specifications of their enlistment, and it was as faithfully performed, by those who remained at home, as if bound upon them by contract or statute. Special provision was necessary, in the second winter of the war.

Suddenly and unexpectedly, one morning in January, 1863, twenty-five wagons, loaded with wood, and one with flour, meal, potatoes, etc., appeared on the streets of Richmond. They were from the farmers in the neighborhood of Middleboro, six miles northeast of the city, and were intended as "aid and comfort" for soldiers' families. A band of musicians volunteered their services, and, hoisting the national flag, the donation was paraded through the streets, and then delivered where needed.

On Saturday, February 14, a delegation came from Boston township, bringing more than sixty cords of wood, three thousand pounds of flour and meal, besides other provisions. A spirit of emulation or rivalry, in this good work, was soon developed, and the various neighborhoods, in the vicinity of Richmond, competed with each other in bringing contributions of this character. On the 28th of February the farmers residing along and near the National road (or Eaton pike), east from town, brought, in a long procession, ninety-two cords of wood, over two thousand pounds of flour, forty bushels of corn-meal, six bushels of potatoes, etc. That procession filled Main street for eight blocks.

The following Monday the rival procession of farmers residing along and near the National road west from town, came in. It has never been decided which of these contributions was the larger. Both parties claimed the palm.

The Middleboro farmers, having started these generous outpourings, concluded to put a finishing touch to the work for this season, so on the 28th of March they came into town with a train of wagons nearly a mile long. Residents of Whitewater and Franklin townships joined their neighbors of Middleboro. The farmers along the Liberty turnpike also brought in a contribution. A new feature attended this demonstration. Fresh beef and poultry were brought in, sold on the streets to citizens, and the proceeds given to the aid fund. In this way $192 were realized. One hundred and twenty-eight cords of wood, over two thousand pounds of flour, and seventy-five bushels of meal, besides other provisions, were contributed, the whole donation amounting, in money value, to nearly $1,300. The influence of these acts extended to other towns and cities. Among the towns in this county, Centerville received a large donation on the 19th of March, 1863.

This commendable practice was revived the following autumn, and continued in the last winter of the war. On the 23rd of December, 1864, four competing delegations entered town from the four sides. The total of these contributions was two hundred and forty-two cords of wood.

Such acts were, indeed, worthy to be the theme of the poet. - M.

CARRIER'S ADDRESS.

TO THE PATRONS OF THE RICHMOND PALLADIUM,
JANUARY 1, 1864.

Dear friends of yore, I come again to greet you,
  Though months have passed since last I sang my song,
And smiling faces that were wont to meet me
  Are missing, and no more to earth belong.

Still, to the dear old friends whom I remember—
  Whose kindly acts have cheered me on my way—
I give my hand, and may a happy New Year
  Be yours, without one sorrow-clouded day!

Since last I sang to you, in jingling numbers,
  A year has rolled its changes o'er the land,
And yet peace hath not spread her snowy pinions,
  Nor yet return our noble, patriot band.

And many, many noble forms are sleeping
  Low, 'neath the sod upon the battle plain,
And many weary eyes to-day are weeping,
  And dim with watching, waiting, all in vain;

And over all our land, where'er we wander,
  Woe's sable garb we meet on every side —
The garb of highest honor to the wearer,
  Whose best-loved, for his country, fought and died.

Though many noble braves have fallen in glory,
  Where the red tide of carnage thickest run,
Many are left to tell the thrilling story
  Of how they fought, from dawn till setting sun.

Bright be their names on glory's scroll engraven,
  And every scar a badge of honor, fair;
No diamond-studded crown, worth half a kingdom,
  So nobly, proudly could our heroes wear!

But through our long-linked months of Polar darkness
  Bright streaks of dawn begin to make their way,
And many joyful messengers of peace
  Proclaim the coming of a brighter day —

When the bright, starry flag that floats above us
  Shall claim its own, and wave o'er all the land,
And we may welcome home our war-worn heroes,
  And join again the broken household band.

But while we tell of brave men on the field,
  We'll not forget the kind and true at home —
Whose generous gifts, to all the needy poor,
  You'll not find equaled, wheresoe'er you roam.

Then a song for the farmers of Wayne,
  For the old and for the young!
A shout as loud, and a song as high.
  As ever in praise was sung!

For never on Victory's battle-field
  Were braver hosts arrayed
Than they, whose offerings, bountiful,
  On their country's altar have laid.

Sound it over the saddened land,
  That other true hearts may know
The way to strengthen the soldier's arm
  To strike the trait'rous foe;

The way to lift from the weary heart
  A weight of burdening care,
And send, with blessings, their name on high,
  In many a thankful prayer.

Long may they live, in plenty and peace —
  The noble farmers of Wayne —
And finally meet their just reward,
  Where peace shall eternally reign!

Our city's in most prosperous condition —
  Improvements, vast, we meet on every side;
In fact, there's not a doubt about the matter —
  'Tis Indiana's highest boast and pride.

Our ladies are most beautiful and loyal —
 Forever working in the cause of right;
Our men are foremost in the field of battle,
 Facing the foe in every deadly fight.

But, lest I tire you with too long a story —
 Which has been sad, I fear, from first to last —
I 'll point you to the brightly coming future,
 Forgetting not the lessons of the past;

And hoping ere next New Year's morn I greet you,
 That peace shall long have dwelt throughout the land;
Hoping and trusting all things, fearing never,
 Farewell, my friends — here is my parting hand.

But, stop! I 'll merely mention, ere I go,
 What, between us, I hope will raise no barrier:
That I accept all fractional paper currency,
 And that — I hope you won't forget

THE CARRIER.

SOME COUNTY HISTORY.

From the Hagerstown *Exponent,* November 19, 1891.

Joseph Williams, aged eighty-five years, and formerly of Economy, died at Richmond, Wednesday last, and was buried at Economy on Friday, funeral services by the Rev. W. C. Bowen, from whom we learn that Mr. Williams was one of the early pioneers of this section, having settled in the woods, in the Jordan settlement, north of here, over sixty years ago. This section received its first settlers in 1822, when Joseph Bowen, Benjamin Parson ; Rev. Samuel Taylor, a Baptist preacher, who died with the cholera in 1833 ; David Miller, a Dunkard preacher ; John Hardman ; Aaron Miller, who settled on the old Petty farm ; John McLucas and Hugh Allen, all came about the same time and bought land at $1.25 per acre, and settled in the woods. At that time there was not a house in all this section ; not even where Hagerstown stands. There were a few Indians here yet, and deer, bears and other wild game was quite numerous. Soon after the first settlers were established in homes, others came in, and it was not long till four church organizations were made. The first organization was composed of a Baptist congregation, started in a log house where the

Baptist church, called Salem, now stands. The second church organized was a New-Light congregation, and held meetings in a log school house that stood two miles south of this place. Among those who were members of that congregation, Mrs. Miller, mother of Sol. Miller, is the only one that is now living. Their first preacher was Samuel Boyd, who was a Revolutionary soldier. The third church to organize was the Methodist; they organized in Joseph Bowen's house, and among the first members were Joseph Manifold, Benjamin Parson and wife, Sammy Pollard and John Doan. The fourth were the Dunkers, generally known now as the "Dunkards;" they organized in John Ritter's house, which is still standing, being the old log house that stands a short distance east of E. B. Reynolds' present home. Among their first members were Ritter, John Hardman and David Hardman; David and Aaron Miller were their first preachers. These were the four churches that occupied the entire religious field from 1822 to 1830. The Methodists and Dunkers all wore plain clothing, and the Methodists would not license a preacher who refused to wear plain Quaker clothing. Class meetings were held with closed doors, and the Dunkers and New-Lights washed feet at church services, regularly, every three months. The Methodist ministers always preached from one hour to an hour and a half, and the Baptist sermons often lasted two hours and a half, and members complained when the sermons were short. The Methodists held a revival every.preaching day. The first "squire" elected was named Bedford, whose first case was a quarrel between two neighbors, over the shooting of a dog ; each man had a lawyer ; Bedford dismissed the case because he could find no dog cases in his law book, and divided the costs of the case between plaintiff and defendant. Old Saulsbury, six miles south of Richmond, was the first county-seat of this county. In those early days there were no saloons, but whisky was used freely in almost all houses, and not even a preacher could get his harvest cut unless he supplied a liberal supply of rum. There were no divisions or classes of society, as now — all mingled, socially, on a common ground. "Big dinners" were common, and every one in the community was invited. At the weddings the preacher kissed the bride, and the old folks all went home soon after supper, while the young people always indulged in sports of some kind, all night. When the organiza-tion of a Sunday-school was first proposed, the idea was strongly opposed by many church members, and on account of such oppositions, there were no such schools till in 1836. In 1840 the Washingtonian tem-perance movement was started, and in 1854 the legis-lature passed the Maine temperance or prohibition law, but it was pronounced unconstitutional in less than a year. The first sermon ever preached in Hagerstown was by John Kiger, a Methodist, who is still living, and is ninety years of age. The second sermon was by John Sullivan, a Methodist minister; he organized a church, among the first members of which were Greensbury Savoy and wife, Bazel Taylor and wife, Worley Williamson and wife, Ezra Doughty and Elijah Castator.

HISTORICAL.

RECOLLECTIONS

AWAKENED IN THE MIND OF A FORMER RESIDENT BY
THE BURNING OF THE CENTERVILLE SCHOOL-
HOUSE.—A BIT OF HISTORY.

SAN MARCOS, TEXAS, NOV. 9, 1891.

Editor the *Telegram:*

I noticed the account in your columns of the burning of the public school building at Centerville. It
awakened many recollections in my mind, and, though
rather too late to give them in detail, as I would like
to, I am unwilling to let the occasion pass without
adding somewhat to the facts given by you, for, as you
say, the building possessed great historic interest.

The name and style of the original building was
"Wayne County Seminary." My first recollection
dates back to 1834, when, a small boy, I accompanied
my oldest brother, John, who was one of the actors, to
witness a performance of the "Centerville Thespian
Society," in the upper story.

Among the early teachers of the Seminary, prior to Mr. Hoshour, my memory recalls the name of Royal T. Wheeler, afterwards Chief Justice of the Republic of Texas; George Fairchild, James B. Haile, Nathan Smith, and G. Smith, a Methodist preacher, brought up a few miles above Richmond.

Mr. Hoshour took charge in 1836, and continued four years. It was to his administration that most of the pupils, of more or less note, whom you enumerate, belonged. But you are mistaken as to one — George W. Julian — he was not a pupil of the Seminary, but, after the usual country school probation, graduated at Friends' school, hard by West Grove meeting-house. I notice in Mr. Hoshour's autobiography an addition to your list, in the person of Mr. Rariden's protégé — the son of a Miami chief — mention of whose death I noticed not long since. I remember him well. I am not sure as to the succession after Mr. Hoshour, but Rawson Vaile occupied that position during several years of the forties; he was, I think, the last teacher in the Seminary.

Of the early teachers, there were, also, editors, viz: Mr. Haile, of the *People's Advocate;* Mr. Hoshour, of the *Wayne County Chronicle*, and Mr. Vaile, of the *Free Territory Sentinel* and the *Indiana Free Democrat.*

I think you are mistaken as to the date of transfer to the Methodists; at any rate, I find the name changed to "Whitewater College and Whitewater Academy," with Thomas H. Lynch in charge, in 1849. In 1850 Cyrus Nutt and James A. Beswick were called to the position, and the institution was known as "Whitewater Female College and Academy." The two following years were the palmy ones of its history. The first commencement, in the summer of 1851, passed off with great eclat. The society of young ladies of the institution, known as the "Sigournean Society," was really quite brilliant in its personale. The first graduates were Misses Gertrude Newman and Kate Woods. The next session turned out about a dozen.

I shall not undertake to trace regularly the further course of Whitewater College. In 1858 A. C. Shortridge was the principal, his chief assistant being Miss Emily Huntington, a Connecticut lady — since, as Emily Huntington Miller, an authoress of note. She resides at Evanston, Illinois. During the early years of the war, William H. Barnes presided. He was a scholarly gentleman, author of a "History of the Thirty-ninth Congress" and other works of value. Having removed to Richmond at the beginning of 1864, my recollections along this line close here.

Isaac H. Julian.

A TRIP TO CALIFORNIA.

HOW IT WAS MADE FIFTY YEARS AGO.

SAMUEL CALDWELL MEREDITH, FORMERLY OF WAYNE COUNTY, RELATES
THE INCIDENTS OF A MEMORABLE JOURNEY — GOLDEN
STATE PRICES.

In the winter of 1849 the late Andrew F. Vaughan, of this city, Daniel Storms, of Hagerstown, and Samuel Caldwell Meredith, of Centerville, agreed to go to California together, aid each other on the way, and care for each other, if any got sick. And now the last mentioned of the trio, who is the father of William H. Meredith, superintendent of the government bureau of printing and engraving, and who had himself been in the newspaper business at Centerville, since 1835, has written up the trip, at considerable length, for the Indianapolis *News*, from which the *Telegram* takes the following quoted extracts :

In 1835 Mr. Meredith started the *People's Advocate* in Centerville. It was Democratic in politics, did not pay, and he changed it to the Wayne County *Chronicle*, which was a Whig paper. Then Mr. Meredith removed to Illinois, and it was succeeded by the *National Patriot*, which failed. Next, in 1841, Mr. Meredith started the Wayne County *Record*, which, old printers say, has never been surpassed, for typographical appearance, in this county. During his absence in California, it, as the Whig organ, was conducted by D. B. Wood and John B. Stitt. Subsequently Mr. Wood went to California, where he was killed, and Mr. Meredith returned to resume the publication of it, but it lost money, and in 1852 he sold it to D. P. Halloway, of the Richmond *Palladium*, and removed to Indianapolis, which has since been his home.

In the beginning of his narration, Mr. Meredith says : "Storms went to see friends in Ohio, and was to meet Vaughan and myself at the Gault House, in Cincinnati. I left Centerville early, on the morning of October 24, in a spring-wagon, for Richmond, and from there went to Cincinnati in an omnibus. On October 26 we procured passage on a steamboat to New Orleans for $20, and left Cincinnati on the 27th, at 3 o'clock, arriving in New Orleans November 5. On November 14 we got a passage on the steamship Alabama, for Chagras, at $45, and arrived there on November 23. We paid $10 each for a canoe to carry us to Gorgonna. * * Here we hired mules or horses to carry our baggage to Panama. We left Gorgonna on November 29, at 8 o'clock. Two trunks and several small packages constituted a load for one horse. We went on foot, and didn't let the baggage get out of our sight. * *

"Arriving at Panama, I met Colonel Elliott, who informed me that Dr. Waymann, Hiatt Jemison and others, who had left Wayne county four weeks before I did, were there. I found that living was high, the health bad, and that there was no chance of getting passage in a steamer for several months, so that we had better go in a sail vessel. The fine ship, Sea Queen, of Dundee, Scotland, was to leave on the next Tuesday. We were advised to purchase second-hand tickets from speculators, and go with all our Indiana friends.

"We procured, from speculators, tickets on the Sea Queen, at $250 each, and on the 4th of December went on board. * * On the 9th of January, 1850, the ship ran into the entrance of the harbor at San Francisco, at 4 o'clock in the evening, and, after the anchor was cast, the passengers manifested their joy by giving three cheers, and three times three. I found a boarding house, the price being $18 a week, the best I could find. I was very thankful that I had been permitted to get on shore, after the many dangers through which I had passed, from home to the Golden Gate.

"In a letter to my family, dated San Francisco, January 14, 1850, there are these expressions: 'By the blessing of Divine Providence I have been permitted to put my feet upon the shores of California. Labor here, of all kinds, is high. One dollar an hour for work on some of the streets, in the mud ; for wheeling sand down hill, in a dry place, 50 cents an hour. Sweet potatoes sell here for 25 cents a pound ; Irish potatoes, 20 cents ; onions, $1.25 ; vinegar, 50 cents a quart ; brandy, $1.25 a quart. I saw a horse, not half as good as James Pritchett's, sell for $150 ; another horse, just arrived from New South Wales, for $1,300, in Centerville would be $60 to $75 ; another horse, from the same place, sells for $700. I have seen better looking sell for $30 or $40. Rent for a house, about like Dinwiddie's shop, but not so good, $4,000 a month. A room, like our smoke-house, $50 a week. Flour, per hundred, $12 ; per barrel, $20 ; fresh pork, 50 cents to 75 cents a pound ; beef, 25 cents to 50 cents a pound ; butter, from $1 to $1.50 per pound ; sugar, 30 cents ; coffee, 12½ cents ; cheese, 30 cents to 40 cents ; tallow candles, 60 cents ; bread, 30 cents for a small loaf ; pies, $1, and not good at that ; wood, $40 a cord, $1 for an armful ; small premium cook stove, $100 ; molasses, $2.50 per gallon. I saw a deer, with the hide on, sell for $40 ; wild geese, $2 ; ducks, $1. Eggs have fallen very much ; they are now worth 25 cents each ; a month ago they were worth $1 each., Tin cups, 25 cents each ; coarse boots, from $12 to $20 a pair, such as I can buy at home for $1.50 or $3 a pair ; silk handkerchiefs, 75 cents to $1, a fine article, and other things in the same proportion. The papers here cost 12, 25 and 50 cents each.'

" I left Centerville October 24, and arrived in San Francisco on January 11, being eighty days, at a cost of $412.

" Now, in 1891, persons can go in a palace car, have all the luxuries of a fine hotel and sleeping cars, for $100."

And now, in 1896, a round-trip ticket may be had for a little over $100, with the privilege of a six months' stay. Verily, times have changed.

WESTERN SKETCHES.

AN OLD-TIME ELOPEMENT.

To the Indianapolis *Journal:*

About the year 1817 there came from Kentucky to Wayne county, Indiana, a young man by the name of John Bailey. He was industrious, active and thrifty, and in those primitive times acquaintances were readily made throughout the entire settlement. It was not long before John was a favorite at corn-huskings, apple-cuttings, quiltings, and wool-pickings, and, what would naturally follow, he was soon desperately in love, the object of his devotion being the daughter of one of his neighbors, Mr. Lamb, whose residence was on Greensfork, between where the towns of Washington and Williamsburg, Wayne county, are now located. But "the course of true love never did run smoothly," and in this case, although John was favored with Patsy's love and esteemed by the best men in the community, he met with a stern and positive refusal on the part of the parents.

He was called away to his old home in Kentucky, a journey which, in those days, required considerable time. As "star routes," like railroads, were then unknown in this State, he could have no word from Patsy during his absence.

> " With many a vow and locked embrace,
>   Their parting was fu' tender."

John was detained at his old home in Kentucky much beyond the time appointed for his return, and when he arrived again at the home in the forests of Wayne county, he learned that Patsy had promised to become the wife of another, and that the day appointed for the marriage was a week from that time, the license having been already procured. If "love laughs at locks and keys," what would it do in a country where locks and keys were all unknown?

John was determined to see, once more, the object of his affection, regardless of father's frown or mother's anger. Accordingly, on Sunday evening, he went to the home of her whom he feared had proved forever faithless. There he met the happy man who had, as he supposed, supplanted him in the affections of the young Hoosier lass. There was but one room in the house, and John had no opportunity to speak with Patsy. Unwilling to abandon so good a cause, however, without one more desperate effort to effect his purpose, he remained over night.

While the family slept, he lay with one eye open. In the stillness of the night Patsy slipped quietly to his bed-side, and whispered to him the story of her thraldom. She was to be an unwilling bride, in four days from that time. John's courage did not fail him, but he said, " Meet me at Billy W.'s to-morrow.'' She promised ; but alas ! when the girl came, her father accompanied her and refused to allow her to see John. The situation was now becoming desperate ; but John proved equal to the emergency, and arranged with a mutual friend to notify Patsy that he would be at a place agreed upon, near her father's house, on Tuesday before the day arranged for her marriage to his rival. He had brought with him from Kentucky a splendid horse, full of spirit, and of great power of endurance.

At the appointed time John appeared at the place designated, mounted upon his good horse, " Ball." Patsy saw him, and picked up a bucket and started to the spring, as all supposed, for a bucket of water. She had not gone half way to the spring, however, until, in her haste and excitement, she dropped the bucket and started to run. It was mid-winter, and a heavy snow covered the ground. She lost her bonnet before she reached the fence, where Ball stood, ready to receive his precious load. But, all unconscious of her loss, with her hair streaming in the winter wind like a flag at half-mast, she continued the flight.

Her mother discovered the fugitive at this time, and started in hot pursuit. John always declared that Patsy never, before nor since, mounted Ball so nimbly as on that occasion, and that Ball never walked up to the fence so readily. The nearest settlement to which they could fly was seven miles distant, and through an almost unbroken wilderness.

When Patsy was fairly mounted behind John, the race began in earnest, Ball taking in the situation at a glance. He laid back his finely formed ears and turned his splendid eyes upon them, as much as to say, '' Hold on to me, and I will carry you safely through the perils of the journey.'' And they did hold on to him, and most nobly did he do his duty. Over hills and through streams he sped like an arrow, '' his nostrils drinking in the breath of their own swiftness.'' With every jump he appeared to laugh defiance at his pursuers, who soon abandoned the chase. Before nightfall they stopped and borrowed such articles of clothing as were necessary for the journey. They then pursued their way through the forest for several miles, stopping over night with the father of the late Jehu T. Elliott, Judge of the Supreme Court of Indiana, and at an early hour the next morning they again mounted old Ball and resumed their way to Salisbury, then the county-seat of Wayne county, but now a well cultivated corn-field, there not being one stone left upon another where once flourished that town. By 9 o'clock the next morning they had procured the necessary license, and were married by a local preacher then living in the place. In the course of a week they returned to the vicinity of the home of the young wife's parents, where they were hailed with greater delight than a hero of a hundred battles would now be greeted.

John and Patsy lived in that community for more than sixty years, bringing up a large family of honest and intelligent sons and daughters, all of whom are married. Their children, grandchildren and great-grandchildren are scattered over many counties of Indiana, and are known as among the good people of the State.   E. B. H.

CAMBRIDGE CITY, IND., MAY 1, 1884.

EARLY RAILROAD HISTORY AT RICHMOND, INDIANA.

[A brief statement of some facts relating to the early history of the Indiana Central Railroad at Richmond, Indiana; written, at the request of an official of the Pennsylvania Railroad Company, to be placed in an exhibit at the World's Fair, Chicago, Illinois. Written October, 1892.]

Mr. J. E. Watkins, Special Agent, Altoona, Pa.:

DEAR SIR — In compliance with your request of a recent date, to furnish such information and relics pertaining to the early history of the "Central road"— now a part of the Pennsylvania system — as I may be in possession of, I have to say that, after a lapse of nearly forty years, there is comparatively little left, of either information or relics, that is obtainable here. Much of the former has been blotted out by time, and few of the latter have been preserved. Most of the older people who took an active part in the affairs of the time have departed to that bourne from which no traveler returns, and of the few remaining ones whom I have seen I can obtain little definite or satisfactory information of value; and as I was then but little more than a boy, struggling to obtain a livelihood on a meagre salary, and all my time occupied in the service of others, I had neither the opportunity nor inclination to become informed about the leading enterprises of the day.

Some time previous to the year 1850, the people of this region of country began to be interested in the construction of railroads, as you will see by the list of names attached to the enclosed ticket of invitation, which tells its own story. The names are leading ones, and on that account, alone, may be of interest as mementos of the past.

The "Central road" was completed to Richmond some time during the summer or autumn of 1853, when James M. Brown, of the firm of Brown & Morrow, pork-packers, temporarily took charge, as agent, here, transacting the business in his own office, which was located in a frame building, I think, on the west side

of Fort Wayne Avenue, about one hundred yards
southwest of the present passenger depot. When I
succeeded Mr. Brown, I continued to occupy his office
for several weeks, until the freight and passenger
stations were ready for use, when I purchased, of
William T. Dennis, Esq.,—our present State Fish
Commissioner, who was then in the hardware trade in
this city—an iron safe, a copying-press, letter-book,
and sundry other matters pertaining to the office. I
also procured a desk and stool, set up a stove, and was
furnished a lot of Indiana soft coal, and concluded by
employing three men to assist in handling freight,
making transfers, and switching cars about the yard,
for such a thing as an engine for the purpose was not
known here at the time. The men employed were:
Henry Koehring, afterwards long employed at the
Hutton Coffin Works, as engineer, and now in the
service of Mr. George H. Knollenberg, dry goods
merchant, of this city, as night watchman. The second
party was one Fred Schultz, who continued in the
service a short time and of whose subsequent history I
know nothing. He was soon after succeeded by
Thomas Clarke, who continued to serve while I
remained in the office; I think he finally became
conductor of a passenger train on the "Chicago
road;" he has been dead for some years. Last, but
not least, is William Zeek—a most faithful and reliable
German—who has continued at his post from the

autumn of 1853 down to the present hour. If any man in the service deserves to be retired and pensioned the remainder of his days, he is that man.

The writer not only furnished and managed the first freight office of the road here, but was also its first ticket agent as well, working faithfully, late and early, and many a time on Sunday, and all for the munificent sum of $33⅓ per month, the men receiving $30 for a like term of service.

Hon. John S. Newman was the first president of the road, and Samuel Hanna its first treasurer — both residents of Centerville, this (Wayne) county. With the former I was well acquainted ; the latter I rarely ever met. I herewith enclose a letter from Mr. Newman, and a receipt from Mr. Hanna, both in their own handwriting. The " contingency " Mr. Newman refers to was my request for an increase of salary, which was not granted, and I soon after retired from the service. I was immediately tendered a position in the Citizens' Bank, as book-keeper, under Morrisson, Blanchard & Co., of this city, where I remained two years, when I engaged — and successfully — in business for myself. My successor in the office was a Mr. John Lynch — for many years past of Washington, D. C. — and he was succeeded by Mr. S. F. Fletcher, of this city [recently deceased].

The first passenger station was a small brick structure, not exceeding twenty by seventy-five feet in size, having a wooden platform extending around it, with extensions at either end for the more convenient handling of trunks and express matter. The old freight depot was not above half the size of the present one.

That you may see what manner of men officiated as the servants of the road here at that time, I send you three photographs — one of the writer, one of Henry Koehring, and another of that very faithful servant, who is still with you, Mr. William Zeek.

I am fully aware that this is a very meagre and unsatisfactory return to your request for information relating to the road's early history here, but to the lapse of time and a general lack of interest in what does not immediately concern us, must be charged both the defects and deficiencies of this showing.

Very truly yours,
GEORGE P. EMSWILER.

POSTSCRIPT. — Since writing the foregoing I have learned that Mr. Fred Schultz — one of the three hands first employed by me, and whose subsequent history I had lost sight of — engaged in the cigar trade after leaving the railway service ; later on was married and removed to Lewisville, Henry county, where he kept a village store and tavern for a number of years, and, finally, purchased and located on a farm on Eel river, this State, where he died, some years ago.

EMSWILER.

ALTOONA, PA., NOVEMBER 16, 1892.

Mr. G. P. Emswiler, Richmond, Ind.:

DEAR SIR — I wish to thank you very much for your
kindness in sending me description of early history of
Indiana Central Railroad, as well as the photographs,
old envelopes, etc., which reached me safely yesterday
morning.   Yours very truly,

J. E. WATKINS,

Special Agent Pennsylvania Railroad Co.'s Exhibit. World's Columbian
Exposition.

OFFICE OF THE CHIEF OF MOTIVE POWER,
PHILADELPHIA, December 18th, 1893.

Mr. G. P. Emswiler :

DEAR SIR — You will find herewith a catalogue of
the exhibit made by the Pennsylvania Railroad Company at the World's Columbian Exposition.   References to the contribution made by you, for which this
company is greatly indebted, will be found on pages
112 and 113.   You will be interested to learn that one
of the seven medals awarded the Pennsylvania Railroad
Company, by the judges in the section of Transportation, was for the Historical Collection of Relics, Models,
Charts, etc., of which your contribution formed an
important part.

Advantage has been taken of the exceptional opportunity following the success of the Exposition just closed, to establish in Chicago the '' Columbian Museum of Chicago.'' Large sums of money and many important exhibits have been contributed to the establishment of this institution. After careful investigation, and at the earnest request of the Directors of the new museum, it has been decided, as will be seen by the accompanying circular of the President, to deposit the Pennsylvania Railroad Company's exhibit in the museum, under certain conditions, one of which is that the exhibit shall be installed, as a whole, in a separate hall which has been assigned for the purpose.

I am directed to advise you of these facts, and, on behalf of this company, to ask your assistance in preserving the historical value of the exhibit by donating to the '' Pennsylvania Railroad Transportation Exhibit,'' in the Columbian Museum, the objects you kindly contributed to the Pennsylvania Railroad Exhibit at the World's Fair, and that you return my receipt endorsed to that effect. It is hoped that you will respond favorably to this request, in which case a label will be attached to your contribution, containing the statement that it was donated by you, and due acknowledgement will be made in a formal receipt, which will be forwarded to you later. Very respectfully,

Approved : J. E. WATKINS.

THEO. N. ELY, *Chief of Motive Power.*

COLUMBIAN MUSEUM OF CHICAGO, MAR. 23, 1894.

DEAR SIR — The notice of your contribution of your exhibit to the Pennsylvania Railroad collection, in the Columbian Museum, has been received in this office.

I assure you of our hearty appreciation of your kindness in this matter, and convey to you our earnest thanks for this addition to the collection.

Yours very truly,

E. W. PEABODY,

In charge P. R. R. Exhibit.

GEO. P. EMSWILER, ESQ.,
    Richmond, Ind.

EARLY RAILROADING.

MEN, LOCOMOTIVES AND CARS, BETWEEN ANDERSON AND RICHMOND.

Anderson *Bulletin.*

Whilst other enterprises have made rapid strides, and the hand of progress can be seen on every turn, the railroads have not been asleep in the last forty years. There is as wide a difference between the railroad equipments and the mode of railroad management now, and forty years ago, as there is between the fine coach drawn on the streets of to-day, and the old wooden axle carriage of that day. The comparison of one is only a comparison of the other. To illustrate : The Pan Handle railroad was constructed from Richmond to Hagerstown in 1853, extended to New Castle in 1854, and reached Anderson about 1855. The equipments of the road at that time would be a curiosity to the present generation. The first engine that ever ran on the road was called the "Swinett." It was a very small affair, not very much larger than one of the large traction engines in use now for the purpose of running threshing machines. It had no pilot or cow-catcher in front, like the engines of to-day. No coal was used in firing an engine in those days, but wood was used entirely. The smoke-stack on the Swinett was a very large affair, spreading out at the top, with a large sieve covering it, to let the sparks and ashes escape. The smoke stack was nearly as large as the engine.

The Swinett, coming down the road, presented much the same appearance of a country boy at a county fair, with his pap's plug hat on. At night, when she was steamed and her fire box stuffed full of dry wood, as she sailed along through the darkness, she left a string of fire coals streaming over her back like the tail of a comet, often setting fire to straw stacks, barns and fences, clearing everything in her way. She had painted, on the side of her "tender," the picture of a man with a pig under his arm, the tail in his mouth, and he picking on the pig like a banjo. Thus it took its name, "Swinett."

The Swinett had a twin sister that came on the road about the same time, named the "Julia Dean." She was rather smaller than the Swinett, but much handsomer, from the fact that her smoke stack was painted red. As she came sailing along she looked like a sugar trough with a stove pipe stuck up in the center of it. She, like the Swinett, had no pilot or cow-catcher in front. If either of these engines ever struck a cow, it was simply a question of which went into the ditch, the cow or the engine.

The people of those days called a locomotive a "Bulljine." It was a great treat for the youngsters to go to town on Saturday and see the " Bulljine " come in. After these rude, ill-shaped engines had served their day, and the road had reached further into the fields of prosperity, new and more modern engines were placed in service. Whilst they were considered, in their day, the finest in the land, they would suffer by comparison with the monsters of to-day.

Every town on the line of the road, of any importance, was anxious to have an engine named for it. The officials, of course, in order to please their patrons, named an engine after the county-seats through which the road passed. There was the New Castle, the Logansport, the Anderson, and the Chicago, all handsome pieces of machinery for their day. Then there was the S. Fosdick, the largest engine of its day, named in honor of some distinguished man ; but of all the locomotives that ever skipped along the rails of the Pan Handle railroad, from the time the road was first begun, up to date, the " Old Hoosier " took the cake. She was the favorite of all engineers who ever traveled the road. Mark Smith was the engineer who handled her throttle. He was as much a favorite as was his engine. Every woman, man and child on the road knew Mark Smith, and loved him. The Hoosier had a whistle on it that out-whistled all others. People used to say that the whistle of the Hoosier, when she was thrown wide open, would shake the beech-nuts off the trees along the road.

John Smock was the first engineer who ever ran an engine on the road. He came to the road with the Swinett, and stayed with it as long as the engine was in use, and for some time afterward. Smock was a terrible swearer. It is said that he could curse the old Swinett until it would begin to move, without fire, water or steam in it. It was his delight to see a team of horses skip out over a corn-field, along the road, when scared at the cars. He often blew the whistle when there was no earthly need of it, just to scare somebody's horses and see them run.

Among the early engineers on the road was a man named Skinner. He, for many years, ran the " Old

Chicago.'' She was a monster for that day, built for a passenger run. Extra large drive wheels, with the gearing or side rods inside of the drivers.

Skinner was an awful man to swear. He made the air blue when anything went wrong. A man by the name of Grimes was also an early engineer. He was an old friend of Jack Daniel's, and visited him a short time ago.

Tom Clark was the first conductor on the road. He was a whole team by himself. He knew everybody on the road, and everybody knew him. He swore, chewed tobacco, smoked, drank good liquor, and had a good time generally. He retired many years ago, and lived on a farm near Richmond, where, it is said, he died some years ago. There was only one train each way, from Anderson to Richmond, then. It was a mixed train of freight.and passenger cars. Tom Clark was the only conductor, and run the whole business. Afterward separate trains, made up exclusively of passenger coaches and more conductors, were needed.

Then came Charley Lincoln and Elijah Holland, of New Castle. '' Lige '' always wore a blue cloth spike-tail coat, with brass buttons, with a beautiful growth of red whiskers, to match. He was a '' Dick.'' Then there were John C. Huddleston, Thomas, Plimpton, Muchmore, Billy Patterson, Bogart, and others whose names are now forgotten. Bogart was a little New York dandy ; looked like he had just come out of a band-box. He was unused to Hoosier customs. The boys along the road used to have lots of fun at his expense. They kided him in many ways. * * *

John C. Huddleston is still living a retired life in New Castle, and is one of the largest land owners in Henry county. He has acres and acres of Blue river bottom land that one can see as they near New Castle on the Pan Handle train. It looks like the Garden of Eden. He had his foot cut off at Knightstown, in 1860, by the cars running over it. It is said he was there on some political business, and did not want it known, but the accident brought it out. * * *

There was no telegraph line on the road then, and a conductor had to be "up to snuff" to run a train. It was no boy's play, in those days, to be a conductor.

The engine "Anderson," named in honor of this city, done service for several years on the road, and was a general favorite among railroaders, as well as the public. She finally ended her existence by suicide, about the year 1860, exploding her boiler while standing on the track, in the town after which she was named, while her engineer was eating a lunch in a small restaurant or lunch room kept by Buff Dehority, situated near where Wellington's flouring mills now stand, opposite the Pan Handle depot. She was blown into fragments. The boiler was completely demolished, and thrown in all directions. H. J. Daniels, the present postmaster of Anderson, kept a grain house near there, and was a witness to the explosion. No one was hurt, but everybody, for a great distance around, was badly scared and shaken up.

MISCELLANEOUS SELECTIONS.

CANAL-BOAT TRAINS.

NOVEL PENNSYLVANIA RAILROAD ONCE IN OPERATION.

CARS RUNNING ON LAND AND WATER BETWEEN PHILADELPHIA AND PITTSBURG.

Editor the *Telegram:*

In your issue of Saturday you mentioned a project, once had in view by the people of Richmond, to build a railroad from this city to Connersville, which, you state, was to have an "equipment different from anything ever before or since carried into effect," which is described as a car with "bed" shaped as a canal-boat. As no date is given, I cannot say such project had previously been successfully tried, but about twenty years before the war — while I was attending school in Chester county, Pennsylvania — it was a daily occurrence to see trains on the Columbia railroad which had the appearance of a half-dozen canal-boats on wheels, running along at a speed of twenty miles per hour.

The boats were divided in the center, two cars representing one boat. These were loaded in Philadelphia, taken by rail to Columbia — situated on the Susquehanna river, about twenty miles below Harrisburg — where they were launched into the Pennsylvania canal, the two sections coupled together, and from thence towed to Holidaysburg, where trucks were again placed under them and they were hauled over what was known as the Portage railroad to Johnstown, where the queer craft again took to the water and went by canal to Pittsburg, at which point the freight was transferred to boats for all points, from Fort Snelling on the north to New Orleans on the south, thus making but one handling of the freight between Philadelphia and all towns on the Mississippi river and its tributaries. These canals and railroads were owned by the State of Pennsylvania, and when, in 1846, application was made to the Legislature for a charter for the Pennsylvania railroad to extend from Harrisburg to Pittsburg, it was vigorously opposed as a possible competitor of the State works. The latter, before many years, were purchased by the Pennsylvania Railroad Company from the State, and the queer-looking boat-cars ceased to be used.

W. F. SPENCER.

NOTE.—The statement here made by Mr. Spencer the author can fully verify, as he has witnessed the same thing, when a boy, at Marietta, Harrisburg and Columbia, Pennsylvania, hundreds of times.

OUR NAVY DURING THE WAR.

ONE OF THE MARVELS OF THE AGE.—MONEY VALUE OF ITS CAPTURES.

[Admiral Porter's Book, 1861 to 1865.]

The growth of our navy was one of the marvels of the age. It cost the government, in round numbers, $480,000,000, or $120,000,000 for each year of the war, $10,000,000 per month, or nearly a third of a million dollars for every day of the war.

It employed over 600 vessels of war and over 50,000 men, which force greatly exceeded that of any other nation in the world.

It guarded over 7,000 miles of coast, including bays, rivers, ·etc., effectually preventing the importation of arms and munitions of war, and so compelling the earlier exhaustion of the Confederate forces.

It captured the immense number of 1,165 blockade-runners, many of which were fine steamers — a ratio of nearly 300 captures per annum, or almost one each day during the entire war. The money value of its captures was at least $60,000,000, or $15,000,000 worth for each year of the war, and $1,250,000 in value for each month of the war, from first to last.

It co-operated with the army wherever there was water enough to float a gun-boat, while on the high seas our navy covered itself with glory. The river work of the navy on the Potomac, the York, the James and the Mississippi, with its branches ; the coast-line work, from the Chesapeake to the Mississippi, and its work on the high seas, totally eclipse, in martial valor and brilliant successes, all other naval achievements of the world. While history records the names of Fort Henry, Fort Donelson, Island No. 10, Vicksburg, Port Hudson, Fort Jackson, Fort St. Philip, Fort Sumter, Charleston harbor, Mobile bay, Hatteras inlet, New Orleans, Port Royal and Fort Fisher, and a score more of such famous names, the American navy will be universally honored ; while such deeds as the sinking of the Alabama, in square naval battle, will ever be named among the most brilliant victories of the age.

It opened the harbors by the perilous work of removing obstructions, torpedoes, etc., and by utterly destroying the hostile batteries which commanded them. It held in check the hostile elements of many a city and rural section while a dreaded gun-boat quietly lay before it ; in short, it displayed heroism of the noblest type, and made our reputation on the seas equal that of any nation.

WAR PRICES IN THE NORTH.

SOME PRICES CURRENT DURING THE LATE WAR.

This list was issued by H. B. Claflin & Co., corner of Worth, Church and West Broadway, New York, August 27, 1864. "For this hour only, 11 o'clock A. M."

These were net wholesale prices, by the case.

PRINTS.			PRINTS.		
Cocheco	$0	50	Windham Co.	$0	36
Merrimac		50	Amoskeag Pink		43
Sprague		46	Amoskeag Purple		42
Sprague, Pink and Purple Frock		46	Amoskeag Shirting		41
			Amoskeag Ruby		42
Sprague, Indigo Blue		47½	Mallory Purple		42
Sprague, German Style		46	Rhode Island		38
Sprague, Turkey Red		46	Suffolk		41
Sprague, Solid Colors		47	Richardson, Freeman & Co.		39
Sprague, Buff and Green Fancy		46	Gamer Swiss		42
Sprague, Shirting		46	Eagle and Neptune		32
Sprague, 4-4 Purple		60	Cohoes Falls, Etc.		25
American		45	York and Amoskeag Mourning		40½
Pacific		46	London and Atlantic Mourning		43
Dunnell		43½			
Lowell, Dark		39			
Lowell, Light		31	GINGHAMS.		
P. Allen, Shirting		41½	Roanoke		40
Duchess B		38	Hampden		40
Wamsutta		39	Lancaster		48½
Arnold		38½	Everett		47½

DELAINES.

High Colors	$0 60
Armures	57½
All Dark	55
All Wool	72, 75 to 85

APRON CHECKS.

Hamilton	45
Whittenden	52½
Star, 4-2	55 and 60
Star, 2-2	52½
Washington	52½

STRIPE SHIRTINGS.

Pittsfield	35
Hudson River	36
Thorndike	41
Anchor	42½
Franklin, A. C. A.	42½
Uncasville, Light and Dark	57½ and 58½

FURNITURE CHECKS.

Park Mills, Heavy	$0 57½
Columbia Mills	45
Star Mills	55
Star Mills, Red	65
Kirkland Mills	40
Hancock Mills	52½
Washington, No. 80	55
Wamsutta	50
Lanark Brown, No. 3	45
Lanark Brown, No. 2	42½
Marlboro Stripes	37½
Hartford Co.	37½

TICKS.

Pemberton Red Awning	72½

(Pemberton X Blue continued)

Pemberton X Blue Awning	$0 75
Franklin, A. C. A.	62½
Merrimac	62½
Hampden	39
Pittsfield	35
Hudson River	36
Massachusetts	42½

CANTON FLANNEL.

Hamilton, X F. Brown	75
Roanoke, A. A. Brown	44
Naumkeag, A. A. Brown	77½
Naumkeag, Bleached	80
Portland, Bleached	72½

COLORED CORSET JEANS.

Pepperell	$0 60
Lewiston	45
Androscoggin	43½
Indian Orcharde	43½
Newmarket	43½

DENIMS.

Hudson River Brown	40
Madison Brown	46½
Warren Brown	55
Oxford Brown	52½
New Creek Blue	42½
Idaho Blue	46½
Franklin, A. C. A., Blue	48
Massachusetts Blue	50
Merrimac Blue	60
Naumkeag Blue	60
Haymaker Blue	70

BROWN SHIRTINGS.

Boot H, 7-8	47½
Boot O, 4-4	54

Boot S, 9-8	$0 60
Nashua D, 4-4	60
Pacific E, 7-8	57½
Pacific L, 4-4	62
Atlantic E, 7-8	57½
Atlantic L, 4-4	62
James, 7-8	52½
Dwight A, 4-4	55
Newmarket A, 4-4	57½
Great Falls S, 7-8	52½
Great Falls M, 4-4	55
Pepperell O, 7-8	56
Pepperell R, 4-4	60
Salisbury R, 4-4	60
Hamilton A A, 4-4	47½

BROWN SHEETINGS.

All Standards, 4-4	72½
Rittsfield, 3-4	45
Atlantic R, 4-4	63
Atlantic R, 4-4	67½
Ethan Allen C, 4-4	52½
Canestogo No. 1, 7-8	50
Burlington X, 4-4	52½
Little Falls D	55
Nashua A	70

LINSEYS.

Park No. 65	87½
Park No. 45	65
Park No. 35	60
All Wool Filling	75
Rob Roy	67½
Wamsutta	67½
Jefferson	57½
Royal Oak	53
White Rock	

7-8 BLEACHED COTTONS.

Portsmouth F	$0 42½
Pawnee A A	50
Canagua River H	38½
Arctic A	40
Waltham X 55	55
Nipunic 38	38
Edward Harris	50
Blackwater	45
Boote O	52½
Langdon	55

BLEACHED CORSET JEANS.

Pepperell	$0 60
Amoskeag	52½
Androscoggin	45
Lewiston	45
Bates	45

4-4 BLEACHED COTTONS.

New York Mills	$0 77½
Masonville	70
Androscoggin	71
Wauregan Water Twist	74
Langdon	63
White Rock	74
Black Rock	65
Arkwright Water Twist	72½
Dwight, D.	68
Hill's Semper Idem	65
Bartlett	65
Durham	62½
Hope	61
Kensington	50
Commonwealth, U.	48
Wauregan, Extra, X X	58½
Wauregan, F	55

Eldon	$0 45	8-4 Pepperell	$1 32½
Plainfield, A.	44	6-4 Pepperell	1 00
Seneca Mills	50	10-4 Waltham	1 55
Wanhoo, A.	49	9-4 Waltham	1 45
Narraganset	48½	8-4 Waltham	1 30
Chattanooga, A	50	6-4 Waltham . , . .	97½
Reynolds, A.	50	9-8 Waltham	65
Chaumont	43½	5-4 Langdon	72½
Newburyport	60	5-4 Androscoggin . .	78
		9-4 Monadnock . . .	1 35
		10-4 Monadnock, Brown	1 37

COLORED CAMBRIC, ETC.

Colored Cambric, 26½, 27½, 30
Paper Cambric, 25, 31 and 32½
Victory Silisias 45
Lonsdale Silisias . . . 43½

SHIRTING AND PILLOW CASE,
BLEACHED.

10-4 Pepperell . . . $1 60
9-4 Pepperell 1 50

SPOOL COTTON, ETC.

Coates' Spool Cotton,
(5 off) $2 00
Willimantic (5 off) . . 1 50
Worsted Braid, No. 53,
(5 off) 1 87½

Dry goods, wool shawls, dress goods, blankets, cloths, cassimeres, satinetts, cloakings, cloaks and mantillas, Kentucky jeans, notions, white goods, hosiery, lace goods, boots and shoes, all as low as circumstances and the times will allow.

Goods are still advancing in price. Your orders — for which I shall be obliged — will receive prompt attention.

B. BARR.

WAR PRICES IN THE SOUTH,

WITH A DEPRECIATED CURRENCY.

Mrs. Jefferson Davis, in her Memoirs, gives the following extract from the diary of Col. Miller Owens, of the Washington Artillery, during the last war. Made on a trip from Richmond, Virginia, to Augusta, Georgia, in March and April, 1865.

1865.		PRICE.
March 11	To meal on the road	$ 20 00
March 17	To cigars and bitters	60 00
March 20	To hair-cutting and shave	10 00
March 20	To one pair eye glasses	135 00
March 20	To candles	50 00
March 23	To coat, vest and pants	2,700 00
March 27	To one gallon whiskey	400 00
March 30	To one pair pants	700 00
March 30	To one pair cavalry boots	450 00
April 12	To six yards linen	1,200 00
April 14	To one ounce sul. quinine	1,700 00
April 14	To two weeks' board	70 00
April 14	Bought $60 gold	6,000 00
April 24	To one doz. Catawba wine	900 00
April 24	To shade and sundries	75 00
April 24	To matches	25 00
April 24	To one pen knife	125 00
April 24	To one package brown Windsor soap	50 00

In July, 1862, the farmers of the South were selling eggs (which now bring but ten or twelve cents per dozen) for a dollar; potatoes for $6 per bushel; chickens, 57 cents to $1 apiece; butter, 75 cents to $1 per pound; cabbage, 50 cents to 75 cents per head. By November they were getting $15 a barrel for their corn, and $4.50 per bushel for their wheat. In February, 1863, prices had risen to a figure that, as one writer puts it, "must fairly make the modern farmer's mouth water:" chickens were $12 a pair, and bacon $8—not a barrel, but a pound! But in 1864, "wealth beyond the dreams of avarice was," the same writer continues, "pouring in on the farmer." Flour then brought $300 per barrel; a turkey would fetch $60; white beans sold for $75 per bushel, and milk $4 a quart. By 1865 the amount of money that a farmer could obtain for his products was almost incalculable. He could name his own price, and the supply of money was inexhaustible. Never before had the farmers of this or any other country so much money in their pockets; in fact, their pockets were not large enough to hold it, and it was said that people took their money to market in their baskets, and brought home their purchases in their pockets.

COTTON MATHER AND THE "FRIENDS."

We are often reminded of the good old times, when men were better than they are now, but we seldom get a glimpse of those better times that we do not rejoice to have escaped them and had our lot cast in the degenerate days of the present. We do not believe that the world was ever better than at present. In government and religion, we think there has been, all the time, a steady advance toward the higher and better, and that the whole people occupy a much higher plane, in morals and virtue, than ever before. Governments are more observant of the rights of the citizen, and the churches more tolerant and more in harmony with the teachings of their great founder than they were ever before known to be. We are led to this moralizing by the recent publication, for the first time, of the following letter, written by Cotton Mather, two hundred years ago. The letter is as follows :

Sᴇᴘᴛᴇᴍʙᴇʀ, 1682.

To ye Aged and Beloved John Higginson :

There be now at sea a shippe (for our friend Elias Hold-craft, of London, did advise me by the last packet that it would sail some time in August) called "Ye Welcome" (R. Green was master), which has aboard a hundred or more of ye heretics and malignants called Quakers, with W. Penn, who is ye scamp at ye head of them. Ye General Court has accordingly given secret orders to Master Malachi Huxett, of ye brig "Porpoise," to waylay ye said "Welcome," as near ye coast of Codd as may be, and make captives of ye Penn and his ungodly crew, so that ye Lord may be glorified, and not mocked on ye soil of this new country with ye heathen worships of these people. Much spoil can be made by selling ye whole lot to Barbadoes, where slaves fetch good prices in rumme and sugar, and we shall not only do ye Lord great service by punishing ye wicked, but shall make gaine for his ministers and people.

Yours, in ye bowels of Christ,

COTTON MATHER.

Had this scheme, which was so earnestly approved by the good and reverend Mr. Mather, been successful, and William Penn and his colony of Quakers been captured and traded to the Barbadoes for slaves — taking rum and sugar in return — we scarcely believe the generation of to-day would approve it as glorifying the Lord or as a credit to the church.

THE OPTIMIST.

If "crime" is the most terrible word which has ever been coined by the lips of man, "ennui" is the most pathetic.

When we read in Gibbon that "neither business nor pleasure nor flattery could defend Caracalla from the stings of a guilty conscience ; and he confessed, in the anguish of a tortured mind, that his disordered fancy often beheld the angry forms of his father and his brother rising into life to threaten and upbraid him," a shudder runs through our hearts.

When we read what Septimus Severus (who rose from an humble station to the imperial throne) said, "Omnia ful et nihil expedit," "I have been all things, and all was of little value," a tear dims our eyes.

"Ennui has made more gamblers than avarice, more drunkards than thirst, and as many suicides as despair."

There is a Persian proverb which says : "When men, passing by a newly made grave, shall say, ' Would God I were there,' the end of the world is nigh."

It is an intolerable thought, that, in this world of wondrous beauty and infinite mystery, the human spirit can ever suffer from mental weariness produced by satiety, and from feelings of tedium and disgust. But such is the case, and ennui is the baneful shadow that dogs the heels of an advancing civilization.

It is the fruit of disease or of dissipation. When life rushes in full tides through the veins, and tingles in the heart, it transforms a desert to a garden without effort, as do gushing streams of water. Beware, those of the impaired digestion, the hacking cough, the feeble pulse! But dissipation is more fatal than disease. The overfed stomach spurns imperial delicacies. The glutted imagination revolts at rainbows. "Enough is as good as a feast," and "too much" is the death of desire.

Didst thou say: "My food has lost its flavor, and the great world its beauty?" Thou fool, thou hast ruined thy palate and perverted thy vision! Rye bread and goat's milk is still "ambrosia" to the hungry swain, and lovers and poets are still intoxicated by the potent spells of nature.

It is no wonder that ennui spreads like a pestilence, when little children are stuffed and surfeited with all the luxuries that money can buy, so that, while they are still in their teens, they have tasted every pleasure and jaded every sense. We make our children drunk with luxuries. We stupify their souls with beauty, as wicked mothers do their senses with beer.

What further charm do you expect existence to have for a man who, before he has reached his majority, has quaffed the cup of life to its dregs? If you find no pleasure in life, do not blame the world. It is still beautiful, and still fills normal souls with rapture. However soft and sweet and caressing a summer breeze may be, it cannot evoke music from an æolian harp whose strings are broken.

The same universe which made the essays of Hazlitt murmur with pain, and those of Amiel with sadness, evoked undying strains of hope from those of Emerson.

There have been men to whom the morning sun, the evening stars, the songs of birds, the bloom of flowers, the laughter of children, were as full of mysterious charm and resistless benediction, when their hairs were white with the snows of life's last winter, as when they whipped the mountain stream for trout, or strummed the light guitar beneath a moonlit window.

CHARLES F. GOSS.

THE CHILDREN OF THE DESERT.

A SYRIAN'S DESCRIPTION OF THE MANNERS AND CUSTOMS OF A ROMANTIC RACE.

[*Courier-Journal* Interview, October, 1885.]

In conversation with a party of Syrians, at the Exposition, one of them gave to a reporter an account of the Bedouins — that mysterious people who have inhabited the desert of the Orient and lived in a nomadic state for centuries. Their origin is veiled in obscurity, and is older than any civilization. They are as much a distinct and peculiar race as the Jews, and have manners and customs, governmental and domestic, that characterized them before the time of the Genghis Kahn, or Tamerlane. The Syrian, who spoke of them, said :

"They number about half a million of different tribes. They never dwell under a stationary roof, but live in movable tents, the fabric of camel hair or goat hair, as the tribe is opulent or indigent. They roam the desert, remaining in a place only as long as the pasturage continues sufficient for their flocks and herds. Each tribe is governed by a sheikh, who has autocratic power over life, liberty and property. Some of the tribes are powerful, and number as many as 15,000 tents, and none less than 200 tents. They are governed by no written law, but are subject, alone, to the will and conscience of the sheikhs, who pay but slight regard to El-Koran. Their wealth is estimated according to the number of their cattle, and their power according to the number of their horses. Theirs are the finest horses on the globe, and they the best riders. Their care and attention for their horses equal the affection of a tender Christian father for his offspring.

"The children of the desert are remarkably quick and intelligent. Their sense of sight is wonderfully acute, and equal to a field-glass of considerable power. They excel the American Indian in the pursuit of stolen or strayed cattle, horses or camels, and can trace them for hundreds of miles across the desert, even though immense caravans have traveled the same paths.

"They are proverbial for their hospitality. I lived with them for four years, and they were necessary to me in protecting my silk farms, some hundreds of miles in the interior from Damascus. They would protect and guard a guest from harm at the expense of their lives and fortunes. Their tents are a sanctuary for any man, no matter what his crime, who invokes their protection. If the host be sheikh or shepherd, it is all the same — the whole tribe would spill the last drop of blood in defense of the guest, though he were the lowest outcast and most miserable beggar that claimed asylum. Breach of hospitality is the greatest of crimes, and they look upon it with emotions of horror. Whoever eats of their salt or their bread, or drinks of their pucketo, or ties a handkerchief to the cord of their tent, is their brother forever. If one's enemy re-captures him after being their guest, they will fight for him to death, or pay their last maravedi for a ransom, though it beggar the clan.

"To enemies, on the other hand, they give no quarter, and in battle they are as savage as they are brave, and commit deeds of atrocity in the hour of victory that makes humanity shudder. They celebrate their victory by feats of horsemanship, on the part of the males, and dances and songs by the females, concluding with a sword dance, in which both sexes participate and in which all are exceedingly expert.

."A Bedouin is never separated from his horse. He claims that his horse is part of his life, and the purer strains have never been sold from the tribes. All the gold of Ophir, all the jewels of Golconda, could not purchase one of the fine strains of noble horses which they possess, and whose purity has been undefiled with colder blood for centuries. Their horses are not large, but exquisitely proportioned for speed and endurance. To strike, or misuse, or speak harshly to a horse, is sacrilege in their eyes. The horse never permits a stranger to touch him, and repays his master's kindness with more than filial love or human gratitude. It is a common feat for one of these horses to run one hundred miles, with a speed equal to the finest Kentucky thoroughbred when making his best time on your race-course.

"The Bedouins subsist on milk, fruits, dates and the flesh of their herds and flocks. I have drank coffee in Constantinople and at Paris, and have imbibed the wine of Cypress and of Portugal, but the coffee as made by these children of the desert is the most delicious beverage that ever greeted my palate, and it is worth a journey to Syria to drink a single cup."

CHRONOLOGY OF PLANTS.

[St. Louis *Globe-Democrat.*]

Indian corn is American. First noticed in 1493.

The rye-plant is noted in Chinese history B. C. 500.

Arrowroot is Central American. Mentioned in 1537.

Tobacco is American. Described by Spaniards in 1495.

The magnolia is a North American. First described in 1688.

Buckwheat is of Siberian origin. First mentioned in 1436.

The pumpkin is Mexican and African. Described in 1527.

Kidney or Lima beans are native in Peru. Described in 1512.

Spinach is from New Zealand. Brought to Europe in 1687.

The pear is mentioned by Homer in the Iliad B. C. 962.

Beans and peas were mentioned in Chinese history B. C. 2700.

Barley is an Asiatic. Mentioned in the Bible B. C. 1900.

The onion is from India. Mentioned in the Bible B. C. 1571.

The olive is an Asiatic. Mentioned in the Bible B. C. 1900.

Flax is mentioned on the Egyptian monuments at least B. C. 2000.

The potato is North American. Taken to England by Raleigh, 1585.

The apricot is Syrian. It was known to the Romans A. D. 30.

The beet is mentioned by Romans, as a table dainty, A. D. 126.

Oranges grow wild in China. Described in Chinese history A. D. 200.

The peach — Persian apple — was mentioned by Romans B. C. 237.

Cotton grows wild in India. Mentioned by Theophrastus B. C. 350.

Apples were known to the Greeks B. C. 900 ; to Romans, B. C. 500.

The pineapple is an American plant. First noted by Spaniards, 1498.

Rice is indigenous to China. Well known in that country B. C. 2800.

About 1,800 varieties of roses have been propagated during this century.

The sugar-cane is native to India. Sugar used as medicine A. D. 600.

The potato was taken to Spain and Italy by the Spaniards, about 1525.

The banana is found wild in Asia and America. First described in 1516.

The tomato is American. First called "love-apple" and noted 1549.

Pliny, A. D. 60, mentions seventy varieties of plums as known in Italy.

The walnut grew in Armenia from the earliest times. Known B. C. 400.

The grape is found in all parts of the world. Mentioned in the Bible B. C. 3500.

The first coffee plants in America planted in Surinam, by the Dutch, in 1718.

Wheat is an Asiatic. Grown by the Chinese B. C. 2700. Called the "gift of God."

The hop vine grows wild all over Europe. German beer noted by Tacitus, A. D. 100.

The fig is universal in all tropical climes. Leaves mentioned in the Bible B. C. 4000.

Mushrooms grow wild in all parts of the earth, and are as plentiful in Siberia as in the tropics.

SHELLS, FOSSILS AND FLOWERS.

O, give me shells, bright, beautiful shells,
   From the ocean's depths below ;
And fossil forms, from the seas of eld,
   Where the matchless corals grow.

For I love them much, and their age is such
   As belongs to the strange and old ;
They've a nameless charm that delights me more
   Than the radiance wrought of gold.

So love I flowers, fair, beautiful flowers,
   On the brow of the bride to twine ;
They please me well, their entrancing spell
   Enchants with a sense divine.

I love all these — they were formed to please,
   And prove that a law, supreme,
Has made not only the shell and flower,
   But the earth and the sun's bright beam.

We thank thee, Father, Almighty of all,
   For the glorious gifts we see ;
And trust, in time, when we pass from hence,
   We may always dwell with Thee.

JANUARY 29, 1897.

TRAVEL.

NOTES BY THE WAY.

On the morning of May 25th, 1896, amidst a pouring rain, the writer left home with the purpose of making a tour of some of the more interesting portions of the East and its principal cities. The program included Niagara Falls and Boston, which he did not, finally, reach, as the time set apart for his stay would have been too greatly exceeded for the interest of business, awaiting his return. For his companion he had Miss Belle May, an interesting and intelligent young lady of eleven — who, though so young, bore her absence from home and friends, during our thirty days' stay, remarkably well, and was greatly interested in whatever we saw that was novel or new, and was readily reconciled to whatever change of circumstance or place might bring about.

Our first stop was at Pittsburg and Allegheny City, where we remained some three or four days, making our home at the Saint Charles Hotel, where we found pleasant quarters, good fare and agreeable people. During our stay here we industriously sought out all the objects of interest, and traversed the two cities from center to circumference, crossing the rivers, ascending the hills, and visiting parks and public buildings. Both cities are well worthy the tourist's attention. Pittsburg is a city of some 200,000 souls, and is one of the greatest manufacturing centers in the world. Situated at the confluence of the Allegheny and Monongahela rivers, and surrounded, as it is, by lofty hills, it is exceedingly picturesque ; while at least three inclined planes are constantly employed in conveying passengers and freight to their elevated summits. To witness the ascent or descent of the cars upon these cable roads — constructed at an angle of some forty-five degrees — is really awe-inspiring. Two of these lines are above six hundred feet in length, and one ascends more than thirteen hundred feet skyward. Even these hill-tops are now densely populated, and well built. The view afforded from above is very fine, indeed.

A citizen whom I met at one of the parks in Allegheny City told me he had known Carnegie for many years, and that he commenced life as an assistant to his father, who was a carpet weaver, in very humble circumstances, and that his home was the merest apology for a cabin. Here, then, is another evidence that poverty, alone, is no bar to the greatest success, provided talent and energy are combined in the individual. No pinnacle is so lofty but ambition and perseverance may reach it.

Our second stop was made at Harrisburg, Pennsylvania, where we were nicely cared for at the Herschey House. We soon began to make the acquaintance of this old capital (laid out in 1787) of a grand old State, and found many points of interest to occupy the time of our brief stay. Among the lesser incidents, which struck me first, was the fact that such a thing as a "tan" shoe was an exceeding rarity, creating in my mind — erroneously, perhaps — the impression that Eastern people get up styles for Western markets, the like of which they never adopt at home. The people with whom we came in contact were remarkably kind and obliging. Industry and thrift are manifest on every hand, but that "up-to-date" condition of things, so omnipresent in "smart" Western towns, is not to be seen. We saw fewer fine carriages, and other similar vehicles, in a population of sixty thousand souls, than Richmond, with its twenty and odd thousand inhabitants, can boast. The people appear to be less given to style and display than we of the West. In our wanderings about town, we saw many handsome residences and other evidences of wealth and comfort, but did not think their stores and business blocks, generally, were the equal of many in some of our smaller Western towns. When a boy, from the age of twelve to fifteen, I had resided here, and in those halcyon days spent many a happy hour upon the bosom of the romantic Susquehanna, which was then spanned

by a single wooden bridge, covered, and projected from
the city's side to a near-by island, and continued from
the farther side to the shore beyond, possibly three-
quarters of a mile in its total length. On the hither
side, near its entrance, stood a rude rock monument,
nearly as nature formed it, bearing upon its face an
equally rude inscription, informing the curious in such
matters that the structure was begun in 1813 and
completed in 1817, and that Theodore Burr was the
builder, at a cost of $192,138. Those dates and the
inscriptions we had faithfully remembered during all
these intervening years, and found them precisely as
we had left them, both in fancy and in fact.

Strolling along the river's bank, one afternoon, we
came upon a lone grave, surrounded by a very high
and substantial iron fence. The gate being ajar, we
entered, and read, upon a plain headstone of marble,
the following inscription :

> " '*A Cruce Salus.*'
> "John Harris, of Yorkshire, England, the friend of
> Mr. Penn, and father of the founder of Harrisburg.
> Died December, 1748, in the communion of the
> Church of England."

In the midst of one of the now busiest quarters of
the city stands a soldier's monument, one hundred and
ten feet high, which is said to have cost eighteen thous-
and dollars, with the following inscription upon a large
stone tablet :　" To the soldiers of Dauphin county,

who gave their lives for the life of the Union, in the war for the suppression of the rebellion, 1861–1865. Erected by their fellow citizens, 1869.''

Of the churches, none impressed me more than did ''Grace M. E. Church,'' a very pretentious and massive pile of stone, erected in 1871. The old ''State House'' still stands as I knew it when a boy, with very little change, except that an addition has been made to it, to increase its capacity.

While stopping at Harrisburg, we concluded to spend a day at Gettysburg, and on the morning of May 29th took passage on a train for that noted and ever memorable battle ground ; the distance from Harrisburg is about forty miles, so that the visit could be easily made in a day. The country intervening, no pen can describe, for beauty of landscape and perfection of cultivation — the fancied paradise of the faithful could scarely rival it. Gettysburg is a beautiful little city, beautifully located, having some good hotels, residences, and public buildings, claiming a population of some thirty-five hundred inhabitants. We were fortunate in making the acquaintance of Mr. Jno. E. Hughes, proprietor of the '' City Hotel,'' for we found in him a thorough gentleman. He furnished us with a team of horses and a guide, who had been a soldier and was thoroughly posted in matters military, to drive us over the grounds, and point out and explain the many localities and objects of interest, which he did, it seemed to me, as only he could do it. The extent of the grounds occupied by troops was many times greater than I had supposed, as you may judge, when I state that it required the better part of half a day to drive us over and around them. Many evidences of the contest still remain, in the way of shot and shell, which have left their impress on many of the older houses and trees of the vicinity. The army of the Potomac, at Gettysburg, was composed of 249 regiments of infantry, 39 regiments of cavalry, and 72 batteries of artillery ; in all, 360 organizations. The Confederate army was composed of 183 regiments of infantry, 30 of cavalry, and 67 batteries, a total of 280 organizations, containing a greater number of troops than the Union forces. The Union losses were 23,003. There is no official data of the Confederate losses at Gettysburg, but it is known to be far greater than the Union forces. New York and Pennsylvania lost most heavily, the former 6,705, and the latter 5,876; Indiana, 552. The monuments erected to noted persons, and marking important positions and events, number about 400, some of which were very expensive. The government intends to convert the grounds into a beautiful public park, and to that end has appropriated money to construct sixty miles of drive-way, at a cost of $5,000 per mile.

Arrived at Baltimore Saturday, May 30, at 6:00 P.M., we found first-class accommodations at the "Eutaw House." On the following day, which was Sunday, pursuing the bent of our inclinations for sight-seeing, we wended our way, first, to "Druid Hill Park," and could scarcely have done better, even had we been worshipfully inclined, and gone to church ; for we found it a magnificent place, extensive and beautiful, crowned and adorned with native forest trees, such as oaks, elms, maples, ash, etc., which reminded me, forcibly, of Bryant's beautiful lines, "the woods were God's first temples." And here were walks, and drives, and lakes, and lawns, and statuary, and inviting seats, and shade and sunshine, and refreshing breeze, with every comfort and accommodation the heart could ask or wish. And do you ask if there were also "cyclists" in the park? Aye, a thousand within sight, of both sexes, and all sizes and conditions. The merriest, happiest throng you ever saw. "The woods were God's first temples," and the parks and the groves are the paradise of mortals here below. Let every human being get out and go forth to the woods and the fields and the streams, and read and enjoy the glorious, open book of Nature — acquire its secrets, and be happy.

During our stay in Baltimore, we visited several other breathing places of this beautiful city, the best of which was "Patterson Park ;" it was also adorned with trees and walks, and lakes and fountains, and great vases and statuary, and an elevated "look-out," from the top of which an extended view of the country, round about, was to be had. The city has many objects of interest, and miles of magnificent residences, all constructed of brick, with basements and steps of pure white marble, which are daily scrubbed and scoured until they seem as immaculate as a soul just shrived from sin.

From Baltimore we departed for a brief sojourn at the capital of the greatest republic on earth —Washington City — and which now boasts a population of more than 200,000 souls. In point of beauty and completeness, it is the realization of a dream. Its streets, its parks, its drives, its monuments, its statuary, its museums, its galleries of art, its public buildings and libraries, its stately residences, and countless other objects of interest, must be seen to be appreciated ; no pen can adequately describe them, and mine dare not attempt the task. During our stay we ascended the towering Washington monument — to the height of five hundred feet ; visited the navy-yard, where we saw great guns, thirty feet in length, "rifled," and the outer surface turned off as we might turn a piece of wood. We also witnessed the transfer of some of these monster guns by what was termed a "traveling crane," extending across the building an hundred feet or more, resting upon wheels at either end, reminding one of a railway truck upon the track. To the body of this truck, or carriage, or "crane," was suspended the object to be transferred, by some powerful contrivance, and in a few moments it was raised aloft and on its journey to some distant part of the building, drifting along, over the heads of men and machinery, like a thing of life — dangerous in seeming, but evidently safe, to all below.

We next climbed the steps of the capitol, and strolled through its halls, and rooms, and chambers, and galleries, and corridors ; admired the rotunda, the paintings and statuary ; reverenced the master mind capable of conceiving and executing such a wonderful temple to Liberty, and beneath the shadow of its wings were awed — we wondered, and admired, and retired.

On Sunday, June 7th, we joined an excursion to '' Bay Ridge,'' Maryland — on the shores of Chesapeake Bay, some fifty miles northeast of Washington. The place proved to be a most beautiful and attractive summer resort. Bathing was indulged in by many, while various modes of entertainment were provided for the multitude preferring other means of recreation. The beach was especially attractive to the writer, as it is one of the very few that is both sandy and pebbly, many of the pebbles being beautifully rounded by the action of the waves, and either a pure white or semi-transparent :

> So that — like a child, in its merriest glee —
> They all became pearls and jewels to me.

Rarely, indeed, has it been my good fortune to spend a few hours more happily than on that beautiful Sunday afternoon upon the beach at '' Bay Ridge.''

We next visited "Mount Vernon," the home of Washington. It is situated on the west bank of the Potomac, sixteen miles below the capital. The trip, by steamer, is delightful. On the way down we passed the Government arsenal, the Government hospital for the insane, the city of Alexandria ; a light-house, on "Jones' Point ;" "Fort Foote," on the Maryland shore ; and Fort Washington, about twelve miles below the city — from this point the visitor gets the first view of Mount Vernon. The river is here nearly two miles wide, and the mansion, as seen across the wide stretch of waters, presents a very fine appearance. As the steamer nears the landing, or passes the tomb of Washington, the bell is tolled. The tomb of Washington is a plain brick structure, with double iron gates ; over these, on a marble tablet, are inscribed the words :

"Within this enclosure rest the remains of
George Washington."

Two antiquated stone coffins are seen within ; the one facing you is that of the immortal Washington, and that to the left contains the remains of Mrs. Washington, and is inscribed :

"Martha, consort of Washington. Died May 21st, 1801,
aged seventy-one years."

The old tomb, where the remains of Washington rested from his death until 1831, is on the right of the path, some two hundred yards south of the mansion, and is the one to which Lafayette paid a visit, in 1824 and 1825. This old tomb is marked " Washington Family." A tablet, on the iron gate, reads :

" Old Tomb,
" Where Washington's remains rested until 183 .
Tomb restored by Michigan, 1887."

At Georgetown we had pointed out to us the former residence of Key, the author of the " Star Spangled Banner "—a two-story brick structure, which may have been 15 x 50, and extremely plain, and built out even with the sidewalk, or very nearly so. We were also shown the cottage of Mrs. Southworth, who has probably written more fiction than any other woman in America. Arrived at " Arlington Heights," we were amazed at its beauty and grandeur. It is now the resting place of thousands of brave soldiers, who sleep the last sleep that comes to us all.

" The storm that wrecks the wintry sky,
No more disturbs their sweet repose
Than Summer evening's latest sigh,
That shuts the rose."

Many beautiful and expensive monuments adorn the place and record the virtues and the daring of the departed. A large, square monument, near the Lee mansion, bears the following inscription :

"Beneath this stone repose the bones of two thousand and eleven unknown soldiers, gathered, after the war, from the fields of Bull Run, and the route to the Rappahannock. Their remains could not be identified, but their names and death are recorded in the archives of their country, and its grateful citizens honor them as of their noble army of martyrs. May they rest in peace. September, 1866."

The estate is on the Virginia side of the Potomac, directly opposite the city. It comprises about twelve hundred acres, and once seen, can never be forgotten. It was purchased for £11,000, or about $55,000, by Jno. Custis, the father-in-law of Martha Washington, early in the eighteenth century. Arlington House is a noble looking structure, and consists of a central building, sixty feet long, with a portico of eight Ionic columns. There are two wings, each forty feet long. In the rear are the slave quarters, kitchen, stable, etc. The house is constructed of brick, and stuccoed. It has, near by, a glorious well of sparkling water, deep and cool, in which are suspended two oaken buckets, one of which comes up as the other goes down, for the purest of nectar that nature can yield. The government paid to Mr. George Washington Custis Lee $150,000 for this property. The portion of Arlington set apart for the cemetery, comprises about two hundred acres. The total number of bodies interred in the cemetery is over sixteen thousand, or about a thousand more than at Gettysburg. The streets of Washington City are mostly paved with asphalt, or concrete, and the sidewalks with cement, and their equal is probably nowhere else to be found. The colored brother abounds, and the older ones almost invariably take to the streets when walking. This custom I suppose to be a relic of anti-bellum days, when he had few rights a white man was bound to respect. The younger ones, however, usurp their full share, and do not hesitate to jostle their white brethren on the way. Meeting a citizen one day, at a corner store, while awaiting a car, I made some remarks concerning the splendid condition of their streets and walks, and said they must certainly be a great boon to "cyclists." He replied by saying that they certainly were, and that there were at least 30,000 bicycles in daily use in Washington City.

On the evening of the 6th of June we had the pleasure of hearing a two hours' performance by the "Marine Band," on the lawn in the rear of the President's house. The music, to my untutored ear, was simply marvelous, and the attendance of citizens and strangers very large. Washington offers so many attractions that months might be spent in the vain endeavor to exhaust them all, and we left the city with regret. On the evening of the eighth of June, we took passage on board a steamer bound for Norfolk, Virginia, and arrived at our destination about 8 A. M. next morning. The city is said to be above one hundred and fifty years old, and the harbor one of the best in the world. We saw many large vessels at anchor here. The population is claimed to be sixty thousand, about one-third of whom are negroes. There are many fine residences here, and many other evidences of wealth, but they are seemingly of a past age. Some good store rooms are to be seen, but the greater number are not up to the ideas of a progressive people. The colored man performs about all the rougher manual labor, raises immense crops of fruits, vegetables and peanuts, for home consumption and for shipment abroad. At the time we were there, we sometimes saw as many as an hundred men, women and children at work in a single field. I cannot say whether they generally own the grounds or not, but the improvements were universally poor. The black man is a slovenly worker and a shiftless creature, and his reward is accordingly. We have seen him drive a buggy into Norfolk with an ox in the shafts. On a Sunday the young bucks, each with his "best girl," may be seen parading the streets in very good attire. They are also very fond of riding in the street cars, to the great discomfort of the more fastidious whites.

I neither saw nor heard anything to indicate an unfriendly feeling toward the North. The war deprived them of their slaves, and left them stranded and helpless, for a time, but I doubt not that they have been gainers in the end, while many a slave, when freed, was greatly the looser in all but principle. He gained his liberty, but assumed new cares and duties for which he was unprepared. But in time, the balance will doubtless adjust itself to the new conditions, and all be better for the change. While at Norfolk we visited two summer resorts on the sea-shore, one of which was "Ocean View," some eight miles from the city; the other was "Virginia Beach," eighteen miles distant. Each boasted good hotel accommodations, good bathing grounds, and such other peculiar inducements as are usually found at like resorts, in addition to a barren, sandy beach, redeemed and relieved, to some extent, by the restless ocean's flow, whose might and majesty no tongue can tell.

> "Roll on, thou deep and dark blue Ocean, roll;
>   Ten thousand fleets sweep over thee in vain;
>   Man marks thy ruin — his control stops with the shore."

The city of Norfolk is said to be but six feet above sea level, and in many parts not so much as even three. The citizens claim a very low death rate, but they have, nevertheless, a very large cemetery within the corporate limits.

We saw many handsome women here, but they were much given to the use of the negro dialect and inflection. A beautiful and apparently cultured young lady would say, in reply to a question, "Yes, sah," or "No, sah," as the case might be, and many other like expressions, borrowed from her colored brother; but, on the other hand, he seems to have profited little by association with the whites; he is too indolent, too animal and too stupid. The people seemed exceedingly kind and obliging, but must be very non-progressive, if it be fair to judge them by what we saw around us. In a city having three times the population of Richmond, we do not recall the sight of a single new building in course of construction, except that of a brewery and artificial ice plant. Norfolk was the only city visited I should not care to see a second time. Its attractions are few and tame. In my opinion, slavery and the negro have blighted it for all time to come.

The 15th of June, towards evening, found us snugly quartered at the Windsor Hotel, in Philadelphia. We had left Norfolk, by rail, via Richmond, Alexandria, Washington and Baltimore, making four transfers on the way, in a distance of some three hundred miles, but were always fortunate in close connections and fast trains. Our hotel was centrally located — on Filbert street — and consequently in the near vicinity of the Broad street station of the Pennsylvania Railroad, the great City Building, the United States Mint, Wannamaker's famous store, and sundry other places of note and interest. The city is nearly six miles wide and twenty-two in length, and covers an area of more than one hundred and thirty square miles. It has thirty-six hundred acres devoted to public parks, the largest of which is Fairmount, which contains over twenty-eight hundred acres. There are three principal and many smaller ones, and for the past six or seven years more than $500,000 per annum has been expended for their improvement. Philadelphia has always been regarded as a slow city, but it possesses vast wealth, is well and substantially built of brick, and to go over it, as we did, by car and cab, and on foot, and behold its well built and ornate business blocks and many magnificent residences, one is simply amazed, and cannot help but wonder and admire.

The Pennsylvania Railroad depot, at Broad and Market streets, is a splendid example of modern Gothic architecture. The main building of the depot has a frontage of three hundred and six feet on Broad street, and two hundred and twelve feet on Market. Beneath it runs Fifteenth street, and on the north side Filbert street. The train shed is a marvel of engineering skill, for it is a single span of iron and glass, three hundred and four feet in width, six hundred feet in length, and one hundred and forty-six and one-half feet in height, and covers sixteen tracks. More than twenty million persons are said to enter and leave this depot by train annually, and this is but one of many great systems of railways entering this city.

No visit to Philadelphia would be complete without an inspection of Wannamaker's great store. We were over it and through it several times during our stay in the city, and always found it a source of renewed

interest. The stock on hand is claimed to aggregate
$4,000.000, and it is next to impossible to inspect its
multitude of objects without making a purchase; we
are not easily tempted, yet we could not do it. We
feel sure that on one occasion we saw, at least, a
thousand persons on a single floor. Lunch is served,
and mild drinks are to be had by any one applying.
For the convenience of patrons, many waiting, reading
and toilet rooms are provided. No description can
convey a just conception of the place — a visit alone
can do it.

On the morning of June 17th we called at the U. S.
mint, and were soon waited upon by a courteous officer,
who showed us over the establishment, and explained
to us all processes employed in making money, from
the bar to the completed coin, several specimens of
which we brought away with us as souvenirs, which
had been struck while we were present. There is on
display, and in the possession of the mint, one of the
largest and most complete collections of foreign and
American coins in the world, numbering many thousands of pieces, from every part of the habitable world.
The mint was first established in 1792, but the present
building was not erected until 1833. Visitors are
admitted daily from 9:00 A. M. to 12:00, noon, except
Sundays.

One of the marvels of Philadelphia is its wonderful
City Building, begun in 1871, and not yet completed,

but which has cost, up to date, $18,000,000, and may cost several more millions to complete it. The tower, which stands at the north extremity of the building, is five hundred and fifty feet high, and, excepting the Washington Monument, is the highest building in the world. The City Hall stands upon Centre or Pennsylvania square. The building is constructed in the form of a hollow square, with passage ways connecting both Broad and Market streets. It is four stories high, in theory, but actually has eight floors, each of which contains a multitude of rooms, numbering, in the aggregate, nearly eight hundred. The lofty tower is surmounted by a statue of William Penn, of heroic size, being over nineteen feet in height, and proportioned accordingly. During the course of our stay in the "City of Brotherly Love," we made it our business, daily, to traverse its various districts, to the extent of our time and opportunity, by cab, car, or on foot, and thus become as familiar as possible with its more interesting features, and the wonderful magnitude of this great human hive, where poverty and riches, love and hatred, happiness and misery, must ever abound.

Our next and objective point was the city of New York, where we arrived June 19, about noon, stopping at the "Saint Stephens" hotel, on Eleventh street, near Broadway, during the remainder of our stay in the East. The location is most desirable, and the accommodations and fare all the most exacting and fastidious could ask. The facilities for getting about the city are, of course, first-class, and the tourist only needs to know where it is most desirable to go, and acquaint himself with the best and most convenient means of attaining the end desired. There are so many objects of interest in a city so vast, that it is no easy matter for a novice, in traveling and sight-seeing, to determine what to see and not to see, or even how to see. At length, however, one becomes accustomed to his surroundings, and shortly feels at home, even in this modern Babylon. Having been a visitor here on many former occasions (though solely in the interest of business pursuits), we had, nevertheless, learned something of its wonders and its devious ways. We were, therefore, not long in putting into execution the plans we had matured. So that, early in the afternoon of the day of our arrival, we entered a Broadway car, destined for City Hall Park, the New York terminal of the great Brooklyn Bridge. Here we ascended a considerable flight of stairs, which brought us, at length, to a landing or station above, where we, for the second time, entered a car, which, for a fare of three cents, or five cents for two persons, promptly transferred us to the other side of East river, where we, for a third time, took passage, this time on an elevated train which must be over thirty feet from the ground, as we were above the third story of the houses, along the way, and thus we traversed the city of Brooklyn, in the direction of

Greenwood Cemetery, our objective point, for several miles. We had a magnificent view, from our car windows, of the city and its surroundings, including New York Harbor and its shipping, and the great Statue of Liberty. Arrived at our destination, we left our car and descended by a covered way to the ground, and on approaching the beautiful and artistic arched entrance to the cemetery, we found a carriage service awaiting the hourly arrival of sight-seers. We soon engaged the services of an intelligent and communicative son of Erin, who, of course, was familiar with all the points of interest, as his business required him to be. He conveyed us over miles and miles of winding ways, amid this indescribable "city of the dead," whose beauties and marvels it would be folly to attempt to describe. The surface is, in many places, undulating, and every opportunity has been embraced to still further enhance, by art, that which Nature here so lavishly bestowed. The original grounds consisted of one hundred and seventy-five acres, which have since been increased to four hundred and seventy-five acres, the present dimensions. The first interment was made September 5th, 1840, and the total number of interments to January 1st, 1894, was 276,577. There is a receiving vault in the grounds capable of accommodating 1,500 bodies. The cemetery has seven lakes, of varying dimensions ; sixty-two hydrants ; twenty miles of drain tile ; ninety-eight cess pools, and one thousand two hundred receiving basins. There are five entrances, the northern or main entrance being at Fifth avenue and Twentieth street. The interments average eighteen to twenty per day, or over six thousand per annum. The monuments, tombs and statuary to be seen here are truly marvelous, and must excite the wonder and admiration of every beholder. The funds of the corporation, on January 1st, 1894, amounted to $1,608,743.

Saturday, June 20th. This morning we walked from our hotel, on Eleventh street, near Broadway, to Thirteenth street, where we entered an omnibus whose trips terminated near the Sixty-fifth street entrance to Central Park, riding a distance of about six miles for the trifling fare of five cents each. As at Greenwood Cemetery, so at the park, also, were carriages in waiting to convey visitors over the grounds, eight hundred acres in extent, and probably the most interesting and thoroughly developed place, of its kind, any American city can boast. We soon engaged seats in one of the vehicles, and, with several other passengers in pursuit of knowledge and objects new, we were driven over and around this veritable "Garden of Eden" for the space of more than two hours, amid lakes and fountains, and flowers, and statuary, and bridges, and rocks, and streams, and lawns, and trees and shrubbery, and walks and drives, innumerable. Returning, at the end of the journey, to the point from whence we started, we alighted, and re-entering the grounds on foot, we sought new sights to conquer, and "their name was legion." Among the more important, we may name two extensive museums, filled with works of art, ancient and modern ; a zoölogical garden, embracing many specimens of bird and beast, from the Arctic regions to the Torrid zone ; and last, but not least, the Obelisk of Sienite, brought from Alexandria, in Egypt, in 1880, at a cost of $75,000 for transportation over a distance of 5,382 miles. It was erected near the Art Museum, and consists of a single shaft sixty-nine feet in height, a pedestal of seven feet, and a base of five, making a total height of eighty-one feet. The base is seven feet and eight inches in diameter, and the whole shaft is covered with hieroglyphics, or picture writing, more than two thousand years old. On the afternoon of the same day on which we paid a visit to the park, we, in company with a merchant friend, of our own city, who was a guest at the same hotel at which we made our temporary home, took a car to the foot of Broadway, and from thence a boat to Coney Island, some ten or twelve miles distant, where we found a great throng of visitors and pleasure-seekers. Some bathing, many strolling along the beach, or diverting themselves in various ways, as inclination led or fancy dictated. Up to this time, no hotel had opened its portals for the reception of the "Summer girl" and her mamma. A little later, however, all would be ready, and the charming creatures would "dance attendance" to the tune of many dollars a day, to flirt with some brainless fop ; while papa was still immured in his dingy office, coining his brain into the almighty "needful," for the maintenance of his fashionable butterfly family at the seaside.

We found many "tricks" and "traps" and questionable devices here, to lure the unwary into parting with their hard-earned dimes. The Eastern "Yankee" seems unusually prolific of schemes, and is not unfrequently a counterpart of the spider that sought to inveigle the fly. Anything but common, every-day labor for him — it is degrading, in his eyes, and, besides, *it makes one tired.*

While still sojourning at the Saint Stephen's, we received a kindly invitation from an Israelitish gentleman, with whom my merchant friend was acquainted, to pay a visit to the Hebrew Orphans' Home on the afternoon of the following day — which was Sunday, June 21st — at which time and place he would meet us, and take great pleasure in showing us through the institution, which is located, if my memory serves me, in the vicinity of One Hundred and Twenty-fifth street, near the banks of the Hudson river. Accordingly, about 2 : 00 P. M. the following day, we sought a car on the Elevated road, and soon found ourselves at the portals of this noble charity, cordially greeted by our new-made friend, who introduced us to the physician and other officials of the Home. The building is charmingly located and constructed of brick, some four stories in height. It consists of two distinct structures, joined front and rear, having an open court between, one side being occupied by the boys and the other by the girls. No child is received into the institution under five years of age, nor over fourteen. At the latter age homes and places of business are provided for them, with respectable and responsible people, where they may grow up to lives of usefulness and honor. At the present time there are about five hundred boys and two hundred and fifty girls being cared for. The types of the boys were distinctively Jewish, and, having come from the lower orders, very few were good-looking, though many were bright. Of the little girls, a considerable number were really handsome, modest and retiring. On our first entrance to the place we found about two hundred of the older boys being drilled in military tactics. We were subsequently shown through the school-rooms of both sexes, and found them graded as in our public schools. Some were being taught type-writing, others short-hand, and so on through the various grades, the supreme object being, as far as possible, to prepare them for the inevitable "battle of life." We were taken through every part of the great building, from top to bottom. Beginning with the laundry, we passed into and through the dining-room, the dormitories, the parlor, reception rooms, library and office rooms, etc., and we must say, most emphatically, that a better kept, more tidy or more cleanly place, we never saw ; the management seemed perfect, the children polite, respectful, orderly and happy. Long may the noble institution flourish, to do good ! In one of the lower rooms we saw an exquisite piece of statuary, in Italian marble, recently donated by a friend of the Home, at a cost, to him, of $3,000. It was the creation of a native of Cincinnati, Ohio, now an artist in Italy. The piece, without the pedestal, may be three feet in height, and represents Pharaoh's daughter holding aloft and at arm's length the infant Moses. The figure is nude, and beautiful to a degree rarely conceived or executed.

Having now gone over most the ground contemplated for the trip, we were not long in preparing for the return homeward. Accordingly, on Monday, June 22d, we wended our way to the Pennsylvania depot, where we secured seats and berths in the palace car "Jouna," of the fast train, No. 21, which leaves New York City at 2 : 13 P. M. for the west, and on this swiftly moving car arrived home, in Richmond, the next day, at 10 : 30 A. M., having traversed the intervening distance of eight hundred miles inside of twenty-one hours — after an absence of thirty days — without any untoward incident or accident, fraught only with pleasing recollections of agreeable experiences, happier, wiser and better for the outing.

August 14, 1896.

PIONEER DEAD

CENTRAL, SOUTHERN AND EASTERN WAYNE COUNTY.

" Beneath those rugged elms, that beech tree's shade,
    Where heaves the turf, in many a mouldering heap,
  Each in his narrow cell, forever laid,
    The rude forefathers of the hamlet sleep.

" Far from the madding crowd's ignoble strife
    Their sober wishes never learned to stray;
  Along the cool, sequestered vale of life
    They kept the noiseless tenor of their way.

" For them, no more, the blazing hearth shall burn,
    Or busy housewife ply her evening care;
  No children run, to lisp their sire's return,
    Or climb his knee, the envied kiss to share."

FIRST SETTLERS,

WHOSE TIME OF COMING IS DEFINITELY KNOWN, BUT WHOSE PLACE
OF INTERMENT IS NOT.

The earliest immigrants to this neighborhood were principally from Kentucky, North Carolina and Ohio.

	CAME.	DIED.	AGE.
Richard Rue	1805		
George Holman	1805	1859	99
Joseph Woodkirk	1805		90
Benjamin Hill	1806		70
Robert Hill	1806	1850	80
John Smith	1806	1838	82
Ralph Wright	1807		94
John McLane	1810	1838	81
James Pegg	1814	1839	71
Thomas Moore	1815	1839	93
John Pegg	1813		
William Williams	1814	1824	61
John Wright	1821	1838	76
Jeremiah Cox	1806	1826	75
John Morrow	1808	1825	60
Andrew Hoover	1806	1834	83
Thomas Roberts		1840	81
Cornelius Ratliff, Sr.	1810		70
John Burgess	1808		70
Andrew Morrow	1809		
John Townsend		1853	90
John Addington	1806		90
Mrs. Addington (mother of John)	1806		103
Jacob Meek	1806	1842	90
John Hawkins	1807		75

	CAME.	DIED.	AGE.
Ephraim Overman	1807	. . .	80
Thomas McCoy	1805	. . . .	. .
Joseph Wasson (Revolutionary soldier)	1806	. . .	85
Peter Fleming	1807	. . .	75
James Alexander	1807		80
Jacob Foutz	1806	. . .	85
Valentine Pegg	1809	. . .	80
Benjamin Small	1807	. . .	80
Richard Williams	1814	. . . .	. .
David Hoover	1806	1866	85
Samuel Charles	1812	1840	91
John Charles	1809	. . . .	. .
William Blunk, or Blount	1805	. . .	

PIONEER DEAD,

WHOSE TIME OF COMING IS NOT KNOWN.

EARLHAM CEMETERY.

	DIED.	AGE.
Timothy Harrison (born in England)	1881	48
Charles Morgan	1864	63
Phœbe Johnson	1863	39
Stephen C. Mendenhall (son of James)	1887	59
James Mendenhall (father of Stephen C.)	1893	88
Millicent Mendenhall	1892	81
Margaret Poe	1853	64
James M. Poe (Teacher, J. P. and City Mayor)	1879	74
Elizabeth Chandler	1851	74
John H. Thomas (early blacksmith)	1884	78
Dr. Ithamer Warner (born 1782)	1835	53

	DIED.	AGE.
Elizabeth B. Johnson (wife of Benjamin)	1887	60
Mary White (born 1800)	1878	78
Fredolin Schlagel	1882	83
Sarah A. Schlagel (wife of Fredolin)	1869	61
Sarah H. Ward (wife of Daniel)	1888	85
Joseph Dickinson (born 1820)	1895	75
Esther G. Dickinson (wife of Joseph)	1891	76
Isaac P. Evans (born 1821)	1882	61
Jesse J. Kenworthy	1864	37
Josiah H. Test	1864	38
Daniel Ward	1864	64
Thos. Mason (born 1812)	1893	81
Burgess J. Legg (born 1826)	1887	61
James Eliason (born 1829)	1884	55
Dr. O. P. Baer (born 1816)	1888	72
Alexander C. Dill (born 1812)	1863	51
Jane Dill (born 1819)	1894	75
Joseph Kern	1875	83
Elizabeth Hunt (wife of Clayton, Sr.)	1881	67
David Vore (early carpenter)	1865	67
Nathan Doan (born 1824)	1891	67
William Baxter (born in England)	1886	62
Samuel E. Iredell (tailor)	1865	55
Joseph Thatcher (born 1799)	1867	68
Rebecca K. Carter (wife of Charles)	1890	69
Abby S. Dennis (wife of Wm. T.)	1882	62
Andrew F. Vaughan, Sr.	1879	53
Lydia L. Hoover (*nee* Vaughan)	1893	91
Jno. G. Fryar	1894	71
Nancy Cole (unmarried)	1877	85
Samuel N. Foulke	1883	84
Jno. Suffrins (pioneer hatter)	1875	83
Henry Adams	1884	81
Mary M. Leeds	1874	45
Joanna P. Laws (wife of Jno. M.)	1894	83
Jno. M. Laws (pioneer merchant)	1867	64
Joseph P. Laws (son of Jno. M.)	1867	36

	DIED.	AGE.
Pamelia McWhinney	1870	83
Milton Hollingsworth (a noted teacher)	1871	47
Allen Z. Fisk	1872	45
Dr. William B. Smith	1856	48
James L. Morrisson	1893	76
Lydia C. Morrisson (wife of James L.)	1893	75
Mrs. C. A. Reeves	1889	62
Nathan Charles (farmer)	1871	64
Mary Charles (wife of Nathan)	1888	82
Anthony Pitman	1875	77
Margaret Pitman	1880	77
Susan B. Erwin	. .	. .
Frances W. Robinson (wife of Francis W.)	1895	80
Edwin Cokayne	1890	61
George W. Vanneman	1878	72
Eliza Vanneman (wife of George W.)	1882	75
Robert Cox (born 1814)	1890	76
John Yaryan (born 1802; lawyer)	1894	92
Sarah P. Yaryan (wife of John)	1895	72
Mary P. Haines (wife of Joshua W.)	1884	58
George S. Thomas	1890	69
Dr. Israel Tennis	1886	80
Mary E. Tennis (wife of Israel)	1891	80
Phineas Lamb (farmer)	1887	62
Timothy Marsh	1874	56
Abraham Earnist (early merchant)	1882	71
William H. Dalbey	1862	57
Mary Ann Dalbey	1886	80
Captain John Hunt	1884	58
Rebecca I. Hunt (wife of Capt. John)	1889	60
Cornelius Bartlow	1885	78
Elizabeth Bartlow (wife of Cornelius)	1885	77
Adna Bradway (born 1814)	1885	71
Margaret Thompson (wife of Benjamin)	1864	88
Richard Jackson (merchant and manufacturer)	1881	54
Mary J. Russell (wife of George W.)	1884	56
Ellen R. Black	1896	67

	DIED.	AGE.
Catharine H. Wilson	1892	86
Nancy Williams	1879	76
Mary B. Birdsall (wife of Thomas)	1894	66
John H. Hutton (tailor)	1873	61
Sarah A. E. Hutton	1888	76
William Norris	1885	59
Levinus King (woolen manufacturer)	1887	88
Eliza Ann King	1885	79
John W. King (son of Levinus)	1881	57
Hannah H. Dilks	1880	64
Agnes Crawford (wife of D. B.)	1887	79
N. Leonard (dry goods merchant)	1886	70
Helen M. Leonard (wife of N.)	1884	60
Abraham Phillips (early undertaker)	1884	64
Jane Gray McGirr	1887	73
Frances Thurston	1884	66
Leonard Wolfer (early grocer)	1893	79
Christina Wolfer (wife of Leonard)	1885	70
Captain Lewis Henchman	1882	89
A. H. Chapman	1878	52
Alfred Dunlop	1892	61
Walker Holmes	1888	77
Mary J. Holmes	1887	69
Frances Newton Scott	1885	63
Ingeborg C. Borscheim (native of Norway)	1893	66
Henry H. Fetta	1892	53
William F. Spinning (liveryman)	1861	37
Naomi B. Henley (wife of John)	1872	54
Edwin A. Jones	1873	43
William Boyse (retired)	1853	64
Mary Boyse (wife of William)	1891	86
James McWhinney	1879	62
Dr. Charles A. Wedekind	1875	82
Amelia D. Wedekind (wife of Charles A.)	1875	78
Sarah A. Burroughs	1882	63
William N. Cammack	1861	64
Julia B. Brady Dormer (wife of R. O.; born 1836)	1878	42

	DIED.	AGE.
Henry Henley (carpenter and builder)	1883	57
Lucy A. Henley	1889	61
Mary J. Hamilton (wife of James)	1890	56
Stiles Dougan	1886	53
William Norris	1885	59
Nathan Kitson	1857	52
William H. Goode (minister M. E. Church)	1879	72
Deborah W. Sutton (wife of David)	1888	53
Ann S. Woodhurst (wife of John)	1884	75
Joseph P. Strattan	1878	79
John J. Roney (early blacksmith)	1895	77
Nancy Ogborn (wife of Wm. E.)	1891	79
Joseph S. Steddom	1888	61
Rev. Charles W. Miller (Methodist)	1872	55
Joseph W. Gilbert (proprietor early stage coach)	1890	91
Elizabeth Gilbert (wife of Joseph W.)	1890	89
Caleb Shearon (hatter, etc.)	1854	58
Elizabeth Shearon (wife of Caleb)	1885	85
Alfred Tullidge (merchant)	1886	71
Belinda Tullidge (wife of Alfred)	1880	60
Martha Scott (wife of Andrew F.)	1888	80
William H. Schlater (county official)	1886	54
William W. Lynde (early grocer)	1876	64
Mary Lynde	1887	79
John Hawkins (farmer)	1891	79
Sarah Hawkins (wife of John)	1887	73
Isaac R. Howard (wholesale grocer)	1887	59
Jonathan Baldwin	1896	81
Mary Ann Baldwin (wife of Jonathan)	1891	76
Henry Study	1882	72
Sarah L. Study	1892	81
Dr. Vierling Kersey	1875	66
Mary Emily Kersey (wife of Dr. Vierling)	1872	54
Rachael Kersey	1868	87
Joseph Strawbridge (farmer)	1862	56
Rebecca Strawbridge (wife of Joseph)	1875	74
Levi Hawkins (farmer)	1888	54

	DIED.	AGE.
Charles C. Polly (trader)	1889	68
Susan Zeller	1877	73
Milton Foulke	1893	67
Jane Foulke	1891	65
Hannah Washburn (wife of William)	1865	46
Margaret Perkins	1880	61
Albert E. Powell	1887	62
Everette H. Winchester	1885	53
Jeremiah Hadley (merchant)	1878	73
Esther Hadley	1861	42
Daniel B. Robbins (merchant)	1882	58
James B. Brower	1881	60
Sarah L. Crocker (wife of Benjamin)	1883	50
Milton Whitacre	1884	57
Sarah B. Whitacre	1891	60
Daniel Jarrett	1872	64
Elizabeth Jarrett	1893	83
Vincent G. Newman	1883	75
Elijah H. Githens (early grocer)	1882	74
Rebecca Morrison (wife of John D.)	1878	82
Mary Elderkin	1891	70
Jacob Shelly	1884	75
Rosannah B. Ruby (wife of Ambrose S.)	1890	81
Mary Roberts (wife of Jonathan)	1888	78
Philemon F. Wiggins	1874	48
Daniel P. Wiggins (tanner)	1875	81
Andrew Finley, Sr.,	1845	80
Andrew Finley, Jr., (brother of John Finley)	1839	30
Mary Petty (wife of E. G.)	1853	50
S. L. Hittle (broker and financier)	1875	58
Anna G. Hittle (wife of S. L.)	1895	72
Malinda Gaar Scott (wife of William G.)	1848	27
Betsey M. Scott (wife of William G.)	1862	40
William M. Thompson (grocer)	1894	56
Sarah A. Hollingsworth	1892	66
James P. Reid	1895	69
Sarah J. Cunningham (wife of J. A., merchant)	1887	56

	DIED.	AGE.
Emily J. Van Uxem (wife of James)	1892	73
Emily L. Strattan (wife of Benjamin)	1879	62
Maria Weist (wife of Andrew)	1892	70
John McWhinney	1845	55
John W. Thompson	1875	55
James B. Hunnicutt, jeweler	1868	41
Andrew Shearon	1889	69
Angeline E. Shearon (wife of Andrew)	1892	71
Samuel W. Gaar (of Gaar, Scott & Co.)	1893	69
Horatio N. Land (of Gaar, Scott & Co.)	1893	61
Fannie A. Gaar Jones (wife of Oliver)	1894	61
William Blanchard, Sr. (merchant)	1881	80
Isabella Blanchard (wife of William)	1883	79
Abram Gaar (of Gaar, Scott & Co.)	1894	75
Jonas Gaar, Sr. (of Gaar, Scott & Co.)	1875	83
Sarah Gaar (wife of Jonas)	1863	70
Maria L. Henry	1881	85
John C. Hadley (early dry goods merchant)	1894	80
Matthew Rattray (weaver)	1872	76
Elizabeth Rattray	1881	72
John C. Whitridge (attorney)	1888	50
Leonard Templeton	1886	79
Rev. O. V. Lemon (M. E. church)	1889	77
Thomas J. Ferguson (early dry goods merchant)	1873	66
Martha R. Ferguson	1887	81
Isabella G. Reeves (wife of James E.)	1861	42
William Brooks (farmer and merchant)	1882	68
Thomas B. Vanarnam	1883	58
George Holland (lawyer)	1875	64
Richard H. Swift	1885	59
Jesse L. Branson	1890	53
William H. Dewey (wagon-maker)	1887	71
M. M. Swayne (wife of E. H.)	1888	55
Dr. J. T. Plummer	1865	58
Sarah O. Plummer	1877	73
Benjamin Paden	1859	64
Joseph D. Fleming	1884	57

	DIED.	AGE.
John Fleming	1844	41
Daniel McCoy (stone contractor)	1860	55
Sarah McCoy (wife of Daniel)	1891	82
Charles A. Dickinson (jeweler)	1885	73
Ellis Nordyke (manufacturer)	1871	64
Jesse M. Hutton (coffin works)	1886	77
Rebecca L. Hutton (wife of Jesse)	1885	63
Rebecca Hutton	1865	91
David Mather	1874	64
Richard Mather	1875	92
Phineas R. Mather (farmer)	1886	68
Ruth Ann Mather (wife of Phineas R.)	1875	48
Jesse P. Siddall (lawyer)	1889	68
Rev. Geo. Fiske (first rector St. Paul's parish, 1837)	1860	56
Sophia Fiske (wife of Rev. George)	1859	56
James Smith (born in Sheffield, England)	1885	80
Sarah J. Smith (wife of James)	1885	74
Levi Eliason	1890	78
Dr. Lewis J. Francisco	1874	54
Nicholas Hudson (grocer)	1876	66
Samuel Lough (farmer)	1882	89
Sarah Lough (wife of Samuel)	1874	74
Rachel S. Lancaster	1873	67
DeWitt C. McWhinney	1882	54
James W. Scott	1873	58
Charles H. Strickland	1875	55
John A. Bridgland (tobacco merchant)	1880	57
Caroline Bridgland (wife of John A.)	1880	57
Samuel Smith	1851	60
Rachel Smith (wife of Samuel)	1845	56
Samuel Francis Fletcher (grocer, etc.)	1894	76
Sarah Cadwallader	1893	94
Lorenzo D. King	1874	67
Abijah Moffitt	1891	67
Hugh Moffitt (farmer)	1885	79
Charles Newman (wood-turner)	1879	70
Jason Hamm (dry goods merchant, etc.)	1873	62

	DIED.	AGE.
Richard Pedrick (farmer)	1880	81
Clayton Brown	1872	69
Lewis M. Baxter (brick-mason)	1891	79
Daniel Reid (merchant and farmer)	1873	74
Wm. S. Reid (dry goods merchant and pork packer)	1890	72
William Kenworthy (tanner)	1877	83
Marcus Y. Graff	1858	81
Marcus Y. Graff (express agent)	1865	71
Esther Starr	1877	82
Rev. Peter Crocker (Presbyterian)	1855	69
Gardener Mendenhall (florist)	1875	70
Paul Barnard (carpenter)	1880	72
Jonathan Hawkins	1866	63
John Valentine (farmer)	1888	76
Rev. Paul Quinn (Bishop African M. E. Church)	1873	70
Cornelius Ratliff (farmer)	1889	91
Mary Ratliff (wife of Cornelius)	1889	87
Sarah Martin (wife of Benjamin L.)	1889	82
Benj. W. Davis (editor *Palladium* and postmaster)	1885	70
Elizabeth F. Davis (wife of Benjamin W.)	1868	54
Joseph Thatcher	1867	68
Henry J. Pyle (farmer)	1865	50
Nathan Doane	1891	67
Abbey S. Dennis (wife of William T.)	1882	62
Dr. J. W. Salter	1886	78
John Souffrain	1856	80
Daniel Burgess	1874	70
William P. Wilson (City Treasurer)	1880	51
Elizabeth Perry (wife of Judge James)	1882	79
John W. Grubbs (pub'd first paper in Henry Co.)	1893	73
Margaret Grubbs (wife of John W.)	1831	58
Frederick V. Snider (dry goods merchant)	1883	87
Mary S. Snider (wife of Frederick V.)	1891	87
Joseph Coffin (retired; Centerville)	1892	87
General T. W. Bennett (attorney and Mayor)	1893	60
Irvin Reed (in business sixty years)	1891	81
Dr. Joel Vaile	1868	63

	DIED.	AGE.
William L. Farquhar (merchant and grocer) . .	1887	71
William H. Bennett (liveryman)	1864	67
Lydia A. Bennett	1892	92
John Haines (established Greenmount school) .	1864	57
Robert N. Cochran.	1870	71
James Hamilton	1872	94
Oliver Brightwell (son of early merchant)	1866	39
Eliza Jane McCullough (wife of George)	1846	37
Rev. Oliver Tillson	1865	60
Sophia P. Baylies	1892	80
Dr. James R. Mendenhall (early physician) . . .	1870	75
Sarah T. Mendenhall (wife of Dr. James R.) . . .	1893	94
Mary M. Thorpe	1881	64
Catharine Rankin	1881	87
Sarah C. Wallace	1881	73
Benjamin F. Deal (grocer and trader)	1887	57
William A. Reddish	1892	77
Henry Farmer	1892	60
Sarah E. Hollingsworth	1889	63
George Buhl (farmer and grocer)	1882	51
Christian Buhl, Sr. (early brewer)	1861	60
Sarah Buhl (wife of Christian)	1879	57
Mary Laflan (wife of William)	1873	54
James C. Rutter	1876	60
Oran Huntington (hotel proprietor)	1880	80
Thankful Mary Ann Huntington (wife of O.) . .	1838	30
Ominda Huntington (wife of Oran)	1891	73
John F. Hugon (furniture dealer)	1894	68
Phebe A. Thomas (wife of William P.)	1893	66
E. F. Bush (principal of first commercial college)	1861	50
John G. Dougan	1873	71
Sarah Dougan	1879	63
Nancy McGown (wife of James)	1862	103
John McGown	1860	59
Laminda G. McGown (wife of James P.)	1871	60
Nancy Holmes	1879	69
David Sands (farmer and pork dealer)	1876	60

	DIED.	AGE.
W. S. Lancaster	1891	89
John E. Posey (builder)	1870	70
Dulcinia Posey	1880	75
Smith Railsback	1875	37
William L. Chatfield	1893	62
Benjamin Paige	1847	68
Mary Ann Paige (wife of Benjamin)	1841	48
Ralph A. Paige (merchant)	1887	62
Hugh S. Hamilton	1844	34
Mariam Roscoe (wife of T. R.)	1886	68
Nathan Hawkins (farmer)	1890	82
Sarah Hawkins (wife of Nathan)	1867	56
Isaac Walker	1867	80
Daniel L. Downing (gardener)	1860	71
William Edmonds	1864	76
Mary Edmonds (wife of William)	1866	76
Francis Mullett (silver plater)	1879	67
Richard Estell (shoemaker)	1871	67
William L. Fryar (carpenter)	1883	75
Mary E. Fryar	1888	78
John Dennis (grocer)	1892	71
Rev. Samuel Lamb	1876	68
Deary Bowers (grocer)	1893	84
Lucy A. Bowers (wife of Deary)	1885	66
Eli L. Rogers	1895	77
Eunice Rogers (wife of Eli)	1895	76
William Gauding	1894	82
Nancy A. Wilson	1879	73
Hannah Farr	1872	81
Robert Moore (farmer)	1887	79
Alice R. Moore (wife of Robert)	1891	82
John Dougan	1842	79
Martha Dougan	1855	91
John K. Iliff (painter)	1867	56
Sarah S. Dougan	1889	82
Jane R. Dougan	1890	79
Phœbe Jane Paden (wife of Benjamin)	1860	60
Christian Zimmer (retired merchant)	1897	79

MAPLE GROVE CEMETERY.

	DIED.	AGE.
Joseph Holman (farmer and politician)	1873	85
Nancy Holman (wife of Joseph)	1873	66
George Holman (frontiersman and farmer)	1859	99
James L. Harris (F. L. T.)	1858	40
John Harvey Tittle (trader)	1871	47
John T. Smith	1856	62
Enoch McCullough (of Delaware)	1843	27
Mrs. Isabella Faulkner (of Philadelphia)	1859	67
Jesse Iden (retired)	1857	75
Susanna Iden (wife of Jesse)	1860	69
Jane Stokes	1869	83
Mary Roberts	1883	77
Catharine Gulliver (colored)	1880	87
Elizabeth J. McClure	1875	58
Thomas Young	1853	75
George Arnold (tailor)	1858	49
John Morrow	1872	78
Catharine Leeds Hibberd (wife of Dr. J. F.)	1868	41
Stephen Elliott	1882	82
Anna Elliott	1885	81
Nancy Nutting (born in Watertown, Mass., 1782)	1862	80

FRIENDS' OLD NORTH SIDE BURYING-GROUNDS.

	DIED.	AGE.
William Williams	1865	74
Jonathan Wright	1862	76
David Roberts	1861	68
William Clawson	1865	75
Jemima Burson	1860	80
Ann Hunt	1859	74
Samuel Charles	1849	90
Gulielma Charles (wife of Samuel)	1847	86
John Pool	1865	88

	DIED.	AGE.
Elizabeth Pool	1848	64
Sarah Tremble	1849	71
Abigail Koons	1850	78
John Starr	1850	72
Mary Starr	1865	79
Lydia Holman (wife of Joseph)	1854	63
Jonathan Wright	1862	79
Nathan Clark	1854	51
John Hawkins (born 1777)	1859	82
Lydia Hawkins (born 1768)	1854	86
Tabitha White	1856	84
Sarah Stuart	1859	89

NOTE.—In these grounds were found hundreds of graves without a stone to tell the story of the departed; and very many more, which had low rude markers, were wholly without inscriptions—thus consigning to oblivion a host of honored, worthy and deserving names. This was especially true of the west side division, recently converted into a public park by James M. Starr.

GERMAN LUTHERAN CEMETERY.

	DIED.	AGE.
Samuel B. Morris	1887	69
Christopher Yurgens	1868	63
John H. Schepman	1889	67
G. H. Snyder	1890	55
Henry Rosa	1883	70
John Henry Drifmeier	1886	77
John W. Snyder	1873	64
William Kehlenbrink	1879	67
Bernhardt H. Knollenberg	1878	59
Miria E. Knollenberg	1884	57
Christopher H. Kemper	1886	52
Ernist Frederick Rosa	1870	55
Catharine M. Sittloh	1894	72
John Deitrich Knollenberg	1876	90
Maria Knollenberg (wife of J. D.)	1874	85

	DIED.	AGE.
John F. Besselman	1867	57
John Henry Landwehr	1874	83
Christopher H. Erk	1882	65
Gerhard H. Schuella	1884	58
Henry Wunker (born 1799)	1877	78
J. Henry Sieweke	1878	79
August Kamp	1883	76
Henry Yurgens	1865	72
Catherine Yurgens (wife of Henry)	1872	78
Eberhard H. Kemper	1870	63
William Koehring (born 1811)	1890	79
Rev. August Mueller	1884	52
Peter Arnold (born 1811)	1890	79
Elizabeth Arnold (wife of Peter)	1876	59
August H. Dunning	1891	54
G. H. Fetta	1874	63

GERMAN CATHOLIC CEMETERY.

	DIED.	AGE.
Barbara Hatmaker	1883	75
John Henry Moorman (born 1816; grocer)	1889	73
George Balling (grocer)	1895	47
John Henry Meyer (born 1825)	1880	55
F. Gauspohl (born 1816)	1887	71
K. Gauspohl (wife of F.)	1891	66
John Henry Brocamp	1880	71
Clement Liss	1887	64
Bernard H. A. Melle (born 1805)	1865	60
H. H. Geers (born 1815)	1890	75
Maria Anna Geers (born 1811)	1875	64
Elizabeth Pardieck (born 1790)	1862	72
Eva Deabert (born 1810)	1878	68
Louis Bedenbecker (born 1800)	1866	66
Maria Anna Bedenbecker (wife of Louis)	1869	74
Peter Shindler	1882	72

	DIED.	AGE.
Gerard Grothaus (born 1822)	1893	71
Catharina Grothaus (wife of Gerard)	1893	71
Joseph Batter	1877	63
Mary A. Batter	1891	67
Kasper H. Kuhlenbeck (born 1806)	1884	79
Elizabeth Kuhlenbeck (wife of Harmon H.) . . .	1882	74
J. W. Schwegman	1865	98
Frances Loehle (wife of Charles)	1878	63
Joseph B. Brocamp	1874	75
A. M. Elizabeth Brocamp (born 1800)	1883	83
Frank H. Rohe	1879	57
Elizabeth Blomer (wife of Henry)	1871	63
H. Anton (born 1808)	1892	84
Anne Rohe (born 1826)	1892	66
J. H. Berheide (born 1821 ; farmer)	1893	72
J. W. Wolke	1891	79
Anna M. Kuhlman	1878	88
Harmon H. Pohlmeyer (born 1810)	1881	71
Frank Heidkamp (born 1816)	1889	73
John E. Hoppe	1884	65
Barnard Lenaman	1866	70
Casper Johannes	1876	61
Bennet Baumer (farmer)	1883	72
Anthony Overman	1890	49
Katharina Kamberly	1883	68
John H. Offenbeck (born 1796)	1872	76
Gerhard H. Imhoff (born in Hanover, Germany)	1882	107
Joseph G. Imhoff (born 1818)	1889	71
M. Elizabeth Offenbeck (born 1801)	1870	69
Herman Bowing (born 1811)	1884	73
Bernard Meggenburg	1875	54
Elizabeth Meyer	1891	83
George M. Theobold .	1891	76
Geneva Theobold	1888	59
Anton Egli (born 1817)	1879	62
Bernard Heilkamp (born 1818)	1869	51
Louis Debus	1886	51
Maria Merkamp (wife of Henry)	1885	56

IRISH CATHOLIC CEMETERY.

	DIED.	AGE.
Margaret Flatley (wife of Thomas)	1885	59
Thomas McShea	1890	73
Susan Ellis (wife of J. F.)	1890	70
Daniel Maloy	1880	58
Dominick McMullen	1890	64
Mary McMullen	1888	57
Annie Kain	1884	58
Maria Whalen Mead (wife of John)	1879	77
Lawrence Mead	1869	62
Ellen Devine (wife of James)	1871	58
Michael Kute	1888	63
Sarah Galvin	1880	68
Joseph Cowhig	1892	78
Ellen Cowhig (wife of Joseph)	1886	69
Peter Mitchell	1885	52
James Carr	1888	69
Julia O'Connor (wife of Edmund)	1877	65
Bridget Carr (wife of Peter)	1865	85
Timothy McHugh	1877	62
John Leonard	1884	61
Catharine Karney (wife of Patrick)	1871	67
Mary Flanagan	1872	73
Margaret Hogan	1888	85
James Gordon	1893	64
Winnie Gordon (wife of James)	1891	60
Anna McManus	1892	55
James Riley	1879	56
Catharine Luby (wife of Michael)	1876	50
Mary Conway (wife of Walter)	1879	63
Michael Kennedy	1881	74
Lawrence Healey	1884	90
Margaret Mullen	1879	80
Michael Grace	1890	90
Thomas Burke	1867	53
Patrick Mitchell	1893	60

	DIED.	AGE.
David Breen	1894	55
John O'Neal (contractor)	1895	57
Johanna Ryan	1894	65
Margaret Breen (wife of John)	1891	58
Mary McIntire	1883	53
Thomas Dunn	1882	55
Russell Turner	1884	65
Timothy Harrington	1885	73
Mary Flanagan (wife of John)	1880	62
Patrick Doyle	1881	60
Dennis Kenney	1871	84
Mary Kenney	1871	73
Patrick Madden	1889	63
Anthony Madden	1893	65
Philip Frazier	1892	72
Patrick Beatty	1890	65
Patrick Mitchell	1891	70

HOOVER BURYING-GROUNDS

	DIED.	AGE.
William L. Brady (harness-maker)	1872	62
Susan Brady (wife of William L.)	1891	79
Henry Hunter (manufacturer of cutlery)	1875	59
Henry Hoover	1868	80
Frederick Hoover	1868	85
David Hoover (very early pioneer)	1866	85
Catharine Hoover (wife of David)	1865	75
Samuel Hoover	1869	60
Jacob Sanders	1864	72
Sarah Sanders (wife of Jacob)	1884	86
Susannah Wright	1862	77
Daniel Bulla	1890	76
William Bulla	1862	85
David Hoover, Jr. (died Jan. 22)	1897	74

McCLURE FAMILY CEMETERY.

	BORN.	DIED.	AGE.
Thomas McClure.	1788	1839	51
Nathan McClure.	1789	1862	73
Isabel D. McClure	1791	1875	84
Nancy D. McClure	1793	1867	74
Polly R. McClure	1795	1861	66
David McClure.	1797	1852	55
Jane A. McClure.	1798	1847	49
Rebecca N. McClure	1800	1869	69
Sarah W. McClure	1803	1883	80
James McClure	1805	1847	42
Holbert McClure.	1808	1820	12
Elizabeth L. McClure	1812	1887	75
Alexander McClure	1814	1847	33
Nathaniel McClure.	1765	1847	82
Jane McClure (wife of Nathaniel, Sr.)	1768	1850	82

(The preceding are parents and children of
one family.)

	BORN.	DIED.	AGE.
Sarah McClure (consort of Nathaniel, Jr.)		1846	58

The McClures were a very peculiar people — ignorant,
honest, unsophisticated and confiding. When the writer first
knew them, there were some half-dozen old maids in the
family, ranging from forty to fifty years in age. They were to
be seen upon our streets, weekly, for many years, until literally
retired by their infirmities. Their home was on a farm about
two-and-a-half miles southeast of the city. They all dressed
as nearly alike as possible, usually wearing some conspicuous,
out-of-date pattern, a showy shawl and large "scoop" bonnet;
each one carrying a great black satchel and large old-fashioned
cotton umbrella, walking invariably in single file — presenting
a most novel and grotesque appearance, so that one might
readily have fancied them to be the quaint representatives of
a past and long-forgotten age. None of their number ever
married, as the parents required that that interesting event
should occur to each in the order of their respective ages — the

eldest first, and so on down to the youngest member—but as no such opportunity ever came, in that particular way, they finally all passed hence in a state of "single blessedness," attaining to very advanced ages. With their demise, the family name became extinct, and their likes will never, here, be seen again.

FRIENDS' "RIDGE" CEMETERY.

	DIED.	AGE.
William Elliott	1889	74
Ezra Smith (carpenter)	1886	73
Margaret Smith (wife of Ezra)	1886	72
J. Micamy Wasson	1884	75
Jonathan Moore (shoemaker)	1884	78
Eliza Moore (wife of Jonathan)	1882	70
Nathan Morgan, Sr. (early undertaker)	1885	92
Margaret H. Morgan (wife of Nathan)	1876	77
Ira Moore	1885	75
Solomon Gause	1880	72
Benjamin F. Horton	1876	65
Lucinda Dowell	1870	78
Dr. William R. Webster (dentist)	1881	64
Samuel Irwin (farmer)	1888	68
John S. Brown (farmer)	1879	68
Stacey H. Wilkins (tailor)	1887	70
Eleanor S. Wilkins (wife of Stacey)	1892	73
John Hughes (early carpenter)	1869	87
Joseph Parry (plasterer)	1870	82
Sarah Parry (wife of Joseph)	1861	72
William Thistlethwaite (farmer)	1871	79
William Cain, Sr. (lumber dealer)	1876	75
Rebecca Hill	1871	79
William Parry (president Fort Wayne Railroad)	1894	84
Mary Parry (wife of William)	1892	79
Charles W. Starr	1855	62
Elizabeth Starr (wife of Charles W.)	1884	86

	DIED.	AGE.
A. Morton Brailey	1886	88
Joseph Gibson	1869	70
Robert Morrisson, Sr. (financier)	1865	75
James S. Hibberd	1894	82
George Hill	1882	57
Aaron Shute (farmer)	1883	76
Thomas Sooy	1867	75
Alma Sooy (wife of Thomas)	1884	83
Edward Kirby (farmer)	1868	47
Susan Wiley	1886	70
David Wiley (harness-maker)	1854	29
Joshua Wiley (harness-maker)	1866	48
Martha Nixon (wife of William)	1864	84
William Nixon	1869	94
Joel Matthews	1877	78
Susannah Wright	1872	84
William L. John (born 1805)	1896	91
James B. Hughes (died Feb. 27)	1897	84

KING'S CEMETERY.

	DIED.	AGE.
Mary Drake (wife of Ephraim)	1875	84
Aaron Pitman	1879	70
James E. Bryant	1871	63
John Wilcoxen	1875	84
B. H. Ivins	1866	59
Frances Embree (wife of John)	1863	77
Thomas Allred	1860	80
Margaret Allred (wife of Thomas)	1855	79
Louisa Bryant (wife of James E.)	1848	35
Hannah A. Ewbank (wife of Thomas)	1873	45
Marjahah Rich (wife of Joseph)	1863	73
Joseph Rich	1858	70
Jane Russell (wife of Vinnedge)	1851	34

	DIED.	AGE.
William Kern	1855	34
Sarah Taylor (wife of David R.)	1853	25
John V. Miller	1836	24
Samuel Russell	1835	64
Elizabeth Russell	1833	57
William Vinnedge	1839	40
Margaret Vinnedge	1839	38
Jacob Miller	1829	64
Julia A. Miller	1878	74
Nancy Davis (wife of William)	1868	66
Mary J. Russell (wife of John)	1872	34
Elizabeth Cox	1880	93
Eveline Cox	1859	39
William Cox	1823	38
Sarah Bulla	1839	24

GOSHEN CEMETERY.

	DIED.	AGE.
Joseph Brown	1877	91
Alice Brown (wife of Joseph)	1884	91
Thomas Strawbridge	1879	58
Joseph Strawbridge	1851	78
Nancy Strawbridge	1852	61
John Morrow	1875	65
John Chapman	1881	82
Kersey Graves (born 1813)	1883	70
Lydia Michener Graves (born 1814)	1889	75
William Wood	1881	75
Catherine Misner (wife of Charles D.)	1876	90
Paul Starbuck	1878	50
Margaret Graves (wife of Nathan)	1862	66
Nathan Graves	1862	78
Joseph Bond	1864	79
Sarah Bond	1848	57

	DIED.	AGE.
Levis Graves	1878	65
Lydia Arment	1869	76
Elizabeth Bond (wife of Joseph)	1885	80
Barbara Terrell (wife of Robert)	1880	67
William Bennett	1876	73
Sarah Selina Grave (wife of Stephen)	1880	61
James P. Thomas	1847	57
Ann Thomas	1880	84
Nancy Thomas (wife of H. W.)	1893	73
Sarah A. T. Hiatt	1865	62
Ilida C. Thomas	1854	73
John Thomas	1855	87
Rachel A. Thomas (wife of George W.)	1879	57
Reason B. Craig	1881	78
Dorcas Craig	1873	59
David Little	1893	83
Mary Little (wife of David)	1882	66
William Hawkins	1887	79
William S. Morton	1893	71
Elizabeth Thomas (wife of J. W.)	1881	59
John E. Willse	1873	83
Rachel M. Black	1885	67
Hannah B. Jeffries (wife of Way)	1870	72
Way Jeffries	1874	77
Samuel Sparklin	1887	64
Elizabeth Jeffries (wife of Isaac)	1877	71
Beulah Satcher (wife of Robert)	1886	85
Thomas Wesler	1882	83
Susan Wesler (wife of Thomas)	1878	72
John Fassold	1885	83
Sarah Fassold	1883	76
Malinda M. Kerlin (wife of Elijah)	1879	72
Phœbe Barton	1894	74
Thomas Marshall	1892	79

ELKHORN CEMETERY.

	DIED.	AGE.
B. Frank Bradbury (farmer)	1885	60
Charles E. Bradbury (tinner)	1873	54
Elizabeth Smelser	1861	75
Jacob Smelser	1875	91
John P. Smith	1885	68
Martha Stanley	1823	87
Nathan D. Farlow	1880	63
Rachel Farlow	1880	87
George Farlow	1873	84
Morton Meek	1894	81
Thurza Burgess	1878	74
Rev. Hugh Cull	1862	105
William Ray	1876	69
Disa McLain	1887	74
Solomon Conley	1871	82
Mary Wood	1848	82
Margaret Sedgwick	1890	72
Joseph D. Turner	1835	80
Abraham Gaar	1861	92
Dinah Gaar	1834	66
Bartlemy Burroughs	1849	69
Barton Wyatt	1870	73
Richard Sedgwick	1849	75
Edmund Jones	1874	85
George Jarrett	1855	72
Zachariah Stanley	1852	70
Thomas Wyatt	1830	77
Charles Hunt	1818	76
David Railsback	1858	85
Abraham Endsley	1850	73
Smith Hunt	1855	72
Mary Nelson	1872	80
Charles Paulson	1858	55
Eliza Paulson	1862	53
Rebecca Clarke (wife of Caleb M.)	1835	25

	DIED	AGE.
John Endsley	1838	66
Peter Smith (father of George)	1866	86
Margaret Smith (mother of George)	1868	80
George Smith (born 1820)		
Clarissa Smith (wife of George; born 1828)		
Joel Railsback	1895	87
Elizabeth Railsback (wife of Joel)	1848	38
Timothy Hunt (born 1771)	1823	52
Isabella Hunt (wife of Timothy; born 1777)	1857	80
Lazarus Whitehead (early Baptist minister)	1816	62
William Whitehead	1814	30
Hannah Whitehead	1809	27
Richard Rue	1844	84
Elizabeth Rue (wife of Richard)	1833	68
Andrew Hunt (born 1807)	1895	88
Hannah B. Hunt	1872	59
Mary H. Smith	1888	55
G. W. Hunt	1869	64
J. P. Burgess	1884	83

"INDIANA,

"*To the memory of Levi Jones, son of Edmund and
Ruthy Jones. Was born May the 31st, 1812, and left
this earthly vale of sorrow and pain June the 14th,
1835. Age, 23 years and 14 days.*" 1835   23

NOTE.—To appreciate the inscription, the stone should be seen.

CHESTER CEMETERY.

	DIED.	AGE.
William Cook	1885	68
Jesse Hunt	1883	76
Wilson Horn	1866	68
Clarkie Horn (wife of Wilson)	1864	66
Robert Higgs	1875	52
Catharine Hunt	1888	82

	DIED.	AGE.
Hannah Ogborn (born in North Carolina, 1805) .	1892	86
Martha J. Pickett	1893	67
James Mann	1891	66
Abigail Kendall (wife of William)	1879	66
Aghsa Baldwin	1865	61
Margaret Baldwin	1864	71
Mary Swain (wife of Francis)	1840	37
Thomas Bunker	1864	59
Rebecca Bunker (wife of Thomas)	1865	59
Jacob Bartenschlag	1876	58
Rebecca Bunker (wife of Samuel)	1892	76
Samuel Bunker	1881	64
Mary Pickett	1890	65
Elizabeth Clark (wife of Jesse)	1874	86
Israel Woodruff	1870	55
Eleazar Hiatt (born 1782)	1872	90
John Gregg	1867	42
Joshua Crampton (born 1807) . . .	1870	63
Elihu Hunt	1872	67
Milton Pickett	1872	46
William Hunt	1885	76
Elijah Roberts	1895	84
Elizabeth Roberts (wife of Elijah)	1880	63
Dr. Henry Ginther	1869	36
Benjamin Carroll	1862	78
Rachel Carroll (wife of Benjamin)	1865	73
Ursly Epps (wife of Richard)	1885	97
Abner S. Searing	1879	60
William B. Carman	1879	81
William H. Carman	1887	59
Elihu Williams	1895	70
John Jeffries.	1876	81
Elizabeth Samms	1862	65
Andrew Hampton	1859	74
Esther Starbuck (wife of William)	1887	69
William Starbuck (born 1788) . .	1825	37
Michael Weesner (born 1788)	1869	81

	DIED.	AGE.
Benjamin Pickett (born 1797)	1876	79
Deborah Pickett (wife of Benjamin)	1864	66
Daniel Fisher	1840	57
Demaris Fisher	1869	83
Phebe Fisher (wife of E. D.)	1875	68
Edward Fisher	1882	76
Benjamin Samms	1857	67
Elizabeth Commons (wife of John)	1850	34
Margaret Carlisle	1859	64
Jehiel Hampton, Sr.	1859	66
Elwood Clark	1877	52

CENTERVILLE CEMETERY.

	DIED.	AGE.
Sarah Hornish	1845	77
Rebecca Test (wife of Charles H.)	1842	34
Minerva J. Barnard (wife of O. M.)	1858	39
Sarah Lamson (wife of J. R.)	1859	61
Jehiel R. Lamson	1861	68
George Kirkman	1853	51
Eliza Williams (wife of Washington)	1848	40
Robert E. Hagerty	1834	23
David M. Hagerty	1833	20
Lucinda Ringo	1841	30
Mary Abrahams (wife of Israel)	1846	61
Joseph Grunden	1855	42
Ann Crooks (wife of Thomas)	1847	41
Daniel W. Conningham	1846	52
Matthew Dill, Sr.	1859	76
Jane Dill (wife of Matthew, Sr.)	1863	76
Lora Dill	1835	20
Thomas Dill	1846	27
James Swan	1844	26
Elvonia Pugh (wife of John E.)	1851	22
Dr. William Pugh	1829	33

	DIED.	AGE.
Henry Dunham	1855	59
Harrison Jones	1844	31
Henry A. Finch	1845	23
Cyrus Finch	1829	34
Jacob N. Booker (born 1785)	1825	40
Sarah Booker (wife of Jacob N.)	1852	60
Samuel P. Booker	1823	34
Lauretta E. Neel (wife of James)	1847	34
John Doughty, Sr.	1842	75
Nancy Adams	1844	78
Emsley Swain	1845	35
Elizabeth Emily Harvey (wife of Isom)	1834	24
Jane Widup (wife of William)	1830	50
Isabella Hart (consort of Patrick)	1830	53
Levi M. Jones	1823	38
Mary Jones (wife of Levi M.)	1848	65
Peter Ringo	1859	68
Margaret Ringo (wife of Peter)	1849	55
Lot Bloomfield	1847	58
William Poston	1835	39
Martha Morris (wife of Owen)	1849	36
Owen Morris	1865	52
Joseph V. Gregg	1850	65
Nathaniel Bell	1845	43
G. W. Stonestreet	1845	45
John Lewis	1825	31
Ann Lewis	1820	27
Robert Dinwiddie	1843	35
George Heagy	1839	54
Levi Crowe	1840	23

BOSTON CEMETERY.

	DIED.	AGE.
Captain Lewis Pigg	1882	64
Nathan Byars	1887	68
Jane Girton	1871	99

	DIED.	AGE.
Jeremiah Girton	1845	72
James Bowles	1854	76
Sylvester Girton	1884	65
Samuel Druley	1822	70
Ann Druley (wife of Samuel)	1845	90
James Stanley	1838	34
Catharine Stanley	1842	88
Martha (wife of John McKinnon and also of Owen Seaney)	1873	82
Jemima Esteb (wife of John)	1839	61
John Esteb	1856	84
Owen Seaney	1871	69
Sinthia Ann Stanley	1837	25
Effie Grimes (wife of William)	1849	58
William Grimes	1853	67
Martha Druley (consort of Aaron)	1842	25
Nancy Parke (wife of Curtis)	1850	42
Nancy Harris (wife of Thomas)	1849	61
Charles R. Stout	1876	82
Nicholas Druley	1849	69
Rosanna Price	1881	76
Samuel Druley	1874	92
William Druley	1851	40
Eliza Steele	1886	79
Luther Garthwaite	1849	63
William Walker	1886	72
Eliza J. Druley (wife of John)	1878	53
Elizabeth H. Druley (wife of John)	1885	51
Timothy Conley	1848	38
Sarah E. Conley (wife of Timothy)	1853	38
Isaac Conley, Sr.	1864	76
Mary Conley (wife of Isaac)	1851	65
Curtis H. Parks	1889	85
Nathan Druley (born 1815)	1895	80
Nancy P. Druley (wife of Nathan)	1893	78
Leah Evans (wife of Owen)	1875	85
Lewis G. Evans (born 1813)	1849	36

	DIED.	AGE.
Rev. Frank Evans	1879	42
Dr. D. S. Evans	1868	56
Emley H. Davenport	1880	54
Smith Druley	1890	72
Anna E. Druley	1896	76
William Bulla	1892	82
Daniel R. Shrader	1878	66
Martha Shrader (wife of Daniel R.)	1877	70
David Fouts	1863	59
John G. Smith	1895	85
Rosanna Smith (wife of John G.)	1886	75
William G. Seaney	1884	57
John Moss (born 1830)	1895	65
Levi Druley	1882	74
Levi Stanley (born 1814)	1891	77
Susanna B. Stanley (wife of Levi)	1887	68

RECENT DEATHS.

	DIED.	AGE.
Harmon B. Payne	1894	76
Jesse Starr	1894	77
Isaac Gaston	1894	65
William P. Hutton	1894	50
Dr. Joseph Howells	1896	80
Mrs. Harmon B. Payne	1895	76
John Brooks (of Greensfork)	1896	89
Mrs. Martha Cates (Olive Hill)	1896	98
John Cates (near Olive Hill)	1896	95
William Goodrich	1896	62
John Heiger	1896	72
George R. Brown (father of Van D. Brown)	1896	85
John Stonebraker (Hagerstown)	1896	100½
Isaac Stonebreaker	1895	87
Jonathan Baldwin	1896	81

	DIED.	AGE.
Isaac Kinsey (Milton)	1896	75
Mrs. Marietta L. Iredell (*nee* Souffrain; born 1812)	1896	84
Dr. Dougan Clark (born 1828)	1896	68
Peter Crocker (carriage maker)	1896	81
John Steele (died Oct. 17)	1896	77
Mrs. Sarah Jessup (died Oct. 29)	1896	92
Eliza A. Earnist (wife of Abram)	1896	75
Rebekah Edwards (born 1810)	1896	86
Susan Thomas (wife of John H.)	1896	89
Charles H. Burchenal (attorney; died Dec. 7)	1896	66
Mrs. Sarah Eliason (wife of Levi; died Dec. 12)	1896	82
Henry R. Downing (twenty years an undertaker)	1896	65
Jacob Hampton (farmer; died Dec. 25)	1896	76
Jeremiah Brown (died Jan. 22)	1897	85

THE SOLDIER DEAD.

The following is as complete a list as we have been able to obtain of such of the dead as are interred in this vicinity, in the cemeteries named.

> " While the fir-tree is green,
> And the wind rolls a wave,
> The tear-drop shall brighten
> The turf of the brave."

MAPLE GROVE CEMETERY.

Casper Zeph, 8th Indiana.
John W. Foster, 16th Indiana.
Silas Clark, 8th Indiana.
Oliver Brightwell, 69th Indiana.
Maj. John H. Finley, 69th Indiana.
Cornelius Hall, 36th Indiana.
Wm. S. Davidson, 2d Indiana Cav.
John Olds, 8th Indiana.
Phil. H. Wiggins, 36th Indiana.
Charles Wright, 36th Indiana.
William Wright, 36th Indiana.
Joseph P. Dempsey, 69th Indiana.
O. J. Hyde, 57th Indiana.
Dr. Joel Vaile, 57th Indiana.
John S. Hollett, 20th Indiana.
Jacob Newcomb, 6th O. V. I.
Joseph E. Bender, 28th Indiana.
Jos. D. Fleming, Co. A, 133d Indiana.
Madison Addington.
A. Emesweiler.
Dr. Alfred Potts.
William Engle, Co. F, 69th Indiana.
Jessup ——
H. Winderling.
John H. Zimmer, 36th Indiana.
Aaron Addington, 84th Indiana.
Dr. Alfred Potts, 16th Indiana.

J. M. Alexander, 8th O. V. I.
Henry Weidner.
Captain Louis Henchman.
Dr. Silas Fisher, 16th Indiana.
Evans Clark, 69th Indiana.
Enos Edwards.
J. M. Bruck.
Charles Shatz.
Shifner.
Hugh Galligher.
John Laker, 8th Indiana.
A. P. Dunham.
William Jones.
Chris. F. Schultz.
John G. Vesper.
James A. Linquthake, 2d Indiana.
Major A. E. Gordon.
John Loheres, 35th Indiana.
Archie Bell.
Lieutenant George Taylor.
William Clark.
Allen J. Fisk.
Cornelius Hall, 69th O. V. I.
William S. Davidson, 36th Indiana.
G. W. Wright.
Captain George M. Graves.
Enos R. Clark, Co. A, 69th Indiana.

Alexander Horney. 69th Indiana.
John H. Popp, Major 18th Indiana.
William P. Payne, 57th Indiana.
John A. Longuecker, 8th Indiana.
John F. Haws, 57th Indiana.
William Engle, 69th Indiana.
William Edwards, 2d Indiana.
Joseph Lintner, 8th Indiana.

Philander A. Scott, 8th Indiana.
John F. Haines.
Theodore Shifner, O. V. I.
Amos Arnold.
Joseph G. McNutt.
Comrade Vogle.
Jerry Hyde, 57th Indiana.

EARLHAM CEMETERY.

Capt. Quinby. U. S. A.
John Mendenhall.
Frank Lewellen.
Capt. Jno. Hunt, Co. D, 57th Indiana.
Jos. M. Strattan, Co. D, 133d Indiana.
Charles O. Wilson, adjutant.
Thomas Viciny.
John H. Cook.
Lieut. Jno. E. Holland, signal officer.
Wm. Wiggins, Co. C, 8th Indiana.
W. P. Wilson, sergeant 19th Indiana.
Paul Griffith, 8th Indiana.
Benjamin F. Schlagle, Co. E, 69th Indiana.
Samuel F. Schlagle, Co. B, 19th Ind.
John W. Schlagle, Co. E, 69th Ind.
Peter Bond.
Henry Nagle, Co. A, 185th Indiana.

Dr. David Evans, surgeon 69th Ind.
Dr. Elisha Fisher, surgeon 16th Ind.
John Mason, Co. A, 69th Ind.
John Turpen, 2d Indiana Cavalry.
Charles Petty, 19th Indiana.
George Ross. Co. A, 133d Indiana.
Geo. M. Bailey, Co. B, 126th O. V. I.
Capt. Joseph S. Stedham, Co. C, 57th Indiana.
Geo. W. Anderson, Co. A, 69th Ind.
Ambrose Lytle (colored).
John Hunt, 1st Massachusetts V. I.
Wm. Overman (colored), 28th U. S.
Mr. Miller. unknown.
Cornelius Pitman, 2d Indiana Cav.
Henry Beckman, 28th U. S. A.
Joseph Werner, 2d Indiana Cavalry.
B. F. Martin. 78th Indiana.

ELKHORN CEMETERY.

Thomas H. Ser, Co. C, 19th Ind.
George W. Beeler, Co. C, 57th Ind.
Reece Swafford, Co. G, 69th Indiana.

Rev. Hugh Oull.
William Hort. Co. A, 133rd Indiana

BOSTON CEMETERY.

Lewis Pigg, 57th Indiana.
Edward G. Stanley.
Wm. H. Stanley.

Jonathan Hill.
Dr. D. S. S. Evans, 69th Indiana.
Rev. Frank Evans. 69th Indiana.

LUTHERAN CEMETERY.

Louis O. Shofer, Co. A, 69th Indiana.
August Posthares, 124th Indiana.
Henry Meyers, 52d Indiana.

John Muy, unknown.
Casper Roll, 124th Indiana.
Fred Beckman, 124th Indiana.

GERMAN CATHOLIC CEMETERY.

Paul Meyers, 8th Indiana.
George Betz, unknown.

William Hutzbout, unknown.

IRISH CATHOLIC CEMETERY.

David Kelley, 124th Indiana.
Michael McAvoy, 2d Indiana Cav.

Lieut. John Dougan, Co. K, 35th
Indiana.

PUBLIC CEMETERY.

Joseph Werner, 2d Indiana Cav.
Henry Beckman, 28th U. S.
C. Pitman, 2d Indiana Cavalry.
J. Goodman, 124th Indiana.

John Hunt, 1st Massachusetts.
William Overman, 28th U. S.
William Sawyer, 28th U. S.

OLD CATHOLIC CEMETERY.

Henry Linneman, 19th Indiana.

KENNEDY'S CHAPEL.

William H. Bailey.

GOD BLESS ABRAHAM LINCOLN.

An Acrostic.

God bless him for his wisdom, for his wisdom blessed his kind;
Often sorely tried was he, in body and in mind;
Devoted, wholly, to the welfare of his race;
Bowed oft in spirit, oft he sought for grace.

Love, led by judgment, ever good and true,
Engaged his soul in what he sought to do;
Serenely, surely and sincerely wrought,
Soundly considered, every act and thought.

A loyal hero none could tempt with gold;
Brave as a lion, strong and just and bold;
Reared in grim poverty, riches he did not crave;
A man of iron will, he freed the shackled slave.

Haughty he was not, though supreme in power;
Armed to do battle — if came such hapless hour —
Manfully, did the evil time require;
Loth to use extremes, he did not thus aspire.

Innocent and tender, he, as a very child;
None could ever gentler be, none was less defiled;
Cool in all his conduct, cautious and serene,
Only he was master, without malice, hate or spleen.

Long live his memory — his life was pure and just;
Naught of guile was in his soul, wrought of love and trust.

January 20, 1897.

FAREWELL POEM.

Not the end of the world has come, dear friend,
　But the end of the book is here;
And we trust that some good has been said or done
　That may add to your weal or cheer.

For this life is short, though the way be long,
　And, ofttimes, not o'er smooth;
So a timely word, or a snatch of song,
　May aid us, the soul to soothe.

So, now, farewell! May we often meet,
　While pilgrims we yet here stray,
As well, hereafter, to know and greet
　Each other, in love, alway.

THE AUTHOR.

MARCH, 1897.